D1526132

MURDER in the ABBEY

Book 8 of the Maggie Newberry Mysteries

Susan Kiernan-Lewis

Other books in the Maggie Newberry Mysteries:

Murder in the South of France
Murder à la Carte
Murder in Provence
Murder in Paris
Murder in Aix
Murder in Nice
Murder in the Latin Quarter
Murder in the Abbey
Murder in the Bistro

1

Maggie put down the binoculars and sighed.

"Is it her?" Danielle sat in the passenger's seat of Maggie's car.

"It is," Maggie said grimly. "Madame Roche."

Danielle took in a sharp intake of breath. "I would never have believed it!"

"You're nicer than I am, Danielle. I suspected her from the get-go."

"What do we do now? Surely you are not thinking of confronting her?"

Maggie tore her eyes from the sight of Madame Roche standing on the corner of the village hardware store with her *tablier* pocket hiding the small mallet she'd just slipped into it.

"I'd just as soon not," Maggie admitted. "But in that case we need to come up with a good reason why we don't let her into the guild."

In the years since Maggie had moved to the little Provençal village of St-Buvard she had come to know everyone fairly well. At first they tolerated her because of their affection for her husband Laurent Dernier, a well-known area vintner, but in the last year she had made inroads on her own account by offering to advertise area artists and shops on her popular blog.

"Perhaps she will not ask to join," Danielle ventured.

Maggie's neighbor and good friend, Danielle was the epitome of the refined country lady. Even now, she wore a fitted tweed jacket over a silk blouse with a choker of pearls at her throat.

"She already has," Maggie said with a sigh. "Or at least her husband has."

"They sell strawberries, do they not?"

"They do."

"But surely strawberries are too fragile to sell to America?"

"Yes, but he said he'd settle for just getting his name out locally. I tried to tell him most people around here don't read my blog."

"What are you going to do? Maggie, you cannot confront her! It would be…" Danielle groped helplessly for the words.

"Danielle, I can't *not* confront her. Is it fair to the other people in the guild?"

The St-Buvard Village Guild, comprised of a select group of farmers, artists and winemakers who advertised their wares on Maggie's blog, had been created last year.

Tucked away between Aix and Arles with no highway linking them, St-Buvard was not conveniently located so the online sales for the many crocks of olives and oil, jams, homemade linens, pottery and artwork of local artisans had made the village a small boon town. The amazing fact at least to Maggie was that, using her skills as a writer to paint a picture of life in a rural village in Provence, she had single-handedly given new life to the town.

Because of the immediate bump in revenue that came from advertising on her blog, there was always a long line of people who wanted to be included. Madame Roche and her husband were no exception.

"Must you give her a reason?" Danielle asked.

"Wouldn't you want one?"

"I cannot believe she is stealing. Are they poor?"

"Pretty hard to eat a hammer."

"*Incroyable.*"

"The people in the Guild are my friends," Maggie said, tapping the steering wheel with a finger as she thought. "It's the first time I've been able to get some level of acceptance in the village."

"All of St-Buvard loves you, *chérie.*"

4

Maggie laughed. "Well, I wouldn't go that far. But I only have so much room for product placement. Why would I bump a hand pressed olive oil for berries that can't ship?"

"*Sais pas,*" Danielle said with a shrug.

"Plus, the first time we met, Madame Roche told me she hated Americans and found us all rude and overweight. Is that any way to make friends?"

"Most certainly not."

"And now she's stealing hammers from the village hardware store. Three strikes."

"I am not knowing this three strikes."

"It doesn't matter. Laurent says I bend over backwards to get people to like me—especially French people because they're all so prickly—no offense. But not this time."

"What will you do?"

"The first thing I'll do is tell her husband that I don't do perishables."

"How will you explain the *profiteroles* you accepted from Madame Benet?"

"Damn. I forgot about that. Well, I'll tell him Madame Benet was grandfathered in. Don't worry. I'm pretty sure I can do this without stepping on anyone's toes."

"And *without* confronting Madame Roche?"

Maggie grinned at her friend. "Yes, Danielle. *Without* creating World War III in St-Buvard."

✵ ✵ ✵ ✵ ✵ ✵

After dropping Danielle at her house, Maggie drove up the long winding drive that led to Domaine St-Buvard, the hundred year old *mas* she shared with her husband and their two children. There was never a time when Maggie drove up to the ancient home that she didn't find herself amazed by its history and its beauty. Especially now with fall breaking out all around them. A splash of vermilion leaves climbed up the entire eastern side of the house.

Their au pair Mimi was outside on the front drive with three year old Jemmy and one year old Mila when Maggie drove up.

Much to Maggie's chagrin, Mila had started walking at eight months and was now running and jumping as easily as her older brother. When the children saw Maggie's car pull into the driveway, they both began waving.

"*Maman! Maman!*"

Maggie got out of the car and dropped to one knee, spreading her arms out wide.

As always Jemmy got to her first and she had a few seconds to hold him close before Mila was on them. Then she pulled the little girl into her arms and held and rocked them both.

"Oh, I missed you so much! And I was only gone an hour!" Maggie said laughing.

The sound of a yapping dog made her look over the shoulders of her children to see her scraggly terrier Petit-Four standing in the drive impatiently waiting her turn.

"All right, come on," Maggie said and Petit-Four leapt into her arms too.

"No fair, *Maman*," Jemmy said. "I want to jump too!"

"No, you'll break Mommy's back if you do," Maggie said, smiling at Mimi.

Mimi was a village girl and quite pretty but didn't seem to know it. It was unusual for teenagers to stay in the village after high school and Maggie and Laurent had been grateful she'd stayed. A grand niece of one of the villagers with whom Laurent did regular business, Mimi had proven a godsend for helping out with the children.

The front door of the house swung open and for a moment Maggie only saw her husband back lit with the dropping sun visible through the house on the rear terrace. A big man of six foot five, Laurent stood only a moment on the threshold before stepping onto the drive to relieve Maggie of her welcoming committee.

"You are late," he said.

"No, I'm not." Maggie put the dog down and picked up Mila before the child could totter off. "What's for dinner?" she asked.

Laurent had always done the cooking for the family.

"Papa is making *coq au vin*!" Jemmy crowed and jumped as if to cheer the fact.

Laurent kissed both Maggie and Mila on the cheeks before going to the car to get the groceries.

"Did Danielle get what she needed?" he asked.

Maggie had driven Danielle to Aix for a doctor's appointment and afterward they'd visited a favorite cheese shop.

"Did she ever. We both spent about a hundred euros at the cheese store."

"Money well spent," Laurent said.

"I knew you'd say that."

Dinnertime was always hectic unless Maggie asked Mimi to stay and feed the children early. She felt like she'd been doing that a lot lately and so opted to send the girl home and put the children at the table. Laurent believed strongly that they would never learn to eat properly if they didn't share the grown-ups' table.

Unfortunately there was usually not enough wine in the whole house to make it a stress free occasion for Maggie—and she lived on a vineyard.

She and Laurent were able to exchange only a few non-child related comments at dinner. Maggie was organizing a wine tour for their label and trying to contact wine experts around the world to donate praise blurbs leading up to the event. She was using her travel blog to showcase the tour. Laurent knew they needed to start doing things like this but it was not his favorite part of owning and running a vineyard and so he left it largely to Maggie.

After dinner Maggie was about to climb the stairs with Mila to begin bath time when Laurent came out of the kitchen and handed Maggie her cellphone.

"Your mother," he said with a raised eyebrow.

Maggie had to laugh. It was his unspoken suspicion that Maggie arranged with her mother to call at certain times—like when it was time to do the dishes or put the kids to bed.

She handed Mila over to Laurent and took the phone.

"Hey, Mom. What time is it there? Two o'clock?"

"Hello, darling," her mother answered. "Yes, early afternoon. I didn't catch you at a bad time, did I?"

Maggie grinned at Laurent as he picked up Jemmy with his free arm and took both children squealing and laughing up the stairs to start their baths.

"No, not at all. What's up?"

Maggie had spent the previous summer in Atlanta with her parents. Her niece Nicole was growing up before everyone's eyes and aside from that nothing seemed to have changed in Maggie's childhood home.

Unless you counted what was happening with her brother.

"It's Ben," her mother said.

When Maggie had been home she'd made repeated efforts to get her older brother to open up to her. But Ben was seriously depressed. He had taken a leave of absence from his law practice and now spent most of his days talking with his therapist or binging on Netflix marathons in his parents' home.

"He's formally quit his job," her mother said.

"Oh, no. Is he talking about it?"

"No, except to say he doesn't want them to expect him back. He says he'd rather die than practice law again."

"Did he use those words?"

"He did."

Maggie could hear the tremor in her mother's voice. She knew it was agony for her mother to watch Ben at such close quarters as he stayed mired in his despondency. Their father was useless at this sort of thing, leaving anything that had to do with emotion or communication to Maggie's mother.

And Maggie's mother was at her wit's end.

"I don't know what to do any more," Elspeth Newberry said.

"It sounds like there's nothing for you to do. The ball's in Ben's court."

"Honestly, Maggie, just wait until you see Jemmy go through something like this and then I'd like to hear you say there's nothing for you to do."

"You're right, Mom. I'm sorry."

"I guess I just needed to talk."

"I'm always here."

"I know, dear. Oh, your father's just back from the club. Let me see if he needs anything. Everything all right here?"

"As rain."

"Good. That's what a mother likes to hear. Hugs and kisses to everyone, darling."

"I will."

When Maggie hung up she sat for a moment holding the phone in her hand and looking out the huge plate glass window that looked out at the dramatic landscape of grapevines.

The sounds of laughter from the children's bath shook her from her thoughts. A smile found its way to Maggie's lips and she got up to join her family upstairs.

Susan Kiernan-Lewis

2

Roger tried to remember the last time he'd driven through the countryside to get to the Abbey. Why was it he was always in a hurry these days?

Especially now.

The sun filtered through the colorful leaves on the trees that lined the English country lane and dappled the road. He glanced at his wife in the passenger seat and felt the pleasure of the splendid fall day begin to deteriorate.

Anastasia was squinting at her smartphone. Her auburn hair was caught back in a long silk scarf. Dark glasses completed the whole Audrey Hepburn look—without doubt the effect she had been aiming for.

Roger refocused on the road. The Daimler handled like butter. At the price the vehicle cost, that was the minimum of what one might expect of it, he thought drily.

"We're going to need to detour," Anastasia said, her voice laced with impatience. "The protest group is staked out in front of the Primrose Inn again."

Roger wanted to ask her how she might know that. Surely they had yet to create an app for where the latest terrorist group waited huddled in ambush? Nigel must have said something to his mother.

A needle of annoyance pierced Roger at the thought of his stepson. Resentful and bitter, the bloke had hated Roger from the moment he'd clapped eyes on him. *Pity really.* Roger had quite fancied the idea of having a son —even a stepson. But there were some stereotypes that really did hold their ground and the animosity between stepchild and step parent definitely was one of them.

"Did you hear me, Roger?" Anastasia said, finally looking in Roger's direction.

"I did."

"It'll make us an hour late at the least but you'll need to turn off."

"Any chance you're wrong?"

"None, darling. You know what they're like. Let's don't chance a strammish, shall we?"

Roger glanced at the dashboard clock. Nearly teatime. He'd hoped to have a proper Devonshire when they got in. Madeline always made the clotted cream just thick enough and she knew he preferred his scones without sultanas. But the only way he was going to make it on time was if he hurried—and *didn't* stop for a bloody protest against the local hunt.

Personally he loved the idea of the hunt and enjoyed watching it from the broad front steps of the Abbey with a strong G and T in his hand. Madeline said nothing made the Abbey more real than watching people on horseback charging over hill and dale consuming large quantities of sherry as they went.

Mind you, none of the Abbey's guests ever actually rode in the hunt. He glanced at Anastasia. His dearest bride had once suggested they arrange for the dogs and riders to mill about the front of the Abbey in their scarlet coats and then go tallyho-ing off to the nearest Starbucks. No drama, no protests, no sky-high insurance premiums.

No charm or imagination either. But then that was Anastasia.

Thankfully, Anastasia wasn't the one with the deciding vote and therefore there was nothing for it: the Abbey would have its hunt and there was an end to it. And for that simple fact, he could thank Madeline. A smile crossed Roger's lips at the thought of Madeline and how stubborn she could be. They were much alike in that way.

And always had been.

"I don't know why you insisted we go this weekend anyway," Anastasia said. "I had a full roster in London, you know."

"You needn't have come."

"Not come?" She looked at him in mock horror. "Go to the Abbey without me? Tongues would wag then, I say!"

Roger forced himself not to roll his eyes. Anastasia had this fantasy that the minute she stepped across the threshold of the Abbey she really did ascend into the upper classes to become among other things fodder for talk and innuendo by the unfortunate underclasses who served her.

No matter how many times Roger suggested that the employees at the Abbey were much more likely to care about the shenanigans at their local than what people with too much money prancing about in fancy dress customs got up to, Anastasia couldn't see it.

She really only saw what she wanted to see.

Frankly it would have been easier on several levels if she *had* stayed in London. Especially with the difficult conversation Roger anticipated having with Will. He hated that it had come to this. It was true he didn't have all the facts yet and he prayed what few facts he did have didn't add up to the result he feared.

As CFO of Roger's nonprofit, the Bentley Foundation Will had every advantage and position of trust. If it was true he'd abused that trust because he thought Roger was too stupid to notice—or too guilt-ridden as an indifferent wealthy relative to mind—he would find out otherwise in short order.

"You can turn down Tarrow's Lane, Roger. It's just ahead."

"I could just barrel right on through, too. Claim I didn't see them."

"Roger!"

"No, you're right. Would be hell getting the dings pounded out of the front bumper."

"I don't enjoy your sense of humor, Roger. I have to say I never have."

In any case it was too late. Roger could see that now. Specifically from the fact that the last turn had revealed a crowd of pedestrians camped on the side of the road straight ahead, and

more generally by the fact that he'd married the one person he'd
been truly mad to marry.

That's what age will do to you, he thought as he downshifted
in an attempt to inch past the group.

No such luck. The crowd of ten surged to its feet and ran,
hands joined, to stretch across the road.

"Bugger," Roger muttered.

"Don't hit them!" Anastasia squealed, thrusting her arms
against the wood burl dashboard.

Roger brought the car to a stop. He could see Nigel standing
in the center of the group. A tall boy—a young man, really—he
wore the jeans and tats of his generation—as if he'd never need to
worry about interviewing for a job. Now that his mother had
married money, that was probably true, Roger thought grimly.

"Oh, there's Nigel!" Anastasia said, pointing out her son. She
waved and even threw him a kiss.

"Do you think you might ask the lad to see if his friends will
get the bloody hell out of our way?" Roger said between his teeth.

"Roger, don't be like that," Anastasia said. "You know the
hunt is very important to Nigel. I would never take a side."

Roger definitely knew that.

A stout young man approached the car. As he neared, Roger
could smell the alcohol wafting off of him. Stood to reason. Only
the unemployed had the time to stand in the road and cause
senseless diversions.

"Got to go round, your worship," the young man said.

"We are not with the hunt, as you can see," Roger said
evenly.

"No matter. We're blocking everyone going to the Abbey.
That's where the hunt starts, ye see."

With visions of his high tea diminishing before his eyes—
only another quarter of a kilometer down the road and he'd be
able to see the Abbey—Roger put the car in reverse.

As he backed up, the group started chanting.

Anastasia waved again. "Goodbye, darling!" she called. "See
you at dinner!"

Roger didn't have to look at Nigel's sullen face to know he
would be ignoring his mother.

How Roger wished it were that easy.

3

Laurent turned the light out in the children's room. Mila was more than capable of climbing out of her crib but Jemmy knew the word *no* and Laurent felt confident he would stay put.

"Watch your sister," he said in an admonishing voice to Jemmy. "If I find her in the hallway, you are in trouble too."

"*Oui*, Papa," Jemmy said seriously, his eyes narrowing as he watched Mila kick her blankets around in her crib.

It was never too soon to instill a sense of responsibility in him, Laurent thought. For his sister, himself, his family. He needed to know from the beginning that it was all connected. What he did, what Mila did—it all reflected on the family.

Of course, if the little sprite did end up running down the hall after Jemmy dozed off, Laurent would return her to her bed—and of course stay with her to make sure she fell asleep. He closed the door and a feeling of satisfaction came over him.

In a million years he would never have imagined how intensely he enjoyed being a father. Was that because of Maggie? Or because raising these two humans was the one thing he'd been waiting to do all this life and never realized it?

Maggie appeared in the hallway in her robe. She was flushed from her bath and Laurent found himself sorry he'd missed that.

"Are they asleep?" she whispered.

"*Non*, they are waiting for you."

She slipped past him in the hall and then stopped and rose on tiptoe to kiss him on the mouth before opening the bedroom door and disappearing inside in a waft of perfume and bath powder. Laurent went downstairs to the kitchen. The *mas* was large and drafty. When they moved in the first thing his American wife had wanted to do was install central heating but they'd never gotten around to it.

Who was he fooling? They couldn't afford it. With trying to get the vineyard up and running—and every season bringing some disaster or setback over the next—money for such luxuries was not possible. Especially since trips to America—and even Paris— were always deemed more important. Now that they were more financially comfortable, he supposed he could revisit the heating question.

True there was always something to spend the money on. Just today he'd received a group entreaty from the St-Buvard village elders asking Laurent to pay for a new bakery.

He began to stack and wash the dinner dishes. Having to travel to Arles or Cabriès or even Aix was not a problem for Laurent. He was always out and about anyway. But the older members of the village keenly missed their daily baguette and their morning croissants. In the eyes of many in the village, the lack of a *boulangerie* was—if not a tragedy—then not far from it.

He lifted his head at the sound of Jemmy's laugh and although he knew the boy should be settling down and not squealing with glee, Laurent couldn't help but smile at the sound.

How did I get so lucky? Could I ever have imagined it would turn out like this? That I would find that rambunctious, maddening, wonderful woman and own my own vineyard?

With children?

He shook his head. Some blessings were undeserved. The mystery of that would always evade him. And perhaps it didn't matter. He didn't need to know why he had gotten more than he'd ever dared to dream when so many others hadn't. He thought of the email he'd received from Roger two days earlier and his good humor began to fade.

"Can't we do this in the morning?" Maggie said as she joined him in the kitchen.

Laurent couldn't help but grin. "That is what you always say when you don't want to see me cleaning the kitchen. But I am done." He turned and brought her into a hug, kissing her quickly and pushing the hair off her forehead.

"Hey, you're frisky tonight," Maggie said, laughing.

Hating to ruin her mood but knowing it was the best opening he'd have with his news, Laurent kissed her again.

"Sherry?" he asked.

Maggie pulled a stool up to the kitchen counter. "Sure. Is something up?"

She knew him too well. This was why his past life couldn't have continued for long. He was already losing his touch by the time he met Maggie.

Or maybe it was just with her. She'd ruined him.

He poured her a sherry and pushed a small dish of cheese and fig jam toward her, then tore off a piece of bread and handed it to her.

"I have heard from Roger Bentley recently," he said. He forced himself not to watch her reaction.

Finally, with no sound coming from her, he turned to look at her. She held the piece of bread halfway to her mouth, her eyes wide. Surely a little dramatic even for Maggie?

"Bentley," she said. "What does he want?"

"You do remember he is a friend of mine, yes?" Laurent tried to keep the irritation out of his tone. It wouldn't help.

"How can I forget? Considering how we met. What does he want?"

"Just to get together. He has married last year. He would like to come to St-Buvard—"

"No."

"Maggie…"

"No way. You can meet him in Paris."

"I do not want to go to Paris."

"Then you can meet him in Aix or Nice."

"Why is it I am not free to meet my friends in my own home?"

"You know how I feel about him! Why can't you respect that?"

He watched her push the cheese dish aside, her face pinched with exasperation.

It didn't matter that she knew how *he* felt about Roger—that Roger was his only real friend in the world. It didn't matter that he corresponded with Roger regularly—and didn't feel comfortable mentioning the fact to Maggie—it only seemed to matter that in the idealized world she'd created for herself Roger didn't exist. And up to now, it hadn't been worth the aggravation to challenge that.

"Laurent? After everything we've been through with Roger!"

"*Oui, cheri*," Laurent said, shoving his long hair out of his eyes with a frustrated hand. "*Exactement*. Roger has been the author of most of the joy in our life. You know this, yes?"

"Oh, give me a break."

"From giving *petite* Nicole a family—and your parents a second chance at Elise's daughter, to meeting me and to that end even the fact of Jemmy and Mila's very existence."

"And the fact that he's a lying con artist who'd just as soon cheat you as look at you?"

"He is my friend, Maggie. I am wondering why *you* cannot respect *that*?"

Maggie groaned and moved from the stool to where Laurent stood and pulled him into her arms.

"Why did you have to put it like that?" she grumbled.

He tilted her chin up and saw the annoyance in her eyes—but also the capitulation—and he couldn't help but smile.

"Is this what love looks like?" he said, kissing her. "Giving me what I want when it is so very much not what you want?"

A corner of Maggie's mouth twitched and he knew the problem spot had been traversed.

"Fine. He can come. They can both come. God. I can't imagine who would marry Roger Bentley. Is she a stripper?"

Laurent grinned and picked her up in his arms.

"Let us discuss the possibilities of that in another room of the house," he said with a smile.

The view from the east wing was breathtaking, there was no doubt about that, Anastasia thought with satisfaction but little pleasure.

She sat at her dressing table, a strand of twinkling diamonds in her lap and her hair pinned up in the old way. The maid Violet stood behind her and sprayed the coif, gently patting it with her hands as if afraid it might explode.

Anastasia had told Madeline to get experienced hairdressing staff but this was clearly the best she could manage.

"You are not supposed to use hair spray," Anastasia said to the girl as their eyes locked in the mirror. "They didn't have hair spray in the twenties."

The maid's eyes went from the can of spray in her hand and back to Anastasia's reflection. She looked absolutely terrified. "Mum?" she said in a stutter.

"And you are to call me *Lady Bentley*. Has Mrs. Mears not trained you?"

"Yes, Mum, I mean, Lady Bentley. I'm sorry, Miladyship."

Anastasia waved her away and the girl literally fled the room, leaving the afternoon tea tray behind her.

Unbelievable!

Anastasia stood and went to the fireplace to yank on the cord that would alert the downstairs staff that she needed someone.

Her dress was a patterned dark silk that flowed to the floor. It was sequined at the seams so that she literally glittered when she walked. Roger hadn't seen the sense of the cost but she had soon convinced him.

How was it possible to stay at the Abbey without proper dinner clothes?

As she returned to her dressing table, patting her hair in begrudging satisfaction at the result, her cellphone began to vibrate on the bedside table. In the early days she'd insisted nobody bring their mobiles with them when they came to stay at the Abbey but they all ignored her anyway. Truth be told, a little modern convenience sprinkled here and there tended to make the weekend experience even more intense.

She saw the number on the screen and flushed with annoyance and a glint of fear.

Idiot! What is he doing calling me?

She picked up the phone and glanced at the door to the hall. Roger was downstairs having cocktails but someone would come soon to take her tea tray away.

"I thought you understood not to call me," she hissed into the phone.

He hesitated on the other line and then spoke. The deep resonance of his voice seemed to vibrate through the phone line and down into her very diaphragm.

"I didn't want to take the chance of missing it," he said.

"*Tonight*," she said, walking to the door to hear if someone was coming yet. "You know it's tonight."

"I wasn't sure you still wanted to go through with it."

"Stop talking! Nothing's changed! Tonight!"

Anastasia disconnected and dropped the phone on the bed just as Madeline Mears, the manager of the Abbey knocked on the door and entered. Madeline was plump and rosy-cheeked. While she quite fit the part of a downstairs housekeeper it annoyed Anastasia that she had to spend so much time upstairs. There was absolutely no elegance or style about the woman.

Anastasia walked to the mirror. Her face was flushed with agitation.

"Yes, Anastasia?" Madeline said. "You rang?"

"Do you think you could stay in character for five minutes?" Anastasia said coldly, forcing herself not to glance at the phone on the bed.

"There's no one here but the two of us."

"What does that matter? Take the tray away, Mrs. Mears and please have a word with the girl..."

"Violet?"

"She has no idea of how to address me. I thought you said you trained the staff."

Madeline picked up the tray and sighed.

"It's not like the old days," she said. "They don't live here full time so when they go back to their lives outside the Abbey, they forget."

"I require you to do what's necessary to remind them such that I don't have to instruct them myself," Anastasia said. "Our guests do not come here to experience life as one of the privileged elite only to have to explain to the ones serving them how it's done!"

"I quite agree, Milady," Madeline said, not bothering to hide her sarcasm. "Will that be all? Or would you like me to charge up your smartphone before I go?"

Anastasia blushed furiously. "Just go," she said.

Madeline left the room and Anastasia went to the bed and snatched up the phone. She scrolled through the recent calls and deleted the call she'd just received before sagging onto the bed.

Tonight was taken care of. There was that. But somehow she didn't feel better.

Not at all.

Susan Kiernan-Lewis

4

Maggie was relieved to see Madame Roche seemed to have opted not to appear at tonight's guild meeting. Maggie and Danielle had arrived early so Maggie could go over some of the photographs scheduled in her upcoming blog post. The wine harvest was weeks past but she'd taken several pictures that were full of color and action. Maggie intended to use most of them in the promotional pieces she was creating for the upcoming wine tour, but there were also a few she could use for the village fete in early December. The fete was basically an outdoor Christmas market where everyone brought their butters, their lavender, their handmade crafts and their homemade brews and oils and soaps.

The meeting was crowded tonight and Maggie wasn't surprised. Everyone was vying for a top position in the blog leading up to the fete and if Maggie's blog comments section could be relied upon there would be literally hundreds more visitors to the village this year from Paris and the UK.

Madame Dulcie of the St-Buvard *charcuterie* waved to Maggie as she and Danielle walked in the door.

"Madame Dernier! Maggie!" Madame Dulcie called. "Come! Come!"

Maggie left Danielle and walked into Madame's quick embrace.

"*Bonjour*, Madame Dulcie," Maggie said. "We've got quite a turnout tonight."

"Monsieur Dernier is not coming?" Madame Dulcie affected a sad expression but Maggie knew she didn't really mind. While the whole village loved Laurent, these meetings had become more about Maggie and how she would represent what they had to sell to the outside world.

"At home taking care of the babies," Maggie said. "Like a good husband."

"*Bien sûr!*" Madam guffawed. "Now I must show you what my nephew has created, yes? I think you will want to put it front and center in your blog, eh? Front and center!"

Maggie allowed herself to be led past the rows of folding chairs that had been set up in the only indoor public space there was in St-Buvard—the back room of the old bakery. Closed now for nearly five years, the bakery sat in the center of the village. All the equipment except for the ovens had been put into various storage rooms around the village—or usurped. There wasn't a time that Maggie came into the space that she didn't feel a twinge of pain for the first year she had lived in St-Buvard and what the bakery had meant to her.

All gone now.

She shook off her momentary melancholy as Madame Dulcie pulled out an oil canvas from a wide satchel. Maggie knew Madame Dulcie's nephew's work and it was always stellar.

She was immensely grateful for that. It was impossible to say no to certain people in the village and Madame Dulcie was one of them. If her nephew's art had been crap, Maggie would still have featured it in her blog—no question about it—but she wouldn't have done it with nearly the enthusiasm.

The painting was a landscape that could be anywhere in Provence. The burnt oranges and muted mustard yellows offset the dusky green hills. Maggie could see the faint black sticks of the omnipresent vineyards in the far background. It was just the thing that any Francophile American tourist would be eager to buy for her "great room" back home.

"It's beautiful, Madame Dulcie!" Maggie exclaimed. "But you know you don't need to bring the actual piece to me. Have Eduardo send me a jpeg of it and the price he's asking for it."

"I wanted you to see it, Maggie," Madame Dulcie said, looking at the painting with pride.

"Maggie! Over here!"

"Well, it's gorgeous and I'm sure Eduardo will sell it quick and it'll lead people to all his other beautiful pieces. Excuse me, won't you, Madame Dulcie? And tell Eduardo to email me. Deadline in three weeks!"

Maggie turned to see Danielle standing with two men. One of them was her husband Jean-Luc. Maggie's good mood began to falter. The other man was Madame Roche's husband.

Crap. It had been too good to be true, Maggie thought, trying unsuccessfully to assess the look on Danielle's face.

She joined them and greeted Jean-Luc. He was a rough old farmer with his share of dirty dealings in his past but he was Danielle's cherished husband and a good friend to both Laurent and Maggie—not to mention a surprisingly excellent acting grandfather for the kids.

"Monsieur Roche was just telling us that he would like to be considered for your blog," Danielle said. "And I was telling him I thought you mentioned that you had a full roster for the next one?"

Maggie turned to Monsieur Roche. He was forty-something with a long draggy mustached and flint-cold grey eyes that watched Maggie. She knew she needed to be careful. It was a small village and if at all possible she needed to try to get along with everyone.

If at all possible.

"Yes, Monsieur Roche," she said shaking hands with him. "I'm glad to know you. But yes, as Madame Alexandre has said, I can only advertise a maximum of ten or twelve products per post and I —"

"I am not asking you to ship my berries," the man said abruptly, surprising Maggie with his high-pitched voice which did not match his appearance. "Simply to include my sales information and a picture of them."

"Well, as I've said I only have room for—"

"I am told you are promoting your husband's wine tour next month."

Maggie stared at him and then glanced at Jean-Luc who was frowning.

"That's right," she said.

"You could include the mention of my berries in that promotion."

Maggie felt a kernel of anger grow in her chest and she took a quiet, unobtrusive breath to keep calm.

"I am not mentioning anything in that promotion," she said, "except my husband's winery."

"I am sure it will not be a problem to include my berries. I will send you my information."

"That won't be necessary, Monsieur Roche," Maggie said firmly. "But again, I'm glad to have met you." She turned and took Danielle's hand and pulled her toward their seats.

"You handled that well, *chérie*," Danielle whispered as they sat down.

"You wouldn't say that if you could see his face right now," Maggie said. "He's shooting me daggers."

"Ignore him. He said what he had to say and you answered him. That is the end of it."

Why is it that somehow, Maggie was pretty sure that wasn't the case at all?

⁂⁂⁂⁂⁂⁂

Laurent threw the tennis ball to Jemmy but Petit-Four got there first. He couldn't help chuckling over Jemmy's howls of outrage as the little dog sped away with the ball.

"Never mind, Jemmy," Laurent said, waving his son over to him. As the sun dropped in the sky pushing the vineyard into shadows, Laurent turned to pick out the au pair with Mila in the distance.

He'd been happy to hire Mimi. She needed the work, and he'd owed her parents a favor—not something that happened often. He'd been afraid Mimi wouldn't stay but so far she seemed happy—and the children loved her.

"Inside now," he called to her. She nodded and pulled Mila out of the baby swing Laurent had hung in the magnolia tree.

"Not yet!" Jemmy whined as he presented himself in front of his father. "Petit-Four took the ball!"

"We have others," Laurent said as he lifted his son onto his shoulders, prompting wild squeals of joy from the boy. He

26

waited until Mimi and Mila had stepped into the house before he brought up the rear with Jemmy, stopping briefly to take one quick look at the scene of his home and vineyard.

He was proud of what he'd built here—and that included the three people he called his family. He knew he was looking forward to seeing Roger—it had been too long—and he knew a part of his anticipation was the fact that he wanted to show his friend how far he'd come.

How far he'd come from what he'd been.

And who more than the one who knew you then to appreciate that?

He set Jemmy down inside the house, made sure the outdoor driveway light was on for Maggie's return later from the village meeting, and then went to the kitchen to start dinner.

After the children were down, fed, bathed and read to—and before his *femme* came home—he would email Roger to extend the invitation. Maggie's jokes of strippers aside, it would be interesting indeed to see who it was Roger had chosen after all these years. While Roger had told Laurent that he'd married, he'd told him very little else about his bride.

Perhaps that is the way of people like us who once made our living in the shadows, Laurent thought as he turned on the front burner to the stove.

But still it was strange.

"Monsieur Dernier?"

Laurent looked over his shoulder. Little Mimi—sixteen years old but small for her age—stood in the doorway to the kitchen with Mila in her arms.

"*Oui?*"

"A phone call for you, Monsieur Dernier."

Laurent frowned. Nobody called the landline. He wasn't even sure why they still had one. He touched his jeans pocket for his cellphone but it wasn't there. He must've left it upstairs in the bedroom. Perhaps someone had tried reaching him there first.

"*Merci*, Mimi," he said, going into the living room and shooing Jemmy upstairs to watch his cartoons in the playroom up there. "Dinner in thirty minutes. Baths first, *oui?*"

Jemmy, Mila and Mimi all three nodded and then turned and ran upstairs while Laurent picked up the receiver from where Mimi had left it on the couch.

"*Allo?*" he said.

"Laurent?" a female voice asked breathlessly.

Laurent knew the voice and a thread of unease stung behind his eyes.

"Jill?" he said.

"I am so sorry to have to call you under these circumstances, Laurent," she said, her voice wobbly with emotion.

"What has happened? Is Roger there?"

"That's just it, Laurent, he's not," Jill said. "I can't believe I have to make this phone call to you. I am so sorry, but Roger's dead."

5

Except for a request to help clean up the village fountain and to ask for any suggestions on finding a way to finance a new bakery for the village, the only reason most of the people at the guild meeting were present to discuss Maggie's blog and what they might expect from their advertising in it.

As soon as Madame Charpentier—the postmistress—opened the meeting up to discussion, most of the questions were directed at Maggie.

How soon did Madame Dernier think they might see the benefits of being mentioned in her blog? When was Madame Dernier going to increase the number of products or services allowed in her blog? What did they have to do to be interviewed for it?

Maggie answered them all with patience and good humor. Five years ago most of these people—with just a few exceptions —had considered her an outsider. Today, they were used to seeing her and the children out and about the village. But more than that —they saw how her writing had helped benefit St-Buvard and everyone who lived there. With her blog now edging on twenty thousand subscribers and connected to all the major travel websites, most of the people advertising with her had increased their revenue fourfold.

Within one year and one simple blog about her life in Provence, Maggie had opened up the villagers' hearts to her and created a life in the village for herself that was fulfilling and satisfying. So they could ask all the questions they wanted. And she would do what she could to make sure she could say *yes* to all of them.

Or almost all of them.

She watched Monsieur Roche on the fringe of the group. He never took his eyes off her. And they were not happy eyes.

As she and Danielle were packing up to leave, a few people came over to shake hands with Maggie and to ask about the children and Laurent. One or two even asked about Grace. Grace Van Sant was Maggie's best friend. For several years, she had lived not far from St-Buvard but the past year had been a rocky one for her and she hadn't handled it well. Now Grace was home in the States trying to put her life back together. She and Maggie were still in contact, but barely.

"I've been meaning to ask you," Danielle said quietly when the last of the village women had left and she and Maggie were alone in the meeting hall. "How is Madame Van Sant?"

"I'm not really sure," Maggie said with a sigh. "I've reached out to her a bit but she's not reaching back. If she's trying to tell me she needs space, I want to respect that."

"A lifelong friendship goes through many stages, I think," Danielle said.

"That's true."

"But I think sometimes if a friend is going through a particularly trying time in her life, they might need us to step out of character a little."

When it came to her friendship with Grace Maggie knew *she* was the one who always reacted emotionally and Grace who was the voice of reason.

Last year that had all changed.

"When our friends are in trouble we cannot always wait for an invitation," Danielle said.

Maggie leaned over and hugged the older woman. "How did you get to be so wise, Danielle?"

"Old age mostly."

They both laughed.

"Is this a private conversation?"

Maggie looked up to see Madame Roche glowering in the doorway of the bakery.

"What is your problem?" Maggie said with annoyance, aware that Danielle had put a firm hand on her arm as if to hold her back.

"You have chosen to exclude my husband and me from membership in your precious guild."

"It's not my place to exclude or not," Maggie said, feeling her temper get the best of her. "It's voted on by the members."

"Do you think I am stupid?" Madame Roche stormed into the room and Maggie had to force herself not to take a step backward.

"Stop it this instant, Madame," Danielle said to the woman. "There has been no exclusion—"

"It is because we are Catholic!" Madame Roche shrieked. "This is racist in its purest form."

Was the woman mental? Half the people in the village were Catholic—Maggie included. In the back of her mind, Maggie saw three people file back into the room as if curious about the raised voices.

"It's not about your religion," Maggie said hotly, ignoring Danielle's tugging on her arm. "It's about—"

Before Maggie could finish, Danielle interrupted her.

"We saw you, Madame," she said breathlessly. "Yesterday in front of the hardware store. We saw what you did. Now we will speak no more of this. Go home."

Madame Roche's mouth fell open and she looked from Danielle to Maggie and then, to Maggie's horror, burst into tears and turned and fled the room, pushing past four villagers—all women—who had heard every word.

✦⋆ ✦⋆ ✦⋆ ✦⋆ ✦⋆ ✦⋆

An hour later Maggie drove up the winding drive to her house, turned off the car and sat listening to the engine ping noisily as it cooled down.

The fact that Danielle had been the one to say it out loud had helped mitigate the damage. Maggie had been a breath away from saying it herself and that would have been ten times worse. All the good will Maggie had built up in the village would've been gone in the time it took to utter the fateful words: *you stole.*

As it was, the accusation felt like it came from Maggie but Danielle had at least softened the blow.

What a mess. What a total titanic screw-up. She'd humiliated Madame Roche in front of just enough people to spread the word throughout the village that Maggie wouldn't have her in the guild because Madame Roche was a thief. Maggie groaned and ran a hand over her eyes.

How was this going to work out now?

At best, Madame Roche's husband would confront Laurent with the accusation and the men would sort it out one way or the other. One of the more unfortunate features of village life was that it was stiflingly provincial about the roles of husbands and wives. On the other hand it occurred to Maggie that this might be one of those times when that worked out to her benefit.

At worse, nothing more would be said about the theft and there would be a pall of guilt and reproach that would hover over the village and the Roche's for as long as they lived there.

Which meant Maggie needed to go to Madame Roche.

Hell and damnation.

One little slip of temper and she'd succeeded in setting village detente back twelve months.

Crap. Crap. Crap.

Maggie got out of the car and trudged up the steps to the house. She hated telling Laurent that she'd screwed things up like this. He'd expect her to put it right. Like she didn't have a thousand other things on her plate without this! She stepped into the house and dropped her leather tote by the coatrack in the foyer.

Tiled with vintage Italian ceramic flooring, the foyer was nearly as big as the apartment Maggie used to live in back in Atlanta. Straight ahead was the large marble staircase that led to the upper level of the house. The first level was comprised of three rooms—the living room was the largest—a square forty by forty feet and anchored by a massive fireplace and two sets of French doors which led to the garden. The other room was a small dining room connected to the second largest room, the kitchen.

Mimi was seated at the dining room table writing in a notebook. Maggie assumed the children were in bed and asleep so it was odd to find Mimi still here.

"Hi, writing a book?" she asked the girl and then looked up at the stairs questioningly.

"No, just my diary," Mimi said. "The little ones are asleep but Monsieur Dernier is outside so I didn't want to leave."

Maggie stepped into the living room to look out to the patio which, in summer, was an extension of their living room. She could see Laurent sitting in one of the chairs outside. She saw the glow of his cigarette. Petit-Four was lying at his feet.

"He got a phone call," Mimi said as she began to pack up her things.

"A phone call? From whom?"

"I do not know, Madame. It was on the house phone."

Laurent was clearly reacting to some kind of news delivered on the phone that only coroners or police officers would call since everybody else called their cell phones. Maggie was sure it couldn't be about her parents or Laurent would have called her.

"I'll drive you home," Maggie said to Mimi, but her eyes were on her husband on the patio.

What in the hell had happened?

"No need, Madame Dernier," Mimi said. "I told my father to come for me when *Maman* returned from the guild meeting tonight."

Mimi's mother, Genevieve Dorset, was a seamstress in town. Maggie advertised the full line of her smocks and children's play clothes and always enjoyed talking with her at the guild meetings.

"That's him now," Mimi said, going to the front door. Maggie followed her and could see Yves Dorset in the car. They exchanged waves.

"Thanks for waiting for me, Mimi," Maggie said. "That was good thinking. Say hi to your mother for me."

"I will, Madame. I hope everything is all right." Mimi hurried down the steps to her father's car and hopped in.

Maggie went immediately to the patio and opened the French doors. Petit Four ran to her.

"What's happened?" she said as she joined Laurent.

It was a cool night but Laurent seemed not to notice. He sat and stared out over his vineyard, a cigarette in one hand and a glass of scotch in the other.

"It's Roger," he said, not looking at her.

Maggie sat down beside him. Whatever had happened, it had to be bad. Laurent wouldn't be reacting this way if Roger couldn't come or was sick or even in prison. No, somebody had died.

"What happened?" she asked gently.

Laurent shook his head. "An accident."

"Car?"

"*Non.* He had a fall."

"I'm so sorry, Laurent," Maggie said. She touched his wrist but he didn't look at her, just kept his focus on the darkened outline of his vineyard. And why should he? He knew full well what she thought of Roger. He knew she couldn't share his grief. Maggie felt a spasm of guilt as she watched her husband.

Roger was the brother he'd never had.

And now he was gone.

And even though all of Maggie's loved ones were safe and well tonight, watching Laurent trying to come to grips with a world without his dear friend in it—made Maggie feel worse than she could ever remember feeling.

6

The next morning, Maggie and Laurent were up early. They would be gone for at least four days and while the harvest was over, there was still a surprisingly long list of things that needed to be done during their absence. As Maggie packed her sweaters in her suitcase, she caught sight of her husband's tall form striding through the vineyard. One of his hunting dogs trotted at his side.

Petit Four barked and Maggie turned to see her dog on the floor watching her. She picked her up and tousled her curly head.

"You're worse than the kids," she murmured to the dog. "We'll be back before you know we're gone."

Danielle and Jean-Luc would move into Domaine St-Buvard to help Mimi with the children for the few days that Maggie and Laurent were away for Roger's funeral. Maggie had no doubt Jean-Luc was secretly pleased to be able to spoil the children full time.

The children themselves were much less secretive about expressing their joy in the fact.

It would be the first time Maggie would be separated from Mila for longer than a few hours. And only the second time she'd been apart from Jemmy—which she swore she'd never repeat.

It didn't matter. They had to go.

Maggie put the dog down and sat on the bed. Out the window, she saw Laurent was talking to Jean-Luc by the far perimeter of the vineyard.

She still couldn't believe what had happened. Roger dead? In the twelve hours since she'd learned that he'd died, she was surprised to realize she would miss him. Even though she rarely saw him over the years, even though she always thought he didn't matter to her, she would miss knowing he was somewhere in the world.

Roger. So worldly, so full of quip and vim.

It was just not possible to think of him gone.

Her heart squeezed in pain. As much as Laurent loved Roger she knew Roger had loved him, too. Loved him like a brother.

Talk about putting petty village politics into perspective, she thought grimly. Here she was getting upset about a woman who didn't like her and now another woman a few thousand miles away was dealing with true heartbreak over the loss of her husband.

And then there was the fact that just the day before Maggie had practically thrown a tantrum at the thought of having to entertain Roger and his wife. And how she'd always made it clear that Roger wasn't welcome.

For what? Had she really thought he'd steal Laurent away? Seduce him with plans of a jewel heist or big con? Hadn't Laurent made his choice?

Maggie grimaced in pain and regret.

And now Roger was gone and there was no way to redeem herself. How could she ever even say his name to Laurent again or share his memories when the last thing she'd said about him was *I don't want him here*?

And now it was too late to make amends.

She looked around her bedroom. They'd be gone only a few days to London. There and back. In and out. She left the bag at the foot of the bed—Laurent would get it later and be annoyed if she tried to lug it down herself. She came downstairs where Danielle was preparing lunch for the children. Jemmy sat at the dining room table quietly coloring. Mila was in her high chair.

Danielle smiled sadly at Maggie as she came into the kitchen.

"How are you, *chérie*?" Danielle asked.

"I'm fine, Danielle. But I still can't believe it."

"Sudden death is the worst kind."

Maggie placed a hand on Mila's head where she sat in her high chair. "I've been thinking about Madame Roche and that whole mess."

"Perhaps you can use this time to *not* think about her," Danielle said. "I'm sure it will all work out."

"That's just it. I think *I'm* going to need to do something to fix it."

"You are thinking of talking with her?"

"Bad idea?"

"I don't know, *chérie*," Danielle said with a sigh. "Perhaps all parties can go to their separate corners for a time, yes?"

The French doors opened and Maggie turned to see Laurent and Jean-Luc enter through the living room. As usual Laurent's face was unreadable but Jean-Luc's face broke into smiles at the sight of Mila and Jemmy.

"*Bonjour, mes enfants!*" Jean-Luc said.

Jemmy tossed his crayons down and ran to Jean-Luc to wrap his chubby arms around the old man's knees.

"Pépère!" he crowed forcing Mila to join in with the cry. "Pépère!"

"All right, you two," Maggie said. "Let Pépère get his jacket off, okay?" She watched Laurent but he didn't meet her eye. He went upstairs to get the bags.

Thirty minutes later in a flurry of kisses and last-minute instructions, Laurent loaded the bags in their car and they set off for the airport in Marseilles.

Taciturn at the best of times, Laurent had said very little since he received the news of Roger's death. The drive to the airport was nearly two hours. Maggie was torn between wanting to allow him his private thoughts—and hearing for herself that he was okay.

She gave him until they passed the far boundary of the village.

"Where's the service being held?"

"In London."

Well, that much she knew but she also knew Laurent wasn't being deliberately remote. His thoughts were elsewhere.

"And it was his sister who called you? Jill Bentley?"

"*Oui.*"

"I'm surprised it wasn't his wife. Does she have your number?"

"I do not know, *chérie.*"

"It just seems so strange that Roger would die falling," she said. "He wasn't rock climbing, was he?"

"*Non.*"

"I didn't think so. Roger was a little too urbane for rock climbing."

Laurent glanced at her and she saw a smile tugging at his lips.

"*C'est vrai,*" he said.

Not wanting to spoil the first hint of warmth from Laurent since he'd heard the news but overcome with curiosity, Maggie pushed her line of questioning.

"Where exactly did he fall?"

Laurent sighed. "At a luxury resort of some kind," he said.

An image of Roger came to Maggie. He was always so dapper and good-humored. Ready for the next martini or the next gambit.

"And the cops are saying it's an accident?" Maggie prodded Laurent.

Laurent sighed and kept his eyes on the road.

"His sister said he fell to the bottom of a twenty-foot dumbwaiter," he said

"A *dumbwaiter?*"

"It appears the resort where he died is an old private estate and the drop from the upper floors to the basement is significant."

"How did he get inside a dumbwaiter? Did he lean over too far?"

"That is what was suggested."

Maggie shook her head in confusion. "Was he drunk?"

Laurent's expression told her what she already knew.

"That does not sound like Roger," she murmured.

But it does sound a whole lot like murder.

7

It had been at least a decade since Maggie was last in London. Then it had been for business. She'd been sent there by her ad agency to work on a jingle for a potato chip client back in Atlanta. Being young, single and on the company credit card for two weeks had left a very pleasant taste in Maggie's mouth for the city although she'd spent much of her time alone, wandering through bookstores, flea markets and going to plays.

That had been summer. When she and Laurent landed at Heathrow, she discovered that London in October was cold. *Really* cold. Wet and cold. While autumn had arrived in St-Buvard most people were still walking around in light jackets. Here it was already deep winter as far as Maggie was concerned.

No wonder the English drink so much hot tea! They needed it to keep warm ten months out of the year.

After Laurent rented the car, they drove straight to the church where Roger's memorial service was being held. Roger's sister had told Laurent that the death was still pending the conclusion of the investigation and so the body had not been released. Jill also said that Roger's widow wanted all loose ends tied up as quickly as possible so they wouldn't wait for a funeral which would require getting the body back.

Clearly, the bereaved Mrs. Roger Bentley was ready to move on.

Maggie scolded herself for the ungenerous thought. She didn't know these people or what their circumstances were. She reminded herself to be careful of jumping to conclusions.

Laurent had been quiet on the flight but Maggie could pick up no indication that he was in any way upset with her. If he blamed her for her less than generous attitude toward Roger, she could see no evidence of it.

Which made her feel even worse.

Holy Trinity Chapel off Lyonsdown road was a beautiful example of Norman architecture. Maggie was pretty sure Roger wasn't religious in any way so the choice must reflect his wife's beliefs. They parked on the street and entered the chapel where a tall man in a dark suit met them at the door. He held a program in his hands and handed one to Laurent as they approached. Maggie saw he was wearing a name tag that said "William Fitzhugh."

This was Roger's nephew. He looked vaguely like Roger but where the impish glint that Roger always carried with him in every code of his DNA, this man seemed to project a dourness that Maggie was sure was there even when he wasn't at a funeral.

"They are just starting," William said solemnly and gestured for Laurent and Maggie to seat themselves.

The pews were largely bare with only a handful of people scattered about them which suggested that Roger had few friends and those he had weren't interested in sitting together.

"Did William know who you were?" Maggie whispered as she and Laurent sat in one of the back pews.

"I have never met him," Laurent said and then turned his attention to the program.

The widow sat in the front pew next to a young man that Maggie assumed was her son. Laurent had very little information about Anastasia Bentley beyond the fact that she had brought a child to the union.

From where they sat, Maggie could only see the backs of the heads of Anastasia and her son. An attractive blonde woman sat in the pew behind them and she had twisted in her seat to watch Laurent and Maggie as they entered. That might be Jill, Maggie thought. Roger's sister. Everyone else in the chapel kept their heads down until the vicar materialized and proceeded to give a very short, very generic eulogy. He ended it with a prayer and invited the congregation to stay behind for tea.

People began filing out before he'd descended from the pulpit.

Roger deserved better than this, Maggie thought. The way Laurent was clutching the program, his eyes on the empty pew in front of him, she was pretty sure he was thinking the same thing.

Maggie watched as Anastasia Bentley walked past them on her way out. She was dressed expensively in a formal suit and wore dark sunglasses. She didn't pause when she passed. Her son walked behind her. He wore jeans and a blazer. Even from where Maggie sat she could hear his iPod playing music through his earphones. She wasn't particularly surprised to see he was disrespectful at Roger's service. After all, the two of them hadn't had much time to become close.

Unlike me who has had five years of opportunity to embrace Roger.

She flushed with guilt and turned away just as Roger's sister walked up and leaned over and kissed Laurent on the cheek.

"I am so glad you're here," she said. "Of all of them, you're the only one who mattered to him."

She glanced at Maggie and smiled. "I'm Jill. You must be Maggie."

"I'm so sorry for your loss," Maggie said. "Truly."

"You are coming to the wake?" She looked from Maggie to Laurent.

"We are," Laurent said.

"Great. We'll talk then." Jill put a hand on Laurent's shoulder and then left.

It occurred to Maggie that Laurent would have every reason to believe that Roger's sister shared more of his grief than Maggie did. That was likely true.

An older woman in her fifties was the last one to leave and as she passed, Maggie was astonished to see Laurent lift his hand to her and the woman take it. It was brief but heartbreaking. Whoever this woman was, Laurent knew her and knew she was hurting just like him.

"I think we will skip the tea, *oui*?" Laurent said to Maggie as he stood up.

41

"Do you know where the wake is being held?"

He nodded without answering, as if his mind was too full of what he had seen and felt today. For once in her life, Maggie didn't push it.

The wake was held in the backroom of a nearby pub. By the time Maggie and Laurent arrived, everyone else seemed to be in full swing of drinking to Roger's memory. Anastasia was standing and greeting people at the entrance to the back room, a glass of white wine in one hand and her sunglasses on the top of her head.

She was lovely, without doubt, Maggie thought. She looked the very picture of the classic English rose. Pale, unblemished skin, golden hair and cerulean blue eyes. It wasn't fair to judge her today of all days, Maggie knew. But there was something off-putting about Anastasia Bentley and Maggie wasn't sure it wasn't something intrinsic to the woman.

"Thank you for coming," Anastasia said coolly as she shook Laurent's hand.

Laurent murmured his condolences and moved to the bar leaving Maggie with Anastasia.

"I'm Maggie," Maggie said. "Roger was a good friend to our family and we'll always be forever in his debt."

Anastasia made a face. "He seems to have had that effect on quite a few people," she said, turning her eyes to the next person in line.

Maggie found Laurent at the bar and he handed her a glass of red wine.

"Will you be fine if I leave you?" he said, looking around the room.

"Of course."

There were definitely more people at the wake than at the memorial service. *Maybe that's as it should be*, Maggie thought. It was an open bar so it was possible some of the people here didn't even know Roger. Maggie caught a glimpse of the stepson Nigel. He was leaning on the bar with a tall glass of whisky in front of him and already seemed drunk.

Thinking of how she had made up her mind about Roger and then never gave him a chance to alter that opinion made her think of Madame Roche. The difference was Roger had all the grace and charm that Madame Roche lacked. And yet in his lifetime, Maggie could never find it in her heart to truly forgive him. Why? Why had she been so hard on him? What exactly had he done to her except try to cheat her and end up enriching her life beyond measure?

"You are Laurent's wife, aren't you?" a voice said at Maggie's elbow. She turned to see the older woman who had held hands briefly with Laurent in the chapel.

"I am," Maggie said.

"I'm Madeline Mears. I own the resort where Roger died."

Maggie thought that was an odd thing to say since Madeline obviously had another connection to Roger or she wouldn't have reached out to Laurent. Her age was closer to Roger's so Maggie's best guess was that Madeline was an old girlfriend. She forced herself not to look in Anastasia's direction who was easily twenty years Roger's junior.

"Laurent and I knew each other ages ago," Madeline said, as if reading Maggie's thoughts. Her eyes glinted meaningfully at Maggie and the rest of her message was delivered silently: *I knew Laurent before he was a respectable vigneron and family man.*

Maggie fought her first reaction to the woman, which was a defensive one—for herself, her family. And for Laurent.

"Well, a lot has happened since you knew him," Maggie said.

"Hasn't it just?" Madeline said, sipping her tumbler of whiskey.

Maggie could see that at one time Madeline might have been good-looking. She had high cheekbones and bright blue eyes. But the years had not been kind. No fillers or skin smoothers for her. The folds around her mouth were deep and the lively blue eyes were today swollen with the evidence of crying.

"So how did you know, Roger?" Maggie asked bluntly.

Madeline paused, studying the depths of her drink. "We did business together. A long time ago."

So she was in on the scams and the heists back in the day? Must have been a pretty hard fall from living on the Riviera scamming tourists and living the high life to ending up old and alone running a country hotel.

"Why was Roger at your resort?" Maggie asked.

Madeline didn't answer. She was watching someone over Maggie's shoulder and when Maggie looked she saw Anastasia was now seated at a back booth holding court. Maggie turned to look at Madeline and saw her face hardened into loathing.

"Did you know Roger's wife?" Maggie asked, watching Madeline's face for a reaction.

"I did and I do," Madeline said bitterly.

Whatever or whomever Madeline had been twenty years ago, she was a dried up old crone compared to the lovely Anastasia.

"She finally has what she's wanted all along," Madeline said, her eyes still on Roger's widow. Anastasia's voice lilted over the crowd as she laughed gaily at something someone said.

"Was Roger rich?" Maggie asked.

Madeline turned her attention to Maggie. "Rich enough. But that wasn't the main thing she wanted."

Maggie held her tongue. In her experience, even the gentlest prompting was often too much to encourage people to speak when they knew they shouldn't.

Madeline's eyes went back to Anastasia. "She wanted the Bentley name," she said softly as if she herself had imagined having that same name many years ago.

"Did Roger have a good name?"

Madeline twisted around as if looking for a waiter. She drained her whisky.

"As far as social climbers are concerned, he did. The Bentleys have been in Burke's for centuries."

Maggie frowned. "Burke's?"

"It's the book with all the families of the Commonwealth that can claim a heraldry of the Peerage."

"Roger was a duke or something?"

"Son of a baronet. Didn't you know? It didn't matter that his family was financially ruined over a century ago. In Britain the name is everything." She looked into the depths of her empty glass.

"In fact, if you think money is the root of all evil, you should see what some people would do to protect their good name."

Maggie felt an unpleasant tingling up and down her arms at Madeline's words.

8

Laurent listened as Jill alternately spoke and wiped her eyes. She and Roger hadn't been close, he knew, but still, to lose a brother was hard. He gestured to the man behind the bar to bring them both another whiskey. He watched Maggie from across the room. She was talking to Madeline Mears.

How many years had it been since he'd seen Madeline? It was unfortunate to see her this way. He had always liked her.

Maggie was looking around the room—probably for him— and he shifted to catch her eye.

"Have you met Maggie?" he asked Jill as he gathered up their drinks to walk toward Maggie and Madeline.

"No, but I've heard about her from Roger," Jill said. "He was terribly impressed."

Laurent hoped Jill wouldn't mention that to Maggie. It would only make Maggie feel more guilty.

Suddenly Anastasia appeared at Madeline's elbow and hissed loudly at her, making several people turn to look. Madeline's face drained of blood as Anastasia addressed her. Then Madeline shoved her drink glass onto an empty tray and rushed out the door.

He and Jill reached Maggie and Anastasia a second later.

"I just think it's jolly bad form, don't you agree?" Anastasia was saying to Maggie. "Strictly speaking, she's the help, you see. Not to mention Mrs. Mears is the manager of the establishment where my husband died. You do see, don't you?"

"I..." Maggie looked from Anastasia to Laurent as if for a clue as to what to say.

"Not to mention Madeline was Roger's ex," Jill said tartly to Anastasia, "so that's always awkward."

"Don't be absurd, dear," Anastasia said coldly. "That was centuries ago. Oh! I see someone I simply must talk with. Excuse me, won't you?" Anastasia disappeared into the crowd to talk to no one that Maggie could see.

"We all hate her," Jill said with a sigh. "My brother lost his damn mind and that's the truth of it." She turned to Maggie. "Can you imagine Roger with her?"

Maggie said, "Well, I haven't spoken to her much."

"She doesn't seem too bloody devastated, does she?" Jill said bitterly. "Oh, well, black widow and all that."

A loud crash made all three of them turn their heads in time to see Roger's stepson Nigel push through the crowd and climb on top of a small stool, bringing him only a few inches above the heads of the crowd.

"Excuse me, I'd like to say a word," he shouted.

Laurent thought the young man looked flushed but whether from alcohol or the occasion it was hard to tell.

"Oh, no," Jill muttered. "We can live without this."

"My stepfather, Roger Bentley, Esquire," Nigel said loudly. "Eh, Mum? Wouldn't want to leave the important bit out, eh?"

Laurent picked out Roger's nephew Will from the crowd. He stood with his wife, Annette, a few feet away from Nigel. Will's face had turned from an impassive stare to a glower and Laurent could only assume everyone knew what was coming.

Laurent had only met Nigel today and even he could guess.

"My stepfather was a unique individual. An original, as me old granny used to say. Isn't that right, Mum?"

Anastasia sat with her back to Nigel as if in a formal display of non endorsement to whatever her son was about to say.

"Unlike just about everybody else I ever knew, Roger succeeded in being the villain in his own story—quite a feat wouldn't you say? A major wanker of the first order."

Laurent walked over and jerked Nigel off the stool. He heard a roar of surprise from the people gathered around him but nobody intervened. Nigel sputtered and pawed at the hands that held him by the scruff of the neck.

"You are inebriated," Laurent said to him, holding his face close to Nigel's. But he smelled no alcohol on the young man. Nigel's tirade wasn't fueled by whisky but by spite. "We will make room for someone else to speak now."

Laurent dragged him to the door of the bar and pushed him into the main bar area. He'd briefly considered throwing him up against a wall to see if that didn't calm him down but in the end decided he couldn't stand the sight of the little *connard*. When Laurent turned around, he saw the entire crowd staring at him with mouths open.

He knew it was Maggie who began to clap. And then the rest of them took it up as he made his way to the bar for another drink.

Maggie kept her eye on Laurent as he stood at the bar, flanked by several people attempting to get his attention. She wondered why it hadn't been Will standing up for Roger—or any one of the people drinking Roger's free booze. She noticed that Anastasia didn't complain about her son being tossed out and Maggie wondered how close the two of them were.

"Nigel's a toad and no mistake," Jill said emphatically. "He's one of the local opponents to the hunt. For a minute that's what I thought he was going to rabbit on about."

"The hunt?"

"The fox hunt. Oh, I forget with you being American and all. The Abbey sponsors a fox hunt on its property every fall. We're all mad for it."

"And Nigel's against it?"

"He belongs to the local saboteur group. He and his lot go around disrupting all the local hunts in the area. It's gotten bloody, let me tell you."

"Do you ride?"

"I do. My horses are at the Abbey."

"I thought the Abbey was a luxury resort?"

"It's a little bit of everything. Do you not know about the Abbey?"

"I guess not."

"It's what they call a Enhanced Experience Vacation. And it's dead popular. People come to The Abbey to live like they're landed gentry from the 1920s. They dress the part, dine the part. It's mad fun. We've been written up in The Guardian."

"We?"

"Well, not *we*, but I'm always there to ride and of course Roger was part owner"

Roger owned the Abbey with his ex-girlfriend?

"I did not know that."

"No reason you should, darling. Anyway, Nigel has been getting more and more belligerent about the hunt and he's put his mother right in it."

"Did Roger hunt?"

Jill burst out laughing. "Oh, goodness, can you imagine Roger on a horse? No, not at all. But Madeline knows the hunt fits the Abbey's brand to a tee. She'd never give it up and before you ask, no, Madeline doesn't ride either. But you do, don't you?"

"How did you know?"

"Maybe it was watching your eyes light up when I told you about my horses."

"It's been a while," Maggie admitted. "But I rode competitively as a teenager back in the States. Just local stuff."

"Hunter jumper?"

Maggie nodded.

"Did you hunt?"

"A little. Mostly drag hunts. They hunted fox in Georgia but I never went."

Jill sighed. "It's illegal here. More's the pity." Jill took Maggie's arm and they began to walk toward the bar where Laurent appeared to be winding up his goodbyes. "Come to the Abbey tomorrow," Jill said. "Let me show you the grounds from horseback."

"I'd love to," Maggie said before she could stop herself.

Laurent gave her a questioning look.

"Jill's asked me to go riding with her tomorrow," Maggie told him. She turned to Jill. "But I don't have anything to—"

"I've got everything you need. Don't worry a sausage about anything. Oh! There's Millie," Jill said looking over Maggie's shoulder. "I must talk to her but here's my number." She handed a business card to Maggie. "Ring me and we'll sort out the details.

Ta, darling." Then she turned and went to embrace a heavyset older woman standing by the bar.

Laurent took the card from Maggie and glanced at it before handing it back to her.

"I did not know you could ride."

"That's me," Maggie said. "Always trying to keep things mysterious for you. Are you ready to go?"

"*Oui.*" They walked to Anastasia who was standing near the door. She was alone, her arms wrapped in a hug around her chest as if she were cold.

"Thank you for coming," she said to Maggie while studiously not looking at Laurent.

"I'm so sorry for your loss," Maggie said, still wondering how much of a loss it really was for her.

"Madame Bentley," Laurent said solemnly as he nodded to Anastasia before he and Maggie left the room. They threaded their way through the main bar area and onto the street outside. It was raining and the temperature had dropped easily another ten degrees. Maggie shivered. She put a hand on Laurent's arm.

These formal gatherings were supposed to help you say goodbye to loved ones, she knew. Had it helped Laurent at all?

"You okay?" she said.

Laurent didn't look at her but squinted down the street as if trying to see their car.

"Roger's nephew told me the police called Anastasia before the funeral," he said.

Maggie pulled her jacket tighter around her as they began to walk down the street.

"Are they releasing the body?" she asked.

"*Non.* They are not," Laurent said, his face an implacable mask. "His death is now being considered a homicide."

Susan Kiernan-Lewis

9

So it was official. Someone had killed Roger.

Maggie shook her head as if to clear it. But, on some level, didn't she already know that? Who—unless they drink like an Olympian—*falls down a dumbwaiter?*

The evening after the wake had been a strained one and any hopes Maggie had that the wake had given Laurent some peace were dashed by the official police announcement. She and Laurent were both tired by the time they checked into their hotel and after a quick phone call to talk to Danielle and the children, Maggie was feeling disoriented and weary.

They were scheduled to fly home in two days. It had seemed like a good idea when they booked the flight to allow themselves a little time together before returning. Neither she nor Laurent had been away from the children since Jemmy was born—and certainly not together. Maggie liked to think of it as Roger's last gift to them.

Just the thought of it made her sad.

She applied body lotion to her elbows and legs—already chapped and dry from even this short a time in the colder weather —and pulled on a warm flannel nightgown. She climbed into bed and watched Laurent. He sat in the room's club chair studying his cellphone.

"Are you okay?" she asked.

"Stop asking me that," he said.

He's right. It's selfish. I'm just trying to make myself feel better. I want him to say he's fine so I can relieve myself of what I know he's going through.

He looked up and smiled softly. "I am sorry, *chérie*. I am tired."

"Then come to bed."

He tossed his phone onto the dresser and pulled his shirt off over his head.

"I didn't know you rode," he said.

"I'm sure I told you."

"*Non*. Never."

"Well, everyone in my circle rode. I was in pony club since I was seven."

"Did you win many medals?" Laurent slipped into bed with her and pulled her into his arms. One thing Maggie knew was that regardless of the effectiveness of funerals or wakes on a broken heart, the secure arms of the one who loved you can often do miracles.

"I was good at it," she admitted, laughing.

Maggie had a gift with animals. They loved her. When she was twelve she once walked through a pack of snarling dogs to retrieve a sweater a friend had dropped—and escaped without a nip to show for the experience. Her experience with horses was the same.

"So Madeline was Roger's ex," Maggie said. "*That* must have been interesting."

"She was his big love," Laurent murmured. The statement was so un-Laurent like that Maggie leaned on her elbow to look at him.

"If that's so, why didn't he marry her instead?"

"I do not know, *chérie*."

"Do you think she was upset to be replaced by such a younger woman?"

"Possibly."

"You know, Laurent, when Grace used to help me out with these cases, she would offer a tad more in the way of reactions and comments."

Laurent gave her a baleful look. "What case?"

"Are you seriously telling me you're not thinking what I'm thinking?"

"I can absolutely tell you I am not thinking what you're thinking."

"Laurent, someone killed Roger."

"Let the police handle it."

"I can't. How can you?"

When Laurent didn't answer, Maggie said, "It's because you know there are a million people out there who'd be only too happy to get a piece of Roger Bentley. Isn't that right? But darling, that doesn't mean they should."

Laurent pulled her to his chest and rested his chin on the top of her head. Maggie felt his sigh come from deep in his diaphragm.

They would figure it out together. They would sort it all out. Together.

Because a terrible injustice had been committed. And Laurent was hurting.

And a part of Maggie knew that she'd contributed to that at least a little.

≈≈≈≈≈≈

Anastasia eased into the back seat of the hired limo. She could smell cigarette smoke. The company said they had a strict rule but obviously that was bollocks.

In fact, it was *all* bollocks unless you owned our own. Only then could you have the assurance that the experience would be as ordered.

She dug out her phone, punched in the number, and waited impatiently for it to be answered.

"Hello?"

"You're done, you know that, don't you?" Anastasia said tightly into the phone. "And now that he's buried, I'm going to start on you."

She snapped the phone shut and stared out the dirty window, waiting for the surge of victory, the feeling of satisfaction. But for some reason it didn't come.

For the price I'm paying, you'd think they could at least wash the bloody windows.

Susan Kiernan-Lewis

10

Madeline stood in the kitchen and faced the twenty men and women seated around the long rough-hewn wooden dining table. A row of gleaming copper pots lined the wall opposite a wall of windows with a view to the back parking lot.

She'd told the cook Gabrielle what she would be saying and how she needed her to react at least publicly to the news.

Although of course, how Gabrielle might react was anyone's guess.

It was unbelievable that Anastasia and Nigel were insisting on staying at the Abbey so soon after everything that had happened. Worse yet that Laurent and his wife would be staying too.

Why? Why was he coming?

Of course she knew she would see Laurent. He and Roger had always been close. His coming to London couldn't be helped.

She supposed she had Jill to thank for that.

But to come to the Abbey?

Was it Laurent's American wife? Did she fancy a bit of a holiday? Was that it? Or a taste of living the upper crust English life? *Americans were usually such fools about that sort of thing. So obsessed with movie stars and royalty.*

Of course. She must be the reason.

"Madame Mears?" Gabrielle said.

Gabrielle was standing hunched over the table as if trying to disguise her height. She was tall for a woman and must have been pretty at one time. But ten bad years and a drug habit can strip the *pretty* off the fairest rose.

"I've gathered you all here," Madeline said, "because the police have asked me to temporarily close the Abbey."

The employees looked at each other and then Madeline.

"Whut? Permanently?" one young man blurted out. He'd been one of the recent hires. Didn't finish school but for raking out horse stables and carrying luggage, he didn't need to.

"No, *temporarily*," Madeline repeated. "Just until the police conclude their criminal investigation. Probably another three weeks."

"And we're getting paid meantime?" a young woman—one of the upstairs maids—asked. Her name was Violet and Madeline was frankly surprised to hear her speak. She was normally very shy.

"Everyone who is suspended for the three weeks will be paid," Madeline said. She hated to do it. With no bookings, she had no idea how she'd managed it. But it didn't seem fair to punish them. Most of them lived paycheck to paycheck. Worse, if she *didn't* keep them on the payroll, they'd find other work.

And with a full summer of bookings ahead at the Abbey, Madeline couldn't afford to lose anyone.

Deciding who would stay for the interim was easy. Madeline knew it had to be Gabrielle and Trevor. For one thing, they both lived at the Abbey.

Besides, Roger would have wanted that.

"That is all. Thank you," Madeline said. "You'll be contacted when to report back."

The employees began to file out happily enough. And why not? Madeline thought. Three weeks paid vacation was not much to grumble about.

Madeline put a hand out to stop Gabrielle. "A word," she said.

They both waited until they were alone.

"We have guests coming today," Madeline said.

"*Quoi*? You are just firing the help!" Gabrielle's English was poor and her accent thick but her face and her manner made for very few misunderstandings.

"It is unavoidable. Anastasia and her son are coming this morning."

Gabrielle made a sound of disgust.

"And two others. A…husband and wife." She didn't have the emotional energy to tell Gabrielle who was coming. She'd find out soon enough.

"*Incroyable*! I am to cook with no help? No sous chef? No prep cook? No *dishwasher*?"

"I know and I'm sorry. Plus it's possible that Roger's nephew Will and his wife will be staying too. That's only four all together," Madeline said quickly. "And you can have Violet stay and help you." Because Violet lived at the Abbey—like Gabrielle and Trevor did—there was a good chance she had no place to go for three weeks anyway.

"The bastard is dead," Gabrielle snarled, "and still I am a pack animal to be worked to death. Nothing has changed."

Gabrielle turned on her heel and left, grabbing her cigarettes as she exited.

No nothing has changed except everything has changed, Madeline thought as she caught a glimpse of the police cars through the back kitchen window as they arrived in the gravel parking lot behind the Abbey.

She watched the Chief Inspector get out of his car and saw him speak briefly to the group of employees as they got into their own cars to leave.

It occurred to Madeline that there might be another reason why Laurent was coming to the Abbey. She might as well face it but when she did a sliver of cold hard steel rammed deep into her gut.

He was suspicious of how Roger died.

And why.

Before stepping into the rental car, Maggie's phone began to vibrate and she saw that Danielle was calling her. Since Laurent was busy checking the front tires of the rental car she walked away and took the call.

"Hi," she said. "Everything okay?" She'd already had a fairly lengthy conversation with Danielle that morning about the change in travel plans. Visions of Jemmy in the Aix emergency room getting stitches in his head came surging into Maggie's brain.

"*Oui*, yes, Maggie," Danielle said. "I just had a moment away from the little ones. Jean-Luc has them out back with the dogs. He enjoys the children so much."

"They love him too."

"I have heard some gossip from the village."

The tips of Maggie's fingers tingled. *Madame Roche.*

"Is it bad?"

"It is not good, *chérie*," Danielle said. "I am worried about where it will lead. She is very angry."

Maggie glanced at Laurent who had finished his inspection of the car tires and was now inspecting her with a frown, clearly wondering why she hadn't gotten in the car.

"Look, don't worry about it, Danielle," Maggie said. "I'll call you later when I have time but I promise I'll settle this when I get back, okay?"

"If you are sure, *chérie*. It is a very unpleasant business."

"Just put it out of your mind. I'll talk to you later, okay?"

She joined Laurent in the car.

"What was that about?" he said.

"Nothing. I have it under control."

"I worry when you say things like that."

"How long is the drive to the Abbey?"

Laurent put his smartphone on the dashboard. His screen showed a GPS map.

"Two hours."

"Good. Should be a pretty drive."

Laurent gave her one last assessing look before clearly deciding he'd be better off not knowing.

She was right. It *was* a pretty drive. Situated outside the village of Compton Abdale, The Abbey was located northwest from London. They took the M40 highway out of the city and turned down a combination of narrow county lanes after that. The pastures along both sides of the road were crisscrossed with drystone walls that seemed to stretch on endlessly over the horizon. Maggie could only imagine how much fun it would be to jump a horse over any one of them.

This was the real thing, she thought with excitement. Not a water barrier or coop artificially devised by a jump designer, but the very thing the course jumps were modeled after: the English countryside. It had been years since Maggie had done cross-country—at least a decade. She knew it was the sort of sport that belonged firmly in the realm of her younger days. But if she wasn't worried about being timed? If she just took the jumps as she came to them, in her own time?

Maggie realized she was already hoping to participate in the fox hunt.

Wow. That was fast. From a simple hack in the woods with a new friend to riding in the annual hunt? Over terrain I've never seen before?

But why not? If she took it slow? Maggie knew from her past experience with the Hunt Club north of Atlanta that there were few things as exhilarating as galloping through the countryside jumping hedges, fences, walls and anything else along the way.

They passed the village on the south side of the Abbey and began seeing signs for the resort. Some of them were marked with mud and Maggie couldn't help but think it would be impossible for a passing car to fling mud up that high.

Did the people of the village not like the Abbey?

"You know we're supposed to dress for dinner every night," she said to Laurent.

He only grunted.

"But they give you the clothes. Jill said it's called an Enhanced Experience Vacation. Everyone comes here to dress up like they belong to upper-class English society in the 1920's."

"*Ridicule.*"

"You know how the Brits love to play dress up." When Laurent didn't respond, she asked, "What did Madeline say when you told her we were coming?"

He shrugged. "They have room."

"I mean, was she surprised we're coming?"

"She did not appear to be."

"I feel bad about how Anastasia treated her at the wake," Maggie said. "But I can't say I really warmed to Madeline either."

"This is not Madeline's best moment right now," he said.

"No, of course. I know that." Maggie watched the road ahead for a moment.

"Are the cops finished with the crime scene at the Abbey?" she asked.

"Madeline said they are." He looked at her. "You are thinking of examining it for yourself?"

"Aren't you curious?"

"What is there to see?"

"You'd be surprised."

She could see he wanted to go back to his own thoughts and so she focused on the beautiful fall scenery as they sped through the countryside.

A final long slow curve showed another sign that Maggie imagined was again pointing the way to the resort. Unfortunately, it was impossible to read what the sign said.

The carcass of an animal had been nailed to the center of it, obliterating the words.

11

The country road straightened out to reveal a long paved driveway between green lawns punctuated with twin cascading fountains. At the end of the road was The Abbey. Although from the descriptions she'd read online Maggie had been prepared for its size, she still had to stifle a gasp when she saw it. A typical English country manor, the Abbey looked like an enormous public library of brick and stone balustrade stretching the length of a full city block.

The front of the mansion had a strongly Georgian feel to it with a series of tall chimney stacks protruding from the top and mullioned windows in the gables.

"It's hard to believe that at one time only one family lived here," Maggie said as they drove down the drive.

"I thought it was a religious house."

"No, usually a private house that's called abbey is one built on the grounds of a former abbey or monastery."

"They tore down the abbey that was here?"

"Don't you remember Henry the Eighth? He had all Catholic buildings destroyed or claimed for himself back in the 1500s. I read on the Internet that this place changed hands many times until it was turned into a hotel."

"When did you read this?"

"This morning at breakfast when you were staring out the window flashing your *leave-me-in-peace* face."

He smiled. "I do not recall flashing you."

"Oh, you did all right. But that's okay. It's beautiful, isn't it? Can you believe Roger owned half of this? I wonder why he didn't live here?"

"It was just an investment for him."

Maggie knew the Abbey had at least three upper floors so the ceilings must be fifteen feet or more. She got an image of how far the plummet would be in a dumbwaiter from the top floor to the hard basement floor below. She shivered.

"You are cold, *chérie?*"

Even distracted by grief, Laurent missed very little.

"I'm good. Are you sad we came, Laurent? I should have asked you before I accepted Jill's invitation."

"It is fine."

They parked in front of the Abbey and three people—obviously watching for their arrival—stepped out to greet them.

Madeline Mears was wearing a black dress. She had her hair pulled back in a bun. She looked like something out of a British period drama. Her face was impassive, indicating no signs of recognizing Maggie and Laurent at all. A young man and woman stood at attention, their eyes straight ahead.

Laurent made a snort and when Maggie looked at him, he did everything but roll his eyes at the display. Before she could open her car door, the young man ran over and opened it for her, then stepped back and stood again looking into the horizon.

"Thank you," Maggie said.

"Missus," the man said, still not looking at her.

Madeline approached with her hands clasped together.

"We try to use every opportunity to perfect our roles," she said. "Welcome to you both. I hope you will indulge us." She looked meaningfully at the young girl who was dressed as an old fashioned scullery maid. "But we need the practice."

The girl blushed to her roots but didn't look at Maggie or Madeline.

"Thank you for making room for us," Maggie said and then realized as she was standing beside the mammoth house how ridiculous that must sound. Laurent pulled their luggage out of the trunk ignoring the young man who attempted to help.

Madeline turned to the maid and said coldly, "Go." Both she and the young man disappeared into the house.

"It's a work in progress," Madeline said. "Come. I'll show you to your room."

They entered the giant double doors of the Abbey's entrance. The foyer was as large as a bank lobby with marble flooring that stretched in pristine swathes up the huge curving staircase. The walls were paneled and covered with gilt-framed paintings of horses, dogs, countryside, and portraits of generic aristocracy.

It was hard to imagine that this was once ever someone's private residence.

"The police had us ask all our guests to leave," Madeline said as she led them to the wide staircase. "I can only imagine what the online reviews will read like after that. I've let most of the staff have the rest of the month off. No sense in keeping them on with most of the rooms empty."

"Is this the floor where Roger was staying?" Maggie asked.

Madeline stopped on the stairs and turned to look at her. She glanced at Laurent and then turned to resume her ascent.

"No," she said. "That section has been closed off."

They walked the rest of the way to Maggie and Laurent's room in silence. The little maid was standing by the door. This time, her eyes flitted nervously as if she didn't know where to look.

"Did you lay the fire, Violet?" Madeline asked as she pushed open the bedroom door.

"Yes, Mrs. Mears."

"Then go help Mrs. duLac in the kitchen."

"Yes, Mrs. Mears."

They stepped into the bedroom. Immediately Maggie could see the four-poster bed anchored the main area of the room. The tall mullioned windows looked out over the front lawn. The fireplace in the room was nearly as large as the one they had in their living room in Domaine St-Buvard. It was marble from floor to ceiling and a full six feet wide.

"It's beautiful," Maggie said.

"Yes, well, it's been updated. It's all very well to live as the landed gentry did in 1922 but today's guests also require central heating, their own en suite bath—preferably with a jetted tub—

and double insulated walls. Our comment cards indicate they'd like coffee makers and a minifridge in the rooms too. Dinner is at eight with cocktails in the American fashion at seven."

Madeline glanced at Maggie's slacks and cashmere twin set. "No need to dress tonight," she said.

"Are we the only ones here?" Maggie asked.

"Mrs. Bentley and her son are here," Madeline said.

Maggie looked at Laurent to see if he was surprised but he was staring out the window, his thoughts far away. "I guess I'm surprised she would want to be here after...after what happened."

"Nothing surprising about it," Madeline said in clipped tones. "She has every reason to be here now that she is the new majority shareholder in the Abbey...as she has taken pains to remind me literally at every turn."

※ ※ ※ ※ ※ ※

"But what are they doing there? Why are they still here?"

"How would I know?"

"They went to the Abbey, William!"

Will looked at his wife with frustration.

"I know, Annette. I heard you the first time. But I don't know why."

"Well, it's morbid, that's all." She turned and yelled down the hallway, "Jamie! Do not dream of turning on the telly until you've done your homework!" She turned back to Will. "They're there with Anastasia. *Alone* with Anastasia."

"So?"

"So! She'll badmouth you to them! You know she will!"

"What difference does it make now? Roger's dead! Who is there left to care?"

"The police haven't arrested anybody yet."

"You think Anastasia will try to lay this at *my* feet?"

"Stranger things have happened. And now that the merry widow is in fact a widow instead of just acting like one, she'd do well to point the blame away from herself."

"A little physical for Anastasia, surely?"

Annette jumped up and went to the hallway. Even Will could hear the sound of cartoons in the sitting room. He was half surprised his wife didn't go charging down the hall to sort out the boys. She tended to be strict with them. Instead, she closed the bedroom door.

"Will Jill be there?" she asked.

"I don't know about tonight but she'll certainly be there tomorrow."

"You've got to call her and tell her to leave those bloody dogs behind. They are a menace, Will! Someone is going to get hurt one of these days."

"Yes, well, I think that's the point, isn't it? She's trained them, Annette, for protection."

"Nobody at the Abbey is going to rape her! She's paranoid!"

Will knew Jill had been attacked one night in London three years ago. Her attacker was never caught. Perhaps she would've been able to sort it all out if the bastard had been apprehended and punished. Although the police said the attack was random—a matter of Jill being in the wrong place at the wrong time—in Jill's mind, he was still out there somewhere. Waiting.

And meanwhile, she didn't feel safe.

"That was unkind, Annette. Jill can't help how she feels. And the dogs bring her comfort."

"Until they rip the postman's leg off. Then they'll bring her a big fat lawsuit! Did you know one of them's a pit bull?"

"She claims not."

Annette let out a snort of disbelief and when she finally sat on the bed, Will used the moment as an excuse to put his arm around her.

"We're dropping the boys off with your mother, right?"

"Yes," she said begrudgingly as if unwilling to give up her bad mood.

"And you're riding in the hunt day after tomorrow?"

That did the trick.

A smile tugged on her lips. "You know I am."

"Is everything ready?"

As Annette began to warm to her subject, Will found himself grateful that there was an obsession he could always shine the light on when he needed to move Annette about the board.

He envied her that. While she was now happily chattering about what bit to try out or which feed was sub-performing, he was left to his own thoughts.

And while Annette's concern about Anastasia talking behind his back was the least of his worries, the fact that Roger's mate from frogville had decided to move into the Abbey for a few days…well, that was right up there at the top of them.

12

Laurent stood at the corner of the estate and watched the sun drop from the sky, transforming the hedges, the gorse and Yew trees into dark amorphous shapes.

It was so strange. He hadn't forgotten these people exactly but until yesterday, he'd pushed all of them so far into the recesses of his mind that it was as if they'd died and it was only now when he stepped into the same room with them that they were resurrected.

He lit a cigarette and stared into the gloom.

If only Roger could resurrect as easily.

It was impossible to believe that he would never hear Roger's voice again. How is it that so much life and energy could be gone so swiftly? So permanently?

It had been a mistake to come here. Roger wasn't here—certainly not the memory of him—and definitely not the Roger that Laurent used to know.

He threw his cigarette down and ground it out into the gravel but his attention was caught by a movement over his left shoulder. He turned to see who might be standing there, observing him without announcing themselves.

She stood with her back to the door that must lead to the kitchen. She glowed bright white in her chef's jacket and even in the dark, he could see the halo of red curls spiraling around her head that made her unmistakable at any distance—no matter how many years had gone by.

The fiery red tip of a cigarette glowed by her face and he could see her eyes watching him.

Merde.

Had Roger totally lost his mind?

Maggie emerged from the shower and dressed quickly. Laurent had opted to take a walk on the grounds while it was still light enough to see. As Maggie ran a comb through her hair she looked out the bedroom window to see if she could catch a glimpse of him but he must have gone the other way.

The only thing remotely dressy that she'd brought with her was a dark wool knit dress. If she added her pearls and wore the kitten heels she was wearing today with her slacks, she would probably not look too casual for a formal dinner in a castle.

Madeline had insisted she would not take Laurent's money for their stay. Maggie found herself wondering how much living like a duke or a king cost on a nightly basis. She checked her watch. She had a good hour before cocktails. Laurent would likely wander back to the room to clean up for dinner. If she hadn't been so eager to shower off the day's travel, she would have loved to have seen the stables. Perhaps it was better to see them for the first time with Jill. She had seemed so enthusiastic about showing the Abbey to Maggie.

Maggie stepped out of the room, noting that there was no lock on the bedroom door.

They update the plumbing but fail to add a deadbolt to the bedrooms? Shrugging off the incongruity of the thought, she set out to explore the floor. She knew that all the bedrooms were on this level—even the ones closed off.

For Roger to have fallen to his death, Maggie knew he needed to be up high. That stood to reason. She wondered where Anastasia's room was and decided stealth was the best plan at this stage. She tiptoed down the hall until she came to a landing that afforded a view of the downstairs foyer. Keeping close to the wall in case anyone should happen to look up, she hurried past the landing to the other side of the hall.

The doors and the paneling were indistinguishable except for the periodic placement of doorknobs to indicate which was wall and which was a room. The hall carpeting was an Arabian design but whether authentic or reproduced, Maggie had no way of knowing. Not that it mattered. The point was to create an illusion for people who were happy to dole out the big bucks to believe it. Real or fake furnishings were probably beside the point.

Maggie had read that many of these older houses had secret panels or hidden passageways leading to back stairwells. She ran her hands over some of the panels but the hall stretched for at least thirty yards. She would have to know exactly where they were to find them.

As she turned the corner heading toward the back of the great house, she saw the yellow crime tape. She paused to listen but could hear no voices. She walked to the tape and ducked under it. Maggie figured the area must have been dusted and scooped and bagged days before. Even so, she pulled a tissue out of one of her dress pockets and felt her heart beat faster. On the interior side of the hallway away from the outer wall there was a conspicuous handle. There was every reason to believe *this* was the so-called dumbwaiter.

Moving quickly now, she covered the handle with the tissue and jerked it open. The panel creaked loudly and fell toward her. It was large. Very large. And it was not a dumbwaiter. Maggie stared at the interior and then leaned over to look inside. All she saw was darkness. It was probably originally a garde robe that had been turned into a laundry chute. The sides were galvanized metal to expedite the expulsion of any object thrust into it.

It was easily large enough to accommodate a body. And the way it was constructed, it would be fairly easy to give an unsuspecting person a healthy shove to do the job.

Maggie closed the panel door and stepped back under the tape.

Had Roger been hit on the head first? Or just caught by surprise and manhandled into the chute? If only she could talk to the detective on the case!

"Well, well. Are you lost?"

Maggie whirled around to see Nigel standing at the corner of the hallway.

"A little ghoulish, surely?" he said to her with a sneer.

"I could say the same to you," Maggie said. "Did you know about the laundry chute *before* your stepfather ended up in it?"

"Oh, well done, you," Nigel said. "Pin it on the stepson. That's what I'd do but unfortunately for you, that's not what the police are thinking."

Nigel was definitely big enough to wrestle Roger into the laundry chute. And mean enough.

"Good alibi?"

"None that you need to know about. My mother likes to have drinkies promptly. She sent me to collect you and the Hulk." He turned on his heel and walked away.

Maggie followed, noticing that Nigel paused at her bedroom door before moving down the hall to the main staircase. When she got into her bedroom, Laurent was looking at his cellphone and wearing only a bath towel.

"Did you have a nice walk?" she asked.

"*Oui*," he said, looking up at her. "*Et tu?*"

"I just had a little look around," she said.

"You went to the dumbwaiter."

"It's actually a laundry chute." She thought about saying more —sharing her thoughts that Roger's murderer could be female as easily as not given the size and access of the chute. But it was hard to decipher Laurent's mood. Maggie knew he wasn't completely on board with her idea of investigating Roger's murder but neither was he doing his usual over-my-dead-body routine. She just wasn't sure where he was coming from.

Her phone dinged indicating she had received a text and it reminded her that she promised she'd call Danielle. She picked up her phone and looked at the screen.

It was from Grace.

It was the first time Maggie had heard from her in five months.

<R u busy?>

Not much as exploratory openings went, but it was at least something.

"Who is it?" Laurent asked as he ran his hands through his still-wet hair.

"Grace."

"You are not answering her?"

"I will later when we're not rushed." Hearing from Grace reminded Maggie of what Danielle had said to her about

70

friendships. If this was Grace reaching out to her, she wanted to make sure she made the right response.

"Are we rushed?" Laurent asked.

"I ran into Nigel in the hall and he said Anastasia blows a gasket if guests are late to cocktails."

Laurent snorted as if to say that was not a concern of his.

"Don't you think it's strange that she's here?" Maggie asked as she put her phone on vibrate so it wouldn't disturb the peaceful 1920's atmosphere of the Abbey.

Laurent shrugged. "She is half owner."

"I know. But staying at the place where your husband was killed just the week before?"

"She didn't love him."

Maggie stared at him. Again, it was such a very non-Laurent thing to say.

"How do you know?"

"I have eyes."

Maggie felt the weight of her guilt press evenly into her shoulders. Roger Bentley had a friend—the best of friends in Laurent—and Maggie had always made it as difficult as possible for the two of them to spend any time together. She could have green-lighted any number of weekend visits with Roger. He'd only met Jemmy once and had never met Mila. And now of course he never would.

And on top of all that, he'd married a woman who didn't love him.

Susan Kiernan-Lewis

13

The table in the dining room was set for thirty.

Maggie peeked into the room as she and Laurent made their way to the salon where cocktails were being served.

"It looks like a castle!" she whispered as she stood at the door to the salon. "The table looks like a runway it's so big and the tapestry over the fireplace mantel is bigger than the area rug in our living room back home."

Laurent was dressed in jeans and a collared shirt. Even in the throes of an English autumn, and without a sweater or jacket, he didn't appear at all uncomfortable.

"You know everyone will be wearing tails tonight," Maggie said with a smile. It didn't matter to her. After all, she thought he looked handsome when he came in from the vineyard, stomping mud off his gumboots.

And she knew for a fact that Laurent didn't care.

He shrugged and held the door open for her.

Inside the comfortably appointed salon, Anastasia sat on a damask wing backed sofa which was flanked by two rigid and uncomfortable looking Georgian arm chairs upholstered in matching toile. Her son Nigel lounged in one of the chairs, his legs stretched out such that anyone wanting to sit in the area would have to step over him.

The facing wall upon entering was crammed with every imaginable hunting trophy and animal hide. Elephants, rhinoceros, lion, tiger and wildebeest all glared down at the salon occupants.

The little maid Violet stood by a nearby credenza holding a silver tray of crystal glasses and an assortment of amber-filled flasks and a pair of silver plated claret jugs. Behind her was an oddly mismatched pair of mid eighteenth century pistols arranged on hooks on the wall.

Violet watched Maggie and Laurent as they entered. Maggie felt sorry for her. She obviously wasn't relaxed in her role. She smiled at the girl but only got a flush of embarrassment in return.

"So here are our unexpected guests," Anastasia said without rising. "I assume you have been made comfortable?"

Maggie sat in one of the armchairs while Laurent went to the credenza to get their drinks.

"Yes, thank you," Maggie said. "Everything is beautiful. Very authentic looking."

Anastasia was dressed in a mid-calf brocaded crepe sheath. She grimaced at Maggie's comment and looked away as if offended.

She does know none of this is real, doesn't she?

Laurent handed Maggie a drink with a lime bobbing in it and Maggie took a healthy swallow. Vodka and tonic. Perfect.

Laurent sat in the chair next to Maggie, forcing Nigel to pull his legs in. Nigel had a bruise over his right cheekbone and Maggie wondered if that was the result of Laurent throwing him out of the wake or if Nigel had run into someone else who didn't care for his brand of politics. He glowered at Laurent but didn't speak. Maggie wasn't completely sure he wasn't already drunk.

Madeline entered the room and glanced around as if ensuring all was as she expected. She wore a floor length tea dress. She nodded curtly at Maggie and Laurent and then approached Anastasia. She held a brochure in her hand.

"I thought you might want to see how it turned out, Anastasia," she said, holding out the piece to her.

Anastasia hesitated but her curiosity clearly got the better of her desire to stay in character. She began to reach for the brochure and then waved it away and pointed to Maggie.

"Give it to the Americans," she said. "They're our demographic audience, are they not?"

Madeline hesitated and looked at Maggie.

"What is it?" Maggie asked. Before she'd become a professional ex-pat with awkward French language skills and two babies clinging to her skirts, she'd worked in advertising on the creative side for several years.

"It's a direct mail piece," Madeline said, handing the brochure to Maggie. "For the Abbey."

Maggie took the small folder that featured a photograph of Anastasia dressed as if she lived in the 1900s. A glittering diamond tiara crowned a coif of intricate curls and carefully crimped waves. Although the picture was black and white, the densely embroidered tunic was dark as if scarlet or forest green. In the photograph, Anastasia looked over her shoulder as if caught by surprise, her expression showing imperious disdain.

The headline read: *Live the country life as Lord and Lady of the manor! Experience the epitome in traditional sporting country pursuits while your "downstairs" staff waits on your every pleasure!*

"What do you think?" Anastasia inquired over the glass of cut-crystal she held in her hand.

Maggie didn't want to be rude. She glanced at Laurent. Normally, if he cared, he'd telegraph his preference to her. Tonight, she wasn't even sure he was paying attention. His gaze was directed out the window of the salon at the darkened garden.

"Hitting those exclamation points pretty hard," Maggie said with a smile, hoping it would soften her words. "Not very subtle."

"I wrote it myself," Anastasia said icily.

Maggie tossed the brochure down on the coffee table in front of her.

"Well, then," Maggie said. "I think you've nailed it."

Madeline snatched up the brochure as if she was sorry she'd let Maggie see it in the first place.

"Dinner is served," she said abruptly, turning on her heel and exiting the salon.

The dining hall was every bit as magnificent as Maggie's first glimpse had teased. Paneled in darkly ornate wood on all three walls, the fourth wall featured a massive stone fireplace flanked by two floor to ceiling windows that looked out over the front lawns. A huge gilt-framed portrait of some anonymous ancestor hung over the fireplace mantel.

An intricate coral Isfahan rug covered nearly the entire
expanse of parquet wood flooring, allowing only a strip around its
perimeter for credenzas, hutches, and servers that were larger than
Maggie's dining room table back home.

The young man whom Maggie had seen when they arrived
was standing with his back to the wall next to an antique
sideboard. He was wearing what could only be described as a
footman's livery. His long muscular legs were in white stockings.
His jacket was immaculate and trim at his waist and held there by
a trio of three gold crested buttons. His tan face looked out of
place above the starched white shirt he wore.

As Anastasia took her place at the head of the table the young
man instantly went to her and held out her chair before returning
to his place at the wall.

Nigel took his seat to his mother's left and Madeline sat
several seats away. Maggie and Laurent took their seats down the
long table.

The place settings were china and crystal and placed directly
on the glossy walnut table without tablecloth or mats. Maggie
reached for her napkin and Anastasia made a soft sound and
glared at her.

"Trevor will do that for you," she said. "I understood that
Mrs. Mears made you aware that your visit becomes less of an
intrusion if we are able to use it as a way to train our staff."

Laurent flapped out his napkin with a loud snap and laid it
across Maggie's lap, his eyes never leaving Anastasia's. He took
Maggie's napkin and dropped it into his own lap.

The tense moment was interrupted by the arrival of Violet and
another woman carrying large serving trays. Trevor hurried to
them and took the tray from the little maid and carried it to the
long server parallel to the table. He was joined there by the other
woman. She was older, and her face was hard, her eyes focusing
on her work.

Sure are a lot of unhappy employees here, Maggie couldn't
help but think.

As the servants organized the silver-domed serving dishes on
the server, Maggie felt Laurent's knee press against hers. She
wasn't sure what, if anything, he meant to convey to her—but the
gesture comforted her.

What was he thinking? Was he wondering why Roger would want to own this hotel? Was he wondering how Roger could have married Anastasia?

Or is that just me wondering all that?

"Jill tells me you intend to go riding tomorrow," Anastasia said as Violet filled each of their wine glasses.

"That's right," Maggie said. "We're meeting at the stables in the morning."

The sounds of silver utensils scooping into dishes were the only noises in the room as Trevor stood to Anastasia's left and held a platter of venison with peppercorn sauce for her to serve herself.

"Why is it you and Roger were here last week?" Maggie asked, hoping to break the ice.

Anastasia waved Trevor away and he moved behind Madeline.

"We are often here. The outdoor life is not my thing at all, really. Horses and so on, but for Roger's sake...."

Madeline cleared her throat.

"Do you have something to say, Mrs. Mears?" Anastasia said tartly before turning to address Maggie. "I don't approve of staff dining with family. I feel it spoils the illusion. Don't you think?" She reached for her wine glass. "I'm afraid there'll be some changes going forward."

The hard-faced servant brought a serving dish to Maggie. It looked like Yorkshire pudding. Maggie took a spoonful and the woman turned and presented the dish to Laurent.

Violet dropped a large serving spoon on the wood floor by the hutch and gave a squeal of dismay. She glanced quickly at Maggie and blushed darkly.

"Go below, Violet," Anastasia said without looking up from her plate.

The girl bolted for the door.

"You must excuse her," Anastasia said to Maggie. "She has seen so few Americans. She thinks you are all Jennifer Lawrence."

"Well, I don't mind," Maggie said with a smile.

"Do you think the foxes mind when they're run to ground— terrified and confused—before they're torn to a bloody pulp?" Nigel glared at Maggie, holding his fork in a fist on the table.

Where did that come from? Maggie wondered.

"Shut your mouth," Laurent said to him in a low voice. Maggie put a hand on his arm. This didn't need to get ugly and she knew Laurent well enough to know he had no problem throwing Nigel out of his own home, and breaking his nose in the bargain.

"Killing a fox is illegal here," Madeline said.

"But everyone still does it," Nigel said, his eyes going from Laurent to Maggie and back again.

"In Georgia where I'm from, we have a lot of foxes..." Maggie started to say.

"Are you saying that fox hunting is a form of conservation or pest control?"

"Not at all. I—"

"Because it's barbaric."

"I agree with you," Maggie replied. "I'm against killing a fox for sport. Absolutely."

Nigel seemed to deflate a bit at that but it was clear he wasn't ready to give it up.

"That's what they all say," he said sarcastically, "until they're caught red-handed."

"Our hunt is legal," Madeline said firmly. "No foxes are killed. The trail is chemically dragged to excite the hounds."

"That's a lie," Nigel said with a sneer.

"How would you know?" Madeline said. "Your lot has never actually discovered a dead fox on The Abbey grounds."

"That's because we create enough of a disturbance to allow them to go to ground before they're slaughtered!"

Madeline turned to Maggie. "Last year they created enough of a disturbance to send one young girl to the hospital when someone jumped out of the bushes at her horse."

"Serves her right," Nigel said.

"She was *fourteen*," Madeline said, throwing her napkin in her plate.

"Would you care to be excused, Mrs. Mears?" Anastasia asked as she selected her vegetables from a dish the sour-faced woman held out to her.

Madeline hesitated for a moment and then stood up, regally. Maggie saw her exchange a quick covert look with the woman serving Anastasia, and then Madeline turned and left the dining room without a word.

"The veal is superb tonight, Mrs. LeDuc," Anastasia said as she pushed her dish away, untouched.

"Milady," Mrs. LeDuc replied. Until then, Maggie hadn't realized the woman was French.

"Do you intend to ride in the hunt, Mrs. Dernier?" Anastasia asked coolly. She appeared to be examining a portrait on the wall over Maggie's shoulder.

"No," Maggie said. "Not at all."

"Wise decision," Nigel said jeeringly. He flinched when Laurent shifted in his chair as if he might stand up.

Then Nigel stood up himself. "I'm done," he said and stalked out of the room.

Anastasia dabbed her mouth with her linen napkin before reaching again for her crystal wine glass.

"You're not very good at small talk, are you?" she said to Maggie.

Susan Kiernan-Lewis

14

"You are *not* riding in the hunt." Laurent pulled his shirt off over his head and tossed it on the four-poster bed.

"I never planned to," Maggie said, her irritation growing. "But by the way, you can't tell me what to do."

"*Bon.* As long as we agree, I do not need to."

Maggie counted to ten and reminded herself that Laurent had a lot on his mind these days and the way he was processing Roger's death was such that it would probably be a miracle if he didn't end up killing someone soon. She would cut him some slack.

"I had no idea that Roger's family life was so horrible," Maggie said. "Anastasia is a piece of work."

Laurent frowned. "Roger had no family life."

"I don't mean family in the sense that you and I have family," Maggie said. She sat down on the bed next to Laurent and kicked off her shoes.

"There is no other sense, is there?" he said. As if to underscore the point, his phone began to vibrate. It was nine o'clock. His face brightened as soon as he heard the voice on the other line.

"Hello, little one," he murmured. "You had a good day, yes?"

Maggie could hear the exclamations of her son from where she sat and she felt a rush of warmth knowing he was happy, safe and loved even when she and Laurent were not there to tuck him in.

A light tap on the door was followed by the little maid Violet popping her head in.

"May I light the fire, Milady?" she asked timidly.

Laurent had already lit it which was evident by the blaze in their fireplace, but before Maggie could point out the obvious, Violet entered the room with a silver tray and two brandy snifters.

"Lady Bentley suggested a nightcap, Milady." Violet put the tray down, curtsied quickly and then left the room.

Maggie wondered how hard it would be to find a lock for the door while they were here.

After Laurent handed the phone to her and she spoke to Jemmy and then Danielle and was assured all was well in Domaine St-Buvard, she joined Laurent in front of the fire with their brandies.

"What do you think of everything?" Maggie asked.

"Poor Roger."

"I know. He deserved so much better than this."

Laurent stared into the fire. "He wanted a son, you know."

"Really?" Maggie tried to imagine Roger as a father. She hadn't known that side of him well enough for the image to gel. Her phone played musical notes to indicate a received text. She looked at the screen.

"*Oui?*"

"It's Grace. She says she's looking for work and did I have any ideas."

Laurent snorted and looked away.

"What does *that* mean?" Maggie said, putting the phone down. "You don't think I should help her?"

Laurent only raised an eyebrow.

"It occurred to me," Maggie said, "that Grace wanted to get her online children's clothing boutique going last year and I could help her do that with my blog."

"That was last year."

"I know Grace got side-tracked last year but with the increased international subscriber base that my blog has now, I could help her advertise her baby clothes and reach twenty times the customers she was able to reach before. Maybe more."

"Let her do it without you."

"But Grace isn't a writer. And she doesn't know anything about marketing either."

"Then perhaps she needs to learn it or go into another line of work."

"I can't believe you're being so hard on her! Don't you want her to get her life sorted out?"

"Of course. But she must do it on her own."

"But *why* if she has a friend to help her?"

"You have enough to do."

"I'm not overworked, Laurent, unless you're leading up to a complaint? Are your shirts not getting laundered? Is dinner not on the table at a reasonable time every night?"

"You have never done any of those things."

"Well, is there something else that's fallen off my radar that I should be paying attention to?"

Laurent leaned over and kissed her, his breath sweet and alcoholic. "*Non,*" he said.

It was the first time he'd truly focused on her since the news about Roger. Maggie did not intend to waste the moment or let a silly argument about Grace Van Sant or worry about no lock on the door ruin the mood.

🎋 🎋 🎋 🎋 🎋 🎋

The pub was more of a back room than a public bar but that's the way Bob and his lot liked it, Nigel thought as he walked in and nodded at the barkeep. The man was fat and glistened with sweat even though it was a cold night and the heat from the small fireplace in the corner didn't reach that far.

Nigel knew this dive was all a part of the experience for Bob Jenkins. Not that the bastard wasn't a frequenter of such places. He didn't have two sous to rub together. The Crow and Oak was probably a step up for him. Nigel moved to the nearly invisible wooden door at the back of the room. He knocked loudly. There was only one old couple sitting by the window drinking lager and staring morosely into their tankards. He could have kicked the door in and they probably wouldn't have reacted.

He didn't wait for a response on the other side of the door. It wasn't locked. Inside Bob sat with Jimmy and Paul around a small wooden table, beers in front of each of them. If possible, the other two wankers were even bigger losers than Bob. He nodded at them but noticed they didn't bother acknowledging him.

"Paul, you can get the C-4, aye?" Bob said to the man who was covered in acne and looked to still be in his teens.

"Aye, no sweat," Paul said. "Me da's got a garage full of the shite from his last demo job. How much you need?"

"Jimmy?" Bob said, turning to the older man at the table. "That'll be your specialty. How much do we need?"

Jimmy stared at Nigel and leaned into Bob to whisper loudly: "I don't trust this bastard. He looks like a poof."

Paul and Bob laughed and turned to look at Nigel for the first time since he'd arrived.

"Aye, you're right," Bob said in his thick Irish accent. "Now you mention it, he does."

Nigel forced down his humiliation and anger and reminded himself of why he was here...why he was doing this.

"I thought we said a bomb was too unstable," Nigel said. "When did we decide otherwise?"

"See how he says 'otherwise?'" Paul said, giggling. "I think you called it, mate," he said to Jimmy.

"We *decided*," Bob said curling his lip at Nigel, "when *I* decided it was the best way to get everybody's attention on the day of the hunt. Which is what we're about, ain't it?"

The silence stretched between them. Nigel had a feeling there was a contest happening and he didn't know what it was but clearly he was one of the combatants.

He swallowed. "That's all I care about," he said evenly. "Screwing this hunt so bad they never even think about doing it again."

"Well, then," Bob said, studying Nigel openly before turning back to Jimmy. "So how much C-4 will we need?"

15

The next morning, Maggie was up early—but Laurent was already up and gone. Madeline had said there was a formal breakfast at seven but both she and Laurent had had enough socializing for awhile.

Laurent hadn't seemed to think the distinction between the dumbwaiter and the laundry chute was important. He seemed content to wander the Abbey grounds and think of his friend— mourn him, remember him—without trying to imagine there was more to his death than what the police would uncover.

Maggie wished she could feel the same level of confidence.

Violet arrived with a tray of tea and toast and a pair of jodhpurs before Maggie was out of bed. Jill had said there were several pairs of rubber riding boots to choose from in the tack room in the barn.

It had been all Maggie could do yesterday not to go there first. If she hadn't been so keen on seeing exactly where Roger died, she would have. Now, as she finished her tea and tucked her shirt into the skintight jodhpurs, she allowed herself the freedom to think of nothing else except a day of riding—the delightful aromas of the barn, meeting the horses and anticipating a morning unrivaled by few other experiences in life than that of enjoying the world from horseback.

She hurried down the broad stairs and heard voices from the breakfast room. Relieved to avoid another meeting with Anastasia and her son, Maggie quickly detoured the front main hallway to the back of the Abbey where a side door led outside.

It was cold and the sky held promise of rain. Even in Georgia, a potentially rainy day wasn't reason enough to cancel a ride. Truth was, as a teenager, Maggie often rode in downpours without a second thought. Jill had hinted that most British riders felt the same. Given their typical weather, Maggie figured that was pretty much a default position if they wanted to ride.

Maggie shivered inside her jacket as she walked across the lawn until it connected with a curving gravel pathway. Madeline had told her to follow this directly to the stables.

It was hard to miss. The stables were adjacent to the house with a cobblestone courtyard between them. Two massive sliding wooden doors were open, allowing Maggie a glimpse in the dim interior of the barn. Stepping to the threshold she saw the usual line of stalls on both sides of the middle walkway. Most of the stalls were empty.

She walked down the center aisle toward the sound of a voice speaking midway down. Approaching, she saw it was coming from a small alcove where Trevor stood next to a large horse, partially tacked. Maggie watched as he ran his hand expertly down the horse's leg and then stood and patted him on the neck.

"You're all right, beauty," Trevor said to the horse.

"Hello," Maggie said. "I see you do double duty."

Trevor turned and smiled. "Good morning, Milady."

"*Maggie* is fine. I'm American and we don't have titles."

"Suits me," he said with a shrug. "I'm getting Diva ready for you."

The horse was an Irish draft, easily twenty-two hands high and without doubt larger than any horse Maggie had ever ridden.

Not to mention, it was a mare and everyone knew mares were usually trickier than geldings—unless they were *way* trickier in which case you had a real problem.

"You've ridden mares before?" Trevor asked, patting the horse on the neck. "She's a beaut, is Diva."

"I have," Maggie said. *Only she was a polo pony and small enough for me to swing up on it from the ground. If I fall off Diva here, I'll go home in a wheelchair.*

Maggie patted the horse on the neck and watched its skin ripple under her hand.

"But never one this big before," she said.

"Oh, Diva is grand," Trevor said. "You'll love her, so you will." He slid his hand between the horse and the girth to check its tightness and turned to Maggie. "You'll be needing boots."

"Jill said there were some in the tack room," Maggie said as she moved past the large animal and into the adjacent tack room.

"So I take it this is what you really do at the Abbey?" Maggie called to him as she found the boots lined up on a shelf. She sat on a wooden bench and tugged them on.

"Oh, aye," Trevor said and grabbed a bridle down from a hook near Maggie's head. "Lady Bentley only has me in the dining room because she sacked everyone else."

"I thought that was just until the police finished their investigation."

"I imagine she'll be wanting to hire her own people," Trevor said.

Maggie went to Diva and stroked her nose. The horse blew warm breath into her hand.

"Did you know...Lord Bentley very well?" she asked.

"He had us all call him Roger. And not that well, no."

"Knowing him, he probably thought all this was a joke."

Trevor gave Maggie an assessing look as if he wasn't sure he could speak freely.

"Roger was best mates with your husband, isn't that right?" he asked.

"He was," Maggie said, again feeling a stab of remorse.

Trevor unbuckled Diva's halter and pulled the bridle on, tucking the bit between the animal's teeth.

"She's dead calm," he said. "You won't need more than a plain snaffle."

"Are you sure?" Maggie couldn't help but think this was an awful lot of horse to be held in check by a plain snaffle. It meant it was all up to the rider. Because if the horse decided it had a different opinion about what to do—without a Pelham or some other kind of stronger riding aid—they would definitely be doing things the horse's way.

"No worries. You'll be fine."

"Were you working the night Roger was killed?" Maggie asked abruptly. When she looked at Trevor, she saw something in his expression. Something startled and afraid.

"We all work every night," he said. "In two week shifts."

"So you were working that night?"

"I was here in the barn."

"Were you alone?"

"I already gave my alibi to the coppers."

"If you were alone, you didn't have an alibi," Maggie said mildly.

"Look, Bentley was nice to me. He's the reason I got this job." For someone trying to say he was grateful, somehow Trevor's words weren't very convincing.

Before Maggie could respond Diva began stamping her feet. Animals picked up on the mood and energies around them. Maggie put her hand on the horse and felt it calm almost immediately.

Maybe she should leave the interrogations until after she got to know the horse she was about to climb onto.

✿ᕗ✿ᕗ✿ᕗ✿ᕗ✿ᕗ✿ᕗ

Laurent stood on the back flagstone patio and looked across the sloping lawns lined in primrose hedges behind the Abbey. He wasn't surprised that Roger had wanted to own this place—even partially own it. Roger had always longed for something solid and ancestral to remind him of his Englishness—his heritage. As long as Laurent had known him, Roger had had no permanent home. They'd shared hotel space in Cannes and St-Tropez on and off for years. After he and Maggie had moved in together, Laurent had been frankly surprised when Roger had gone home to England.

An English autumn and an English vista. An English estate too expensive for anyone to actually live in. And this Abbey—surely a joke that Roger was in on? Was it imaginable on any level that Roger came here to feel like a member of the upper class?

Did he not know his old friend even that well?

None of it made sense.

Not the charade of an English estate, and certainly not the beautiful widow without an intelligent thought or kind bone in her body.

Was it possible that the strangers Laurent had seen at Roger's wake yesterday were people Roger knew? Or had he left this world friendless, unloved, and steeped in the delusions of his own lies?

Who was the man that Laurent had known? What had become of him?

Laurent had not told Maggie the truth. He hadn't realized it himself before but now he knew.

Coming here had not been a good idea.

Seeing Roger as these people saw him—as someone to mock or cheat or resent—was worse than seeing Roger's body.

The door behind Laurent opened and a large man in a dark suit stepped out onto the veranda. He wore a heavy wool coat and polished shoes. He squinted at Laurent and cocked his head.

Laurent had always been very good at identifying police. He nodded his head in acknowledgement and the man came forward. Instead of putting his hand out to shake, he reached into his coat pocket and pulled out his identification which he showed to Laurent.

"Chief Inspector David Bailey," he said in a deep voice.

Laurent's natural instinct was to give nothing—or as little as was comfortably possible. It was a habit from his past he was still struggling to break.

"Laurent Dernier," he said. "I was a friend of Roger Bentley's."

It cost him a lot to admit that last. Not that it wasn't true. But it was more than he would ever have told a stranger—and certainly more than he would reveal to a cop.

"I am sorry for your loss, Monsieur Dernier," Bailey said. "You've just arrived?"

"Yesterday for the funeral," Laurent said.

"And then here on holiday, one presumes?"

"Of course," Laurent said tightly. "As is the British custom. Bury and then celebrate."

To his credit, Bailey took the insult well. Perhaps he was already regretting his barb about the holiday. In the end it didn't matter. Laurent knew the man was attempting to discover who had taken Roger's life.

And for that reason, if no other, Laurent could endure him.

"May I inquire if you are close to making an arrest?" Laurent asked.

"All in good time, Monsieur Dernier," Bailey said. "Meanwhile, enjoy your holiday."

Susan Kiernan-Lewis

16

It was like walking next to a moving house.

The horse was so large that when Maggie pulled the stirrup leathers down the ends only came to her shoulder. Trevor had escaped to the interior of the stables so Maggie didn't know if Diva was head shy or spooky or easygoing. She didn't know if she needed a crop to budge the horse out of a trot or a shotgun to keep her from running away with her.

She did know that her mood was being transferred directly to the big horse by her touch. Maggie took a steadying breath and reminded herself that she had ridden nearly every day of her life at one point and even had her own horse when she was competing in the local pony shows around Cumming and Alpharetta.

She patted the horse to instill confidence in both of them.

"Just you and me, Diva," she said as she led the animal to the mounting block. Gathering the reins in one hand, she climbed the block and hopped onto Diva's back. The horse didn't move.

First hurdle cleared, Maggie thought as she patted the horse again and leaned down to adjust her stirrup leathers. Once she slipped her feet into the stirrups, she tightened her legs around the horse and it moved forward at a walk.

So far so good.

She heard the sound of an approaching car and walked the horse to the perimeter of the front courtyard. Diva must have been used to noises—especially cars. Only an ear flicked to indicate the horse had even heard the vehicle. Maggie sat in the saddle, drilling her spine straight down to remind the horse to stay put.

From this height, Maggie could see over the eight foot stone enclosure wall that surrounded the courtyard. A sporty black car drove slowly past the front of the Abbey and made its way to the gravel parking lot outside the stable enclosure.

Jill emerged from the car dressed for riding. If Maggie had thought Jill looked smart yesterday at the wake in her sleek black sheath dress, today she looked like she just stepped out of *Vogue* magazine. The snug fitting breeches revealed there was not an ounce on her that shouldn't be there—unlike what Maggie had seen in her own dressing mirror that morning. Jill's hair was thick and glossy blonde and pulled back in a youthful ponytail.

Jill strode through the gate in the courtyard wall with a large English Mastiff at her heels.

Instantly, the dog charged Maggie on the horse.

"No! Maximus! No!" Jill shouted. But the dog ignored her and ran to Maggie. Diva pranced away from the dog and Maggie forced herself to keep her hands relaxed on the reins.

The dog slammed to a stop and sniffed Maggie's boots. Maggie was pretty sure the rubber would be no match for one of the jagged canines in the dog's mouth.

"Did a serial killer wear these boots before me?" Maggie asked breathlessly. "Because I think Maximus isn't too sure."

"It's not you or the boots, trust me, darling," Jill said, pulling a leash out of her pocket and running to the dog. "Maximus is trained to distrust everyone. It's his breed and I encourage it." Before she could snap the leash on him, the dog jumped on Maggie's foot and began licking her boot.

"Hello, sweetie," Maggie said. She reached down to give the dog her hand to sniff. "I thought pit bulls were illegal in England."

Jill stood speechless, her fingers at her mouth.

"Max isn't a pit bull," she said. "He's a mastiff."

"Well, he's vewy vewy scary," Maggie said as the dog wagged his tail and barked at Maggie. His tongue lolled out of his mouth.

"This is highly unusual," Jill said, frowning. "Maximus is not an affectionate dog."

"Oh, animals like me," Maggie said. "Some people can write sonatas or fix a kitchen drain. Me, I've got a way with Jack Russell terriers and guinea pigs."

"And horses?"

"Well, it's been a while. Two kids and about ten pounds ago, frankly."

"You wear it well."

"Was Diva the one you intended for me to ride?" Maggie asked, patting her horse on the neck. "Trevor had her tacked up."

"Yes. She's a sweetheart. You'll be fine on her."

Out of the corner of her eye, Maggie saw Trevor approaching and leading another horse fully tacked. Jill gave Diva a pat as she passed.

"Thank you, darling Trevor," she said as she took the reins of the horse. He looked like an Arabian mix to Maggie, and much smaller than Diva. Maximus approached Trevor with a low threatening growl in his throat. Trevor handed the reins to Jill and backed away.

"Now *there's* the dog I know and love," Jill said with a laugh. "Don't worry, Trevor, he'll come with us when we go and Demon is in the kennel."

She turned to Maggie. "I have two beasties. I like to work them separately. I find they aren't as attentive to me when they're together and I don't want to take the chance of anyone getting hurt —at least not accidentally." Jill faced her horse and bent her knee so Trevor could boost her into the saddle.

"Oh, it feels like ages since I've ridden," Jill said. "Trevor, be a darling and grab a couple of hard hats for us, will you? You can never be too careful," she said to Maggie.

Maggie felt the butterflies stir in her stomach and Diva began to paw the cobblestones. Trevor returned and handed Maggie a helmet and then held Diva's bridle while she put it on and tightened it. As soon as he let go, Diva moved off without being asked to by Maggie.

At least it looked like she wouldn't need the crop.

The weather was cold but it wasn't raining and Maggie was warm in her wool-lined barn jacket. She had worried about riding a horse as wide as Diva but the horse was every bit as responsive to

Maggie's leg aids as any of the smaller horses she'd ridden. Maggie followed Jill on the gravel path that eventually turned to dirt. By the time they'd cleared the last patch of lawn, they were both moving into a rising trot that took them to the first knoll overlooking the Abbey.

Approaching it by car was one thing—and it was impressive to be sure—but looking down on the Abbey provided an almost omniscient point of view. It reminded Maggie that this was how the original owners of the Abbey—the ones who'd called it home—had seen the property. She imagined all the Misters Darcys and Bingleys of the time who must have sat just where she and Jill were now sitting on horseback and looking down at the estate. No wonder they acted like they were gods.

"Magnificent, isn't it?"

"It is. You're so lucky to be able to ride here."

"I know," Jill said almost wistfully. "It's been a dream."

"Will you be able to stay now that Anastasia's taken over as majority owner?"

Jill grimaced. "I don't know. It might not be worth it. Might just be best to remember it as a golden time and move on."

"I'm so sorry about Roger," Maggie said. "I feel bad that we didn't see him more than we did."

"You have a life," Jill said, pulling her horse's head back toward the pasture and away from the house. "Roger understood that. How's Diva feel?"

"Good," Maggie said. "I'm seriously rusty though. I'm probably going to be on crutches for the rest of our visit, I'll be so sore."

Jill laughed. "Thank God for endless hot water and jetted hot tubs. Before the cops freaked out and made Madeline send her away we even had an onsite masseuse."

"That must have been wonderful."

They rode in silence for the next twenty minutes and Maggie marveled that they didn't see a single highway or any other indication of twenty-first century life. Not even a cell tower.

The clouds had finally grouped together and begun to empty their contents on them and Maggie was amazed and pleased that Jill didn't use the rain as an excuse to cut their ride short.

"If I curtailed a hack on account of a sprinkle," Jill said, "I'd never ride."

"Good point."

As they rode, Maggie concentrated on the scenery and the feeling of the horse between her legs. After thirty minutes she knew Diva would respond to her. The few times that the horse attempted to test Maggie, she'd been quickly corrected. Being on horseback again reminded Maggie of all the horse moms back at the barns in Atlanta who managed their daughters' equestrienne activities—the shows, the lessons, the day rides along the Chattahoochee. Until now it hadn't occurred to Maggie that she might be able to do that with Mila. She smiled at the thought of little Mila in jodhpurs and paddock boots.

They came to a large clearing fringed by a small forest of beech and yew trees. Jill pointed to a break in the grouping.

"That's where the hunt goes through," she said. "We go tearing across there, the hounds barking like maniacs, and then boom! into the opening where there are three jumps right in a row. Boom, boom, boom! It's brilliant!"

Maggie rode to the center of the clearing and tried to imagine how it would be tomorrow during the hunt with all the pulse-racing excitement of it all.

"Is it a real fox?" she asked.

Jill grinned. "Of course not. You've been listening to that psycho Nigel. Why would the Abbey take a chance on chasing a real fox? Can you imagine the bad press?"

"Why does he think it's a fox hunt, then instead of a drag hunt?"

"Because he's barking? Gabrielle told me the cops interviewed Nigel the longest. Not surprising."

"You think Nigel wanted to hurt Roger?"

"He hated Roger."

"Why?"

"Who knows?"

"Do the police have a suspect?"

"If they do, they're not telling me."

"Do you think they're telling Anastasia and she's not passing along the info to you?"

"Probably."

"Are they limiting the suspect pool to the group who was staying at the hotel at the time?"

Jill gave Maggie a curious look.

"I know they interviewed all the guests but nobody knew Roger except for us. I'm sure the cops think one of us is more likely to have a motive."

"And you were all staying at the hotel last week?"

"All except Will and Annette. They live nearby. But they were here for dinner most nights."

"Any guesses on your part?"

"God, it could have been anyone. I don't know what your relationship was like with Roger but it was a little trickier closer to home."

"In what way?"

"In every way. Honestly, he and I weren't especially tight and except for the business he almost never spent time with Will. Anastasia is a money grubbing bitch. Nigel is a loathsome cretin who hated him. Hmmmm, let's see. Oh, you know about Madeline, right?"

"His ex-girlfriend?"

"Exactly. Anastasia always put it out there that Madeline was pining for Roger. Like he was the one who got away or some such rubbish. But my take on it has always been that Madeline's never forgiven him."

"Forgiven him for what?" *Did Madeline have a motive to kill Roger?*

"I shouldn't have said that. Besides, it's not my secret to tell."

Maggie didn't push it. In her experience, the best way to get secrets was from the one who'd do anything to keep them secret.

"There's a place just up there that's jolly fun to gallop. Are you up for it?"

"Yeah, sure," Maggie said, not at all sure.

"If she gets away from you, don't try to stop her. Just get into two-point and hang on. She'll stop when Dexter and I do."

Sounds like a plan, Maggie thought nervously as she pushed Diva into a trot behind Jill.

When they crested the hill, Maggie could see why it was a good place for a gallop. It was flat with no major turns or curves.

On a dry day it would probably be ideal. Today was wet and the ground looked treacherous with slick leaves.

"Ready?" Jill said over her shoulder and then, without waiting for Maggie's reply, she tucked her shoulders and put her horse into a gallop straight from a walk.

Maggie felt a lightness in her chest and all her senses heightened as Diva gathered her strength beneath her and then shot off behind Jill. The wind sliced through Maggie as they thundered down the path. She bent into two-point to cut the resistance, and let the reins snake through her fingers as she held onto Diva's mane. She was still in control—and some part of her knew that—but probably only as long as she and Diva were on the same page.

Maggie realized that in just a moment she'd pass Jill and her horse. She checked Diva with her hands and then sat up in the saddle. She had no idea if the horse would respond. But Diva slowed and as soon as she did, Maggie knew she'd been in control the whole time. And Diva had known that even if Maggie wasn't sure. She cantered the horse into a wide circle, bringing her in tighter and tighter until she was trotting again on the path.

"That was brilliant!" Jill said gasping as she rejoined Maggie.

Maggie didn't trust her voice to speak but she nodded. She reached down and patted Diva's neck.

They turned their horses back toward the Abbey.

"I want to thank you for inviting me to come out today," Maggie said. "It was amazing."

"Oh, no worries, darling. You know how hard it is to find people with your same brand of obsession. I can never have enough people to ride with."

That had never been a problem for Maggie. She had been a teenager in a group of horse-crazy teenagers. There had always been someone to ride with.

"I have girlfriends whose husbands hate their horses," Jill said. "They're always ragging on them that the horses are too expensive, too smelly, or take up too much time."

"I imagine it's like any hobby," Maggie said. "It's hard if you don't share it." She thought briefly of Laurent and his vineyard.

Almost as if reading her mind, Jill said, "Have you never gone riding with Laurent?"

Maggie laughed. "Until this week he didn't even know I rode."

"Well, I know how stubborn he can be," Jill said. "I never could get him on a horse."

A trickle of apprehension moved down Maggie's spine.

"When was this?" she asked, keeping her eyes on the horizon ahead.

"Oh, you know," Jill said. "Ages ago in Paris."

When Maggie didn't answer, Jill said. "I'm sorry, darling. I thought Laurent would have told you."

"You know, I don't think he did," Maggie said, trying to keep her voice light.

"He didn't tell you we once lived together?"

17

Laurent paused outside the kitchen door. Enough was enough. He knew she recognized him. What she was doing here...well, it was madness but obviously it was Roger's madness.

How was it he and Roger had never spoken of it?

The sounds of normal kitchen activity came through the heavy wooden door.

Gabrielle duLac, native of Nice. Laurent had no memory of her culinary credentials at the time but then that was ten years ago. Her English had been nonexistent if he remembered correctly.

What was she doing here in the middle of the United Kingdom in a resort for rich Brits and Americans? What was she doing anywhere near Roger Bentley?

Motion caught the corner of his eye and he instinctively moved away from it.

Hard habit to break, he thought with chagrin.

Madeline Mears appeared in the hall and stopped when she saw Laurent. She glanced at the kitchen door and her shoulders sagged with recognition at what Laurent must have been contemplating. She held out her hand.

"Please," she said in a low voice. "Not here." She turned and walked down the hall. Laurent followed her into the salon. It was not even mid morning yet but he saw her waiver by the drinks trolley before marching to the north facing window with a view of the front drive. She stood with her back to him looking out. Laurent joined her at the window.

CI Bailey was getting into his car. So *that's* why Madeline wasn't at breakfast, Laurent thought.

"He is still interviewing you?" he asked.

"It seems I am of special interest to him," she said, not looking at him.

"Because of your past relationship with Roger?"

She turned around to face Laurent. "I didn't kill him."

"I believe you."

Her face was laced with pain but also fear. Laurent knew well that fear often had little to do with reason.

"It's been so long," she said. "I don't know whether I hate him now or whether I've hated him for years."

"Probably not something you want to reveal in conversation with the Chief Inspector."

"I never really knew him," she said, her eyes filling with tears. "Not for a minute. Did you?"

"I thought I did."

"Could you imagine he would marry a woman like that? Or would leave her the one thing I cared about?" She waved a frustrated hand to encompass the Abbey.

"You thought he would leave his share to you," Laurent stated.

Madeline snorted and wiped her eyes. "It was a reasonable assumption," she said bitterly.

"I'm sorry, Madeline." What more could he say? That he knew Roger loved her? He thought he had. But in the end he hadn't married her. In the end, he'd given his half of the Abbey to the one woman in the world Madeline could not do business with.

Madeline pushed past Laurent to the drinks tray after all and poured herself a weak gin and tonic.

"Will and Annette will be at the Abbey tonight. And Jill of course." She gave Laurent a side glance which he ignored.

"Is that unusual?"

"Is *anything* that's happening right now *usual?*" Madeline drank down her drink and glanced back out the window but the Inspector's car was out of sight. "Will knows you are here with Anastasia. Perhaps he's afraid someone will reveal a secret or two."

"Me? Or Anastasia?"

Madeline laughed without mirth. "Either, now that you mention it."

She held her empty glass tightly, her eyes filled with misery.

Madeline looked at Laurent.

"We have seven for dinner tonight not counting staff. I was going to speak to Gabrielle but I am not up to going into the village if she needs something."

"I will ask her."

"Thank you." Madeline put her empty glass down with a decisive thud and moved past Laurent to leave the room.

"And Laurent?" she said, half turning to look at him. "There is no need to speak with Gabrielle about anything else. You understand me? It would only make things worse."

Laurent hesitated and then nodded.

But given what he knew about Gabrielle's past and the fact that she was here at the Abbey, he seriously doubted that.

❄⊹❄⊹❄⊹❄⊹❄⊹❄⊹

The effort to finish the ride and act as if she had not just been hit with a wrecking ball to the solar plexus had been nothing short of herculean. After thanking Jill profusely for the riding invitation, Maggie handed the animal back to Trevor, and hurried to her room to track down her husband with the demand he explain why he had neglected to tell her something he had to know she'd discover the hard way.

Unbelievable!

When the roiling nausea of Jill's words had had a chance to sift through Maggie, she was gripped with a burning fury.

He'd lived with her? How had that little piece of history never come up before?

Their bedroom was empty. Maggie stripped off her clothes and stepped into the shower, using the force and heat of the water to blast away the worst of her anger. She felt a little better when she left the bathroom. On the bed she discovered someone had left a pink silk tea dress. Maggie hesitated to put on the costume. She didn't want to appear silly—especially not when she was going to confront Laurent in about five minutes with justifiable wifely indignation. But the dress was beautiful and would no doubt be flattering. There was no harm in looking good, she thought, when taking one's battle stance.

She pinned her long wet hair up into a quick chignon and slipped the dress on. She looked at her image in the mirror and was glad she'd decided to play along. She didn't even look like herself. And maybe that was a good idea right now. Until the bombshell this morning Maggie hadn't assessed Jill Bentley in any sort of personal reference to herself. But the fact of the matter was that Jill was sexy and slim with all the bright energy and easy flirtation of a single woman who knows she looks good.

And Maggie was still working on getting rid of those last five pregnancy pounds.

As she looked in the mirror, she realized she looked calm. The fact was, Laurent was entitled to have a past. Maggie certainly had one. He was entitled to have a beautiful ex-lover. The point of contention would come in his failure of bringing it to Maggie's attention but even then, she had a strong image of Laurent's face as she confronted him. He wouldn't understand—since he wasn't sleeping with Jill at present—why Maggie was upset.

But it didn't take away the fact that up until this morning everyone but Maggie knew what the truth was.

And Maggie did not like being the last one to know.

After one last reassuring look in the mirror, she left the room to find her husband. She had no idea where he'd gone off to. But she had plenty of time and nothing better to do than look in every single room at the Abbey if she had to.

As it happened she didn't have to.

She reached the bottom step of the massive staircase and saw Madeline and Laurent emerge from the salon where they'd all met for cocktails the night before.

Madeline looked as if she'd been crying.

"Are you all right?" Maggie asked, her eyes going from Madeline to Laurent.

Laurent leaned in and kissed Maggie on the cheek—surprising her.

"Madeline has had a bad morning," he said. "And I have an errand to run. Will you stay with her, *chérie?*"

Maggie nodded. "Of course." The sight of Madeline so distressed immediately pushed her agenda with Laurent down the priority list.

"I'm fine, really," Madeline said but she hesitated and then put a hand out to the wall as if for support. Maggie took her arm and led her back into the salon where she and Laurent had just emerged.

"I suppose I am feeling a little vulnerable at the moment," Madeline said.

"You have every right to," Maggie said. "Under the circumstances."

"As I was telling Laurent, I worry that the police are looking at me rather closely."

Madeline sat in one of the straight-back Edwardian chairs and Maggie went to the drinks cart to pour her a glass of water.

She remembered Jill saying Madeline had a secret that would make her a natural suspect in Roger's murder. Did the police think so too? She handed the glass of water to Madeline.

"What you must think of me," Madeline said as she sipped the water.

"I don't think anything at all. Except you've had a horrendous two weeks."

"Did you enjoy your hack with Jill?"

Maggie flushed at the memory of the morning but forced a smile. Of course Madeline would know all about Laurent and Jill.

Take the high road take the high road take the high road.

"The Abbey is every bit as magnificent as advertised," Maggie said.

Madeline looked appraisingly at Maggie.

"Laurent mentioned you used to do advertising as a career."

"The operative phrase being *used to.*"

"We could use a little help."

"Are you not filling the rooms?"

Madeline shrugged. "Mostly," she admitted.

"If it's not broke..." Maggie said.

"I am not sure we will be able to do so after all this," Madeline said bitterly. "An accident is one thing but *murder...*"

"Really kills re-bookings, I imagine."

Madeline gave Maggie a sharp look. "You know about Roger's nonprofit? The Bentley Foundation?"

Maggie nodded. "Laurent told me a little."

"It was supposed to assuage the guilt he had about the life he'd led up to then. Of course you know all about that."

She was referring to the life Roger—and up until he met Maggie—Laurent too had spent in the south of France cheating tourists and anybody else with money who might trust them. Yes, Maggie knew about that life.

"Did his wife know?" Maggie asked.

Madeline snorted. "My guess is no. That would involve trust. I'm not even sure how much Jill knows. Will and Annette are completely unaware of how Roger made his money."

"But Roger hired Will to run his nonprofit. So it sounds like he tried to do his best by him."

"There are some who think it was more like penance."

"For a crime committed against Will?"

Madeline shook her head. "You shouldn't listen to me."

It sounds like you are exactly the person I should be listening to, Maggie thought.

"It must have been a serious shock when Roger took up with Anastasia," Maggie prompted.

"You have no idea."

"Was it because he wanted kids?"

Madeline looked at her as if startled. "What?"

"Something Laurent said made me think that maybe Roger was hoping for…a child."

Madeline looked at her and a veil of wariness descended across her features.

"Is that what Laurent thinks? Well, the two of them were close. I suppose he would know."

"But that surprises you?"

"Let's just say if it's true it would be the most pathetic example of irony ever."

"How so?"

Madeline stared out the window as if seeing something out there.

"Because twenty-two years ago I became pregnant."

Maggie's stomach contracted painfully. "And Roger wasn't happy about it?"

"You could say that," Madeline said bitterly, "since he made me get rid of it."

18

Will waited in the cab of the horse trailer while Annette kissed, hugged and handed over their two small sons to Will's mother at her house in Bourton-on-the-Water. Will waved to them from the driver's seat.

Annette kept referring to this visit to the Abbey as a much-needed mini-break. Although Will was pretty sure that if relaxing was part of the program, going back to the Abbey—especially after what happened—was a serious miscalculation.

He knew the real reason had more to do with Annette and the damn hunt than anything else. As usual, when it came to horses, Annette would have her way.

Making matters worse was the fact that Madeline had let the masseuse go for the rest of the month ensuring that the only "retreat" Will would enjoy would likely be the time he spent throwing a line in one of the Abbey ponds or aimlessly wandering the Abbey lawns and gardens while Annette spent her time in the stable.

He marveled as he watched her turn back for one more kiss for the littlest one, Ned. Horses could cure any pain for Annette. They could gloss over any damage and soothe any wound.

How he envied her that particular benefit of her obsession.

In all other ways, it was all just one giant pain in the arse.

Annette joined him in the car and they both waved to their sons and Will's mother.

"Do you think your mother will be okay?" Annette asked. "The boys can be a real handful."

"She raised me, didn't she?" Will said as he backed the trailer out of his mother's roundabout driveway.

"My point precisely," Annette said with a smile.

Annette was in a good mood. And why wouldn't she be? She'd been looking forward to the hunt for a year.

"Why don't you board your horse at the Abbey?" he asked as he merged onto the M-4 heading toward Compton Abdale and the Abbey. "Trevor said there's more than enough room."

"Oh, darling, I would love that," Annette said, "Are you sure? I mean, now that it belongs to Anastasia, will she be okay with that?"

"I don't really know," Will admitted. "But I'm pretty sure beautiful horses prancing about the place is part of the brand she wants to maintain for the Abbey."

"Do you think she might not charge us board?"

Will laughed without mirth. "Don't hold your breath," he said.

"That reminds me, Will," Annette said, pulling out a tube of lip gloss from the glove box. "It's all very well to rent a trailer when we need it but wouldn't it be easier to buy our own?"

They'd had this discussion before. A horse trailer was dear—at least two thousand quid and that was *used*. For the five or six times a year Annette needed to trailer her horse, it just didn't make sense. Will knew what *did* make sense of course. And that was the embarrassment Annette felt with her equestrian pals being the only one without her own trailer.

He'd have to see. Have to see how this whole Roger thing played out. There was a possibility—a slim one to be sure—but at least a possibility that Roger's death might actually benefit them.

"Jamie says your mother smokes," Annette said.

"She told me she quit."

"Well, he says she sneaks out to the back garden and smokes. Will, I can't have her smoking around the boys!"

Will sighed. "I'll talk to her. Although, technically, it sounds like she's not smoking around them if she's going outside."

"What about serving as a credible role model? She can hardly say *don't smoke* if she's lighting up fags right in front of them!"

He wanted to say that the boys were eight and five years old. It was a little early to start worrying about a smoking habit. But he knew what Annette would say. That it was never too soon to reinforce the message.

"I'll talk to her," he said.

She reached over and squeezed his hand. "Thank you, darling," she said and then hesitated. "Are you okay, Will? You know, about Roger?"

"Of course."

"Really?"

"Annette, I'm fine," he said firmly. "And it's not like Roger and I were that close."

"Darling, you know that's not true! You ran the nonprofit for him. He depended on you."

They were getting into dodgy territory here and if Annette weren't so focused on the excitement of the upcoming hunt, she'd see that. But as usual, she had other things on her mind. Things that took priority over him.

"I don't know what's true any more," he said.

Annette applied her lip gloss and directed her attention to the passing countryside.

"Do you think running the business will be easier with him gone?" she asked.

He felt a heavy weight descend on his shoulders the closer they drove to the Abbey.

"It could hardly be harder," he said, aware that his wife was no longer listening.

⁂ ⁂ ⁂ ⁂ ⁂

Anastasia went to the armoire and jerked open both doors. She began pulling open drawers and flinging the contents about the room. Silk lingerie and nightgowns took flight and then softly parachuted to the thick carpeting underfoot.

Her nostrils flared and her breathing was coming in loud pants.

"That tiara has twenty-five two-carat diamonds in it!" she screamed, turning to stare at Violet who stood frozen by the door like a deer trapped in the headlights.

"Do you hear me?" Anastasia shouted as she shook bunches of silk underwear in both fists. "And it did not just stand up and walk out of here."

"No, Mi-milady," Violet stuttered, her eyes going to the pools of pastel colored silk on the floor.

"Where is it? Look at me, damn you!"

Violet looked into the face of Anastasia's fury.

"I…I put it back right where it—"

"Liar! Madeline! Where is that woman?"

"Shall I go and—"

"Don't you dare leave this room! I will tear the Abbey apart brick by brick and stone by stone and when I find it—in your room, no doubt—I will see you in jail for the rest of your life. Do you think Lord Bentley is the only one with the power to destroy lives? Just you wait and see!"

The door to the bedroom pushed open and Gabrielle put her head in the gap.

"*Y-a-t-il un problème?*" she asked, looking at Violet.

Violet just shook her head.

"Get someone in here who speaks English!" Anastasia shrieked. "I want Mrs. Mears immediately. And you!" She pointed a long lacquered fingernail at Violet. "You are not going anywhere until we get this sorted out."

Violet's lips trembled but she did not speak. The sound of dripping water made Anastasia look toward the bathroom and then out the window before she realized where the sound was coming from.

It was coming from the small puddle of yellow forming on the spot where the little maid stood cowering on Anastasia's sixty pounds per square foot imported Persian carpet.

19

The scream came from one of the upstairs bedrooms. Madeline jumped to her feet.

"What is it?" Maggie asked, standing too.

Madeline took in a long breath and straightened her dress jacket with a sharp jerk as if to put herself in order.

"It's nothing," she said. "Just Anastasia up to her usual. You will excuse me?"

Without another word, she turned and marched out the door. The hallway erupted with another wail made louder by the brief time that Madeline had the door opened. She shut it firmly behind her.

What a madhouse, Maggie thought as she went to the drinks cart to pour herself a glass of water.

Madeline's words still buzzed in her head. She'd aborted her baby to please Roger—only to lose them both? Surely that would make Madeline a serious candidate for Roger's murder?

Did the police know about the pregnancy?

But just because Madeline hated Roger didn't mean she killed him. Maggie knew for a fact that the list was practically never ending for the number of people who hated Roger. Besides, Madeline was in business with Roger. Even if she hadn't gotten over her bitterness—and it was pretty clear she hadn't—she'd obviously come to terms with it sufficiently to run a business with him.

Maggie stood at the floor to ceiling window and watched their rental car as it navigated the Abbey front drive. Laurent was coming back from his errand.

What errand?

Did he know about Madeline's abortion?

The door to the salon opened and Gabrielle entered carrying a heavy silver tray.

"Madame," Gabrielle said, acknowledging Maggie without looking at her.

She set the tray on the fragile-looking antique coffee table. The corners of the table were fluted as if no small detail was too small for perfection. Maggie tried to imagine the world that the original owners of the Abbey must have lived in.

The tantalizing aroma of freshly baked scones permeated her thoughts and she realized she'd gone off this morning without breakfast. She was starving.

"Wow. That looks amazing," Maggie said as she watched Gabrielle set out china plates, teacups and saucers and bowls of clotted cream and jam. Gabrielle poured a cup of tea from the large silver teapot and set it on one of the side tables with a saucer.

"White, Madame?" she asked.

"Yes, please," Maggie said. "And sugar too." *Screw those last five pounds. I need my strength.*

Nigel entered the room with Will and Annette.

"Oh, jolly good," Annette said. "We're just in time. Hello there," she said to Maggie. "We didn't get a chance to meet properly yesterday. I'm Annette and this is my husband Will."

"Hello," Maggie said as she helped herself to one of the hot scones. There was even a dish of butter cubes in case the cream and the jam weren't enough calories. "I'm sorry we had to meet like this."

Nigel snorted in derision and piled a plate of scones for himself made obscene by scooping a huge pile of clotted cream on top. He took his plate to the window and sat there, staring outside.

"When did you get in?" Maggie asked as she sat on the couch.

"About an hour ago," Annette said. "I heard you went riding with Jill this morning? How did you like it?"

"It was amazing." Maggie forced herself to remember the ride, and not the last thing Jill told her before the bottom dropped out of her morning. "Do you ride too?"

"You could say that," Annette said as she selected a large scone studded with giant golden raisins. Maggie noticed she didn't slather butter or dollop cream on her scone. Probably how she kept so trim. Maggie looked in dismay at her own plate with its half eaten scone. Laurent encouraged a healthy appetite at home with all his cooking. She wondered how happy he'd be with the inevitable results of that appetite. She pushed her plate away and reached for her teacup.

"In fact, we're really here for the hunt," Anastasia said.

"I hope nobody gets hurt this year," Nigel said from his window seat. "That would be such a shame."

Annette rolled her eyes and turned her back on Nigel. She lowered her voice.

"Are you going to ride? You should."

"I don't think so," Maggie said. "For one thing, I don't have any clothes."

"Oh, the Abbey has everything in every imaginable size. For the guests, you know. There's even a sidesaddle for the truly committed," Annette said. "Or maybe you just need to *be* committed if you try and ride in it." She giggled.

"Have you ever ridden a sidesaddle?" Maggie asked.

"No! Can you imagine? Balancing on a horse with nothing to hang onto? It's hard enough when you have your legs wrapped around him!"

Maggie smiled at Will who was studiously ignoring everyone in the room.

"Do you ride, Will?" Maggie asked.

Annette laughed. "Oh, Will could not care less about horses. It's strictly my thing. Who did you ride this morning?"

"Diva. The big Irish draft cross?"

"Oh, I know Diva well. How did you like her?"

Maggie nodded. "She behaved herself."

"Diva is dead calm. At least as much as any horse can be. You're not having the full Devonshire?"

Maggie looked at her plate and shrugged. "Watching my calories."

"Oh, don't I know! Those breeches are hideously unforgiving, aren't they?" Annette laughed as she scooped up a large spoonful of cream and topped off her scone with it.

The door opened and Jill entered. Maggie was surprised to see her in period costume. She would've thought Jill was too cool for that. Her hair was dressed in curls and swept up under a beaded headband. Her gown skimmed her hips in a swath of silk which fell straight to the floor.

She looked absolutely stunning.

"Hello, darlings," she said as she went to the tea service. "Have you heard the palaver upstairs?"

"We heard Anastasia screaming," Annette said, making a face. "Now what is it?"

"She seems to believe the help has stolen her tiara."

Annette gasped. "Oh, no! Not the one with all the diamonds that Roger gave her?"

"Well, dearest," Jill said. "Since Anastasia didn't have a pot to wee in before she met Roger, *of course* it would be the one he gave her."

"That's terrible!" Annette said.

"And not really believable either, is it?" Maggie said.

Jill looked at Maggie.

"Servants don't steal where you come from?"

"Not big ass diamond tiaras they don't have a prayer of fencing, no," Maggie said, her face flushing.

Jill let her gaze linger a moment longer on Maggie before she turned to drop a single sugar cube into her teacup. She didn't even glance at the scones.

Maggie couldn't help but think the gaze wasn't a very friendly one.

꙳ꙅ꙳ꙅ꙳ꙅ

After parking behind the mansion, Laurent hefted the box of groceries onto his shoulder and pushed into the back entrance of the Abbey. A narrow hallway led to the kitchen where Gabrielle and Violet were sitting at a long wooden table drinking mugs of steaming tea. When he entered the kitchen, Violet—who appeared to be in tears—jumped to her feet as though she'd been doing something she shouldn't.

"Excuse me, Milord," she squeaked and ran from the room.

Laurent put the box of groceries down on a long work table. Gabrielle didn't move but Laurent knew she was watching him.

Earlier when he'd come down to ask what she needed from the village, she'd treated him as if he were a vendor from town—which suited him fine. No conversation, just a list of her needs.

He could smell the scent of baked goods in the air. A quick look at the large Agfa stove showed two large iron pans with a dozen just-baked scones cooling on them.

"They are having their tea upstairs?" he asked her in French.

"If you hurry, you won't miss it," Gabrielle said with venom dripping from every word.

Ahhh. So she's had time to think.

He began to pull the groceries out of the box, prompting her to stand up.

"*Non*, Monsieur. I need no more of your help."

"It is no trouble," Laurent said, ignoring her as she stood by him and clenched her hands into fists. He knew it had nothing to do with her not wanting to inconvenience him. She wanted him out of her kitchen and out of her life.

"I am happy to help. You are making *Oysters Mignonette* tonight, *oui*?"

"This is not a culinary vacation school, Monsieur. You are to be upstairs with the others."

Laurent unpacked the groceries on the table. The kitchen was spotless. The floor was a dark slate with not a speck of flour on it. The walls were covered with copper pots and pans of every size and shape. For someone who loved to cook, it was not a terrible place to spend your life.

"Roger sent for you?" he asked mildly.

"Do not say his name to me," she hissed.

When Laurent turned to look at her, he was surprised to see the knife in her hand.

Susan Kiernan-Lewis

20

Maggie looked for Laurent to join them for tea but he never showed and by the time Violet—with red and swollen eyes—came to take away the dishes, everyone else had disappeared to do other things.

"Mostly getting dressed for dinner," Annette said with a giggle as she headed out the door a good twenty minutes after her husband and Nigel had left. "You'll find that's largely what we do here—get dressed, get undressed, get dressed again."

Jill stopped Maggie as she was about to leave.

"I hope I didn't upset you this morning. You have to know I had no idea Laurent hadn't shared our past with you."

"No problem," Maggie said. "He probably didn't think it was important."

"Oh, touché, darling," Jill said with a laugh. "And no doubt you're right. We women often build these things up into something much bigger than they actually were. See you at dinner."

Maggie hurried up the stairs to her bedroom. It wasn't that she'd forgotten the morning's bombshell exactly but between the stolen tiara and Madeline's abortion—it had been pushed to the back of her mind.

When she got to the hallway outside the bedroom door, she hesitated. She could hear Laurent talking inside. His voice was low and firm. She pushed open the door and he looked at her and smiled before bringing his attention back to his phone conversation.

"*D'accord*, Jean-Luc. Thank you. Yes, I will handle it."

"Everything okay with the kids?" Maggie asked.

"*Oui.*"

"Vineyard stuff?" Maggie went to her dressing table and sat down. Her hair was pinned up but that was about all anyone could say about it. She wondered how Jill had gotten hers to look so gorgeous in the short time since their ride this morning?

"Danielle is upset," Laurent said.

Uh-oh. Maggie turned to look at her husband.

"I have that all under control," she said.

"Danielle doesn't think you do. Perhaps you will tell me what happened?"

"It's nothing," Maggie said with frustration. "Danielle and I saw Madame Roche...take something out of the bin in front of the hardware store in St-Buvard."

Laurent's eyebrows shot up. "She stole something? What?"

"Does it matter? And so at the Guild meeting the night before we left town, there was a...a confrontation with Madame Roche."

Laurent groaned. "Why? *Why* was there a confrontation?"

Maggie shifted her stance. "There just was. I didn't ambush her, Laurent. Is that what you think? I was minding my own business."

"This I do not believe."

"Well, it's the truth. You can ask Danielle."

Laurent waved his hands as if to erase Maggie's arguments. "Did you accuse Madame Roche of stealing?"

"Not *directly*..."

"Why?" he said in frustration. "Why did you do that?"

"I think you're focusing on the unimportant part here."

"I am focusing on the part that has created a problem in the village. You know it is not just between you and Madame Roche, eh? You know how small communities operate?"

"What did Jean-Luc tell you? That she's telling lies? So what?"

"Yes, lies. That you are sleeping with Monsieur Picou."

Maggie's mouth fell open. "That's...that's absurd. He's eighty years old."

Laurent arched an eyebrow. "Is that the reason it is absurd, *ma chérie*?"

"No, of course not. I mean, it's a lie and it's absurd."

"It is a lie that we must now deal with. You see this, *oui*? You, me, even our children. Can little Jemmy go to the park now and not hear the whispering about his mother and the *boucher*?"

"I'll get Monsieur Picou to stand up with me and denounce this as the lie that it is."

"Even if Monsieur Picou would allow you to embarrass him to that extent, I will not. Besides it would only open the door for Madame Roche's next lie."

"Fine. I'll just quit the guild then."

"You cannot do that. You must deal with this."

Maggie turned from him and stamped her foot in frustration.

A tap on the door distracted both of them for a moment.

"It is open," Laurent called out.

Violet entered, her arms full of clothing for the dinner that evening. She went to the bed and laid out a complete tuxedo for Laurent and a long lavender gown with a glittering headband for Maggie. The girl's face was still blotchy.

Maggie went to the bed. "Oh, it's beautiful, Violet," she said.

"I will return to prepare Milady's hair before cocktails," Violet said. "If I am still here."

Then she turned and silently let herself out of the room.

Laurent went to the bed and looked at the suit. "Why was she crying?" he said.

"You didn't hear? Seems Anastasia lost her tiara this afternoon. Violet is the prime suspect."

Laurent looked at Maggie. "The tiara she was wearing at dinner last night?"

"I imagine. It had twenty-five huge diamonds in it. Is it real do you think?"

"*Oui*, it's real," Laurent murmured.

Maggie had no doubt Laurent would know the value of the tiara. She also wasn't surprised that he'd noticed it to the degree he had.

"She probably just misplaced it," he said.

"You don't think it could have been stolen?"

"Madeline has done extensive background checks on all her employees."

Maggie glanced at Laurent. Was he covering for someone? Was that even remotely possible?

"Where did you go today?" she asked.

"Madeline asked me to pick up extra groceries for tonight's dinner." He pulled his shirt off. "I am taking my shower now, *ma chérie*," he said. "And if there is time before dinner, a nap."

"Sure. Good idea."

Maggie hung the clothes in the standing armoire and then relit the fire in the hearth. It was only a little after five o'clock but already the shadows had leeched the light from the room. There was also a chill in the room that was not related to the secrets that she now knew without a doubt stood between her and her husband.

118

21

Laurent stepped into the shower and put the spray on full force and as hot as he could stand it. His interaction with Gabrielle had been very telling. He hadn't needed to disarm her in the kitchen since the knife was little more than a message to him not to come any closer or press any deeper. Even after all this time, her bitterness was still raw, still very much alive.

This was not his battle to fight but he still felt compelled to enter the fray. What had Roger been thinking? Had he seriously not left a note—not a single message that would make clear any of this? Had he changed so much in the last few years to have made himself totally unrecognizable as the man Laurent had known?

He scrubbed his skin until it stung and then stood with the hot water blasting down his head and felt his shoulders began to throb, half in pleasure and half in pain.

And then there was Maggie. There was something she wasn't saying. Laurent didn't know if it was a discovered secret she was trying to process on her own—never a good idea—or something else. She would talk about it when she was ready. He could only hope in the meantime she didn't commit to action based on something that lived only as a fact in her own head.

⁂⁂⁂⁂⁂

Maggie pulled the dress over her head and stood in front of the full-length mirror. Her hair still wasn't right but Violet seemed to think she could perform a miracle with it. Maggie heard the shower in the other room and tried again to determine what kind of mood Laurent was in. He was quiet during the best of times.

Which these definitely were not.

She'd made up her mind that she wouldn't confront him about Jill. First, it just made Maggie look insecure and second, Laurent probably had a very good reason why he hadn't mentioned that he had lived with Jill once. And even if he didn't—or at least not up to Maggie's standards—what difference did it make? She and Laurent had two children together and a vineyard!

Maggie had had just enough time between hearing the news from Jill this morning and this very minute to decide that taking the high road meant knowing Laurent had nothing to hide with regards to Jill. Maggie rubbed the goosebumps from her arms and stepped closer to the fire.

No, she would let it go, she thought with determination. In the first truly unMaggie-like thing she'd ever done, she would just let it go.

As she was inspecting her makeup in the mirror over the fireplace to see how much more she'd need to pile on to get the desired effect, the bathroom door opened and Laurent stepped into the bedroom with a large bath towel around his waist.

Steam from his shower followed him into the room. Instantly, Maggie shut the bathroom door behind him. She was sure there were some things even professional hairdressers were not able to rectify and damp frizzy hair was likely one of them. Besides which Violet hardly looked like a professional hairdresser.

That last thought made Maggie pause. It was true. Violet didn't look like the kind of person to take on the job she had. She was way too shy for this kind of work. She found herself wondering why Violet was at the Abbey.

"Do you need help getting out of your gown?" Laurent said as he reached for her.

Maggie laughed. "Ask me again in about four hours. Are you going to wear the tux?" Maggie knew Laurent thought the dressing up part of the Abbey was silly—but that didn't automatically mean he wouldn't play along.

"Do you want me to?" He cocked his head at her.

"I would love to see what you look like in white tie and tails," Maggie said.

He smiled. "*D'accord.*"

As he dressed, Maggie sat on the bed, careful not to wrinkle her gown.

"The way I see it," she said, "the cops must be looking at Anastasia, Nigel, Madeline and Will the most. Don't you agree?"

"I don't know, *chérie.*"

"I figure Anastasia is suspect number one since anyone can see she is not an unhappy widow—no sign of mourning and she clearly wants her hands on the Abbey...*and* she stood to gain financially. So that's motive. What about Nigel?"

"Nigel hated Roger," Laurent said as he raked his fingers through his long hair, bringing some semblance of order to it. "He told me that Nigel once attacked him with a knife but Roger refused to report it.

"That's terrible! Okay. So that's two viable suspects. Three if you throw in Madeline which, much as I hate to, we probably should. I wonder who the police like."

"Perhaps one or two more."

"Do you know something?"

Laurent shrugged. "Roger mentioned last spring that his nephew had a secret. Roger was waiting for Will to share it with him."

"What kind of secret?"

"Something about the business."

"Was he afraid that Will was doing something shady with the business? Skimming profits?"

Laurent didn't answer.

"Well, if he was, that's motive, Laurent," Maggie said. "I mean it's horrible to think his own nephew might have killed him, but if Will didn't want Roger to find out what he was doing..."

"Madeline told me that this was the weekend Roger was to have examined the books on the business."

"Oh, snap."

"*Exactement.*"

"Where was Will the night Roger was killed?"

"*Sais pas.*" *I don't know.*

"We need to find out. Madeline said she was in bed with food poisoning which frankly sounds fake."

"You *asked* her?"

"Of course. You can't be shy about these things, Laurent. And I'm pretty good at telling when people are lying to me too." She leaned in close, her nose nearly touching his. "I learned from the master."

He placed his hands on her hips and drew her onto his lap—*not* what she was expecting.

"I like it when you call me that."

She pulled back to claim some level of control over the situation. She was always thrown off when he had his hands on her and dammit, he knew that very well.

"Anything you want to tell me?" she asked.

The penny dropped and he narrowed his eyes. "What is it you think I have not been truthful about?"

"You do know I went riding with Jill this morning, don't you?"

She saw something flinch in his eyes and her heart sank. A very large part of her was hoping that Jill had been lying.

"I should have mentioned my relationship with Jill to you."

"You think?"

While it was true it had been her own vow not to say anything but that was before Laurent seemed to react to being caught out with such insouciance. Was it possible she'd married someone who didn't know that this was a major breach? That allowing your wife to become even temporary pals with the woman you'd slept with—let alone *lived* with—was wrong on every level there was to be wrong on?

Suddenly the image of Jill in her slim jodhpurs, her small tush and not-at-all small boobs came rushing back to Maggie like a steam locomotive. The woman had set her cap for Laurent and that was as plain as the wary look on Laurent's face right now or as true as the fact that Maggie needed to lose five—*oh hell, let's get real*—ten pounds.

And men were so naïve. Laurent would walk right into Jill's trap, eyes wide open and oblivious right up to the point where he and Jill were trying to decide what the kids would call her: stepmummy or Auntie Jill?

So much of what Maggie was thinking must have passed across her face because she felt Laurent's hands tighten on her hips.

"Stop it, *chérie*," he said in a low voice. "It was a long time ago and has nothing to do with us now."

"Is that so?" Maggie said, warring with herself—the half of her that knew Laurent would never cheat on her faced down against the other half of her that knew he'd made his living lying to everybody in sight for years before he met her. And the demon that is insecurity and jealousy jumped on the side of the bad half and Maggie pulled herself out of Laurent's hands.

"Anything else you want to come clean about?" she said. "While we've got the door open?"

When he hesitated, she blanched. It had just been something to say. Not in a million years did she actually think he was holding something else back!

"What?" she said in disbelief. "What is it? There's more?"

She saw him clamp his mouth together in stubborn refusal.

"When you are rational," he said.

She sprang to her feet, nearly losing her balance in the long gown.

Had he really just said "*when you are rational*?" She ground her teeth and felt her face flush. She knew the cords of her neck were standing out in what was not her most attractive look. She turned with as much drama as she could muster without tripping and stormed out the bedroom door.

How dare he? Did he really presume to tell her that *she* was the one acting badly? That he would determine when he would tell her the truth—as one might a willful child? Maggie stomped down the hallway—made much less satisfying by the fact that she was barefoot and made no noise whatsoever.

That was probably the reason she was able to turn the corner in the hallway and see the two shapes standing in the dark portion of the alcove tucked into the landing overhang. She stopped, confused and without thinking why, stepped into the shadows and out of sight.

The sound of the blood pounding in her ears subsided and she held her breath to listen.

And watch.

Immediately she heard the unmistakable sounds of kissing and then a moan. Maggie knew if whoever was in that alcove came this way, they would see her. She could retrace her steps without detection. But she had to know who was there. Was the little maid carrying on with Annette's husband? Or Nigel? Perhaps Annette and her husband were enjoying a little role-playing of their own? Slinking around the upper levels of the Abbey and pretending to enact a tryst? Maggie had heard of married people peppering their love life with such antics. It didn't seem too out of bounds considering where they were.

A voice. The man was speaking, murmuring. It was followed by a woman's low giggle. A final kissing sound, loud and unmistakable was followed by another giggle. Seconds later, Maggie saw him. The groomsman Trevor emerged from the shadows. Maggie stifled the gasp that found its way up her throat. He walked silently away in the opposite direction from Maggie.

That just left the woman. Even though Maggie stood a fifty-fifty chance of being discovered depending on which way the woman left her hiding place, Maggie would not have broken cover for anything. She started to count, wondering if the paramour in the shadows was counting too. And then the woman peeked out of the shadows, looked both ways down the hall, and chose the route away from where Maggie stood—her mouth open in astonishment.

It was Anastasia.

22

Will looked in the mirror and tried for the fourth time to tie the stupid tie. If it were up to him, he'd go down to the kitchen and make himself a sandwich. But Annette wanted the whole to-the-manner-born experience. She didn't ask for much. It was little enough to give.

He threw the tie down in frustration.

"Why did you talk to the American so much?" he said in irritation. "You were a positive chatty Nancy."

Annette stood up from her dressing table. She wore a long to the floor gown that sparkled at the neckline—drawing Will's attention to her breasts like a laser beam.

"Why wouldn't I?" she said as she picked up the discarded tie.

"You know she's the wife of Roger's best friend?"

"So?" She stepped in front of him and began to tie it on him herself. "Here, let me do it."

"So? Are you seriously asking me that? I know you only have enough room in your head for your beloved horses, Annette, but even you can understand why we don't want to chum up with them."

"It seems to me that chumming up with them is probably the best thing we can do," Annette said. She gave the ends of the tie a sharp pull and stepped back to look with satisfaction at the finished product.

"We want them to leave as soon as possible," Will said in frustration, "Not ingratiate ourselves to them! Why do I have to tell you this?"

"Darling, are you all right? Let's get you a drinkie, shall we?"

Will stomped to the door.

"I'll be more all right when you stop trying to talk to people who are suspicious of me for the murder of a man who's death did not...not benefit me."

"Darling, you're feverish," Annette said. "Nobody is looking at you as a suspect in Roger's murder! That's preposterous. If anyone looks guilty here it's Anastasia or that dreadful son of hers. You are all wrought up over nothing."

"Really, Annette?" Will said, dragging a hand over his face coated with perspiration. "Then why do I feel like every time that frog bastard looks at me I have a neon sign on my face that says *It was me. I killed him*?"

✻ ✻ ✻ ✻ ✻ ✻

Maggie stood in the shadows listening to the soft tread of Anastasia moving away.

Anastasia is carrying on with Trevor?

Maggie shook her head. Is there any other way to interpret what she just saw? Could Trevor possibly have just been consoling her?

By smothering her with kisses? And giggling?

Looks like I just added Trevor to the growing list of people who would benefit from Roger being dead.

How long has it been going on?

If Anastasia was Roger's murderer, Trevor could easily have done any necessary heavy lifting.

Should Maggie go to the police? Was Trevor complicit? Or was he being used?

But if he's only being used, why is Anastasia still carrying on with him?

Unless she's afraid he'll blab what he knows if she doesn't?

Wait until I tell Laurent!

The thought of Laurent gave Maggie a stab of guilt. She'd not behaved well. And after she'd specifically said she wouldn't get all jealous and insecure about Jill—or at least not where Laurent could see.

She began walking down the hall toward her bedroom. There were two turns so if Laurent had already gone downstairs, she wouldn't have seen him leave. She hoped he was still in the room.

Apologies were so much more difficult when they were deferred.

She reached the bedroom and found the room warm from the fire...but empty. She went to the window to see if she could see him walking but it was too dark. She found her phone and sent him a quick text. *<Sorry. Got carried away.>* As apologies went, it wasn't great but Laurent was the subtle sort himself. He'd appreciate it for what it was.

She tossed the phone on the bed just as the door opened. Whirling around with hope that it might be her husband, Maggie's face fell when she saw it was just the little maid Violet. She had a curling iron and two hairbrushes in her hands and a grimly determined look on her face.

※※※※※※

"Can you believe that bitch threatened Violet?" Gabrielle said. "Accusing one of us of stealing her jewels! Ironic, no?"

The French woman stood in the kitchen with her hands knotted into fists on each hip as she stared down Madeline. A baking pan of *gougères* had just been taken from the oven. They would be served with cocktails. *A stupid American habit*, Gabrielle thought. *Ruin your appetite with spirit alcohol and snacks just before sitting down to dinner. Only the Americans would organize it so.*

"Will it never end?" Gabrielle asked tiredly, sitting down with a hard thump on one of the stools by the long table. Even when they were fully staffed, there weren't ten employees to gather around the table. It was just the way the fantasy went. Just one more charade to aid in creating the mirage.

Madeline sighed. "I would have thought it would now with Roger gone, Gabrielle."

"And yet his legacy lives on. Perhaps we should kill *her*, eh?"

"Don't joke about it," Madeline said, her eyes snapping. "What if someone should overhear?"

"Are we being recorded?" Gabrielle looked around her kitchen with fearful eyes. "I wouldn't put it past him."

"Did you talk with Laurent?"

Gabrielle snorted. "I suppose I have you to thank for that."

"I just knew he wouldn't give up until he'd approached you. What did he say?"

"He asked me why I was here," Gabrielle said, her mouth twisted in revulsion. "The same question I have been asking myself for seven years."

"He doesn't know," Madeline said. "Laurent doesn't know."

"That is a lie, *mon chou*," Gabrielle said. "But believe it if it comforts you. The two of them worked together, Bentley and Dernier. Always they were together."

"Not always."

"What does it matter? What does any of it matter? You were wrong, Madeline. You thought Roger would settle his half of the Abbey on you and instead he gave it all to her."

"We don't know that," Madeline said tiredly.

"Trust me, he has screwed us all. Again. As always."

"We'll know as soon as the will is read. No use speculating before then."

"And then what, Madeline? Because from where I'm standing it looks like we risked everything and got nothing. And wherever the bastard is, he is laughing. On that you may be sure."

"It's not over yet," Madeline said but Gabrielle could see she didn't believe her own words.

It *was* over. Their only hope now was that the flic didn't make one or both of them pay for the crime.

23

It was like something out of a very corny but very satisfying old movie. When Maggie stepped off the final carpeted step of the grand master staircase she knew the very essence of what it felt like to make an entrance.

And let's face it, making an entrance is the main reason a grand staircase was created. If Maggie hadn't had the fight with Laurent she wouldn't be stepping off the stairs with butterflies in her stomach full of awareness that she was making a spectacle of herself.

It wasn't that she wasn't sure of her effect on him. She knew her husband. He might have been annoyed with her petty jealousy but in the end it wouldn't have mattered much to him.

She stepped into the salon as covertly as she could without actually slinking into the room. All heads turned toward her; all eyes were on her.

The one that mattered—Laurent—examined her from top to bottom with a smile on his lips until their eyes locked. Maggie flushed at the covert attention, the unspoken but undeniable promise in that smile and those eyes, and went to the drinks cart where she selected a crystal cut glass of bourbon. When she turned around, Laurent was at her side.

He wore a black tailcoat over a white starched shirt with an impeccably perfect white bow tie. It was all Maggie could do not to gasp.

"Tu es belle, ma chérie," he said. "We will have to play this game back home, I think."

Maggie cleared her throat and had to force herself not run her hand across Laurent's chest. It had been a long time since she'd seen him dressed up and never like this.

Will, Annette and Anastasia were sitting together on the couch. Nigel was back in his corner, slouched in a chair and already looking seriously inebriated. Jill hadn't arrived yet.

"Lavender is your color," Anastasia said without smiling.

Maggie smiled her thanks at Anastasia while trying not to let her face give away her feelings. Skulking around dark corners of the upstairs bedrooms with the hired help could only mean the two of them had just *used* one of those upstairs bedrooms. And yet here Anastasia sat—lady of the realm—looking down her nose at the help, the guests and anybody else unfortunate enough to pass before her.

Wait until I tell Laurent. She glanced at him in his starched white shirt. It was a miracle they'd had a tux big enough to fit him. He wore it naturally—as if he dressed for dinner every night. He looked in fact like royalty.

Really, really bored royalty.

One thing Maggie had taken the time to do while Violet was dressing her hair was to remind herself that horseback riding and fox hunts aside—*Laurent* was the main reason they were here this week.

That and finding out who had killed his best friend.

"I got your text," he said.

"I'm sorry," she said.

He leaned down and surprised her with a kiss on the mouth. Laurent was not one for public displays of any kind.

Madeline entered the room with a tray of baked *hors d'oeuvres*. She wore a dark skirt and jacket and a white starched apron. Her manner indicated she was not playing one of the guests today. She was firmly in servant mode.

"Everything looks wonderful, Madeline," Maggie said as she seated herself in one of the plushly tufted Edwardian armchairs.

Madeline nodded noncommittally. "Milady," she said. She turned to Anastasia to offer the tray of *gougères*. Anastasia selected one and nibbled it delicately.

Madeline went to stand by the door with her gaze straight in front of her but ready to move in the direction of anyone who might act as if they wanted a cheese puff.

This is just painful, Maggie thought.

Dinner wasn't much better.

Jill never did make it to the salon for drinks. Maggie thought uncharitably that it might have been because she knew the value of an entrance. By the time Jill waltzed into the main dining room people put down their forks to gaze at her. She wore a devastatingly beautiful gown that looked like it was cut to hug every curve of her body. Slim but full where it counted, Jill set off the dress to its best advantage.

Jill kept her distance from Maggie, only nodding briefly in greeting when she entered the dining room. She also seemed to make a point of not sitting next to Laurent. Maggie wasn't sure what Jill's game was but she knew that acting suspicious or openly wary of her was not the way to find out. If Jill was trying to rub her past relationship with Laurent in Maggie's face, then Maggie could ignore that.

But if something else was going on—*that* Maggie would need to discern and sooner rather than later.

After dessert was finished, Anastasia stood but held her hands out to the men to indicate they should stay seated.

"Violet will bring in cigars and brandy," she said to them. "We ladies will meet you in the salon when you are ready."

Will seemed amiable enough for anything whereas Nigel was clearly too drunk to care one way or the other. Laurent caught Maggie's eye and she shrugged. *Why not? When in Rome.*

She followed the other women out of the dining room to the drinks salon. Someone had built up the fire and laid out a silver coffee service. Maggie was already stuffed from four courses plus dessert but found herself putting a generous slice of pound cake on her dish and spooning fresh berries over the top before settling back into the settee.

Jill and Annette sat at one of the game tables and began to play cards.

"Madeline," Jill said without looking from her cards. "Be a darling and open up a bottle of Veuve, would you? You don't mind, do you, Anastasia?"

Jill resumed her conversation with Annette obviously comfortable in the assumption that the champagne would be forthcoming.

Anastasia nodded at Madeline before sitting down next to Maggie.

"Well, I suppose you heard all the excitement today?" Anastasia said, pouring her coffee.

"About the stolen tiara?" Maggie said. "I did. When did you discover it missing?"

"This morning."

"You're sure you lost it at The Abbey?"

"I didn't *lose* anything, Mrs. Dernier," Anastasia said icily. "It was stolen from my room."

"I wondered why you don't have locks on the bedroom doors."

"Are you attempting to say it's *my* fault that someone broke in and stole my jewels?"

Maggie wanted to point out that without a locked door there really was no "breaking in" involved but decided not to.

"I've had to call the police about it," Anastasia said. "Such a bother. And the last thing I wanted to do this week of all weeks."

Anastasia acted more upset about the loss of her tiara than she did losing Roger. An image of Anastasia and Trevor snuggling in the upstairs hallway alcove flashed into Maggie's head.

Maggie heard enough from Annette and Jill's conversation to tell that it was largely about horses and the hunt coming up in two days.

"I was wondering if the police had any leads about Roger's murder?" Maggie asked.

Anastasia spilled her coffee in the saucer, cursed, and placed the cup on the table.

"They are doing everything they can to find the guilty party," Anastasia said.

"Madeline said they interviewed her for a long time—and she thought they also talked to Nigel."

"They talked to everyone who was here that night."

"The servants too?"

Anastasia narrowed her eyes and Maggie could almost visibly see the woman's guard go up.

"Of course," Anastasia said.

"I talked to Trevor this morning and he said he was in the barn at the time of the murder," Maggie said.

"Hardly a surprise."

"He also mentioned that Roger got him his job here."

"I didn't realize you would be interrogating the staff during your stay."

"I was just wondering how Trevor knew Roger."

"My husband did not know Trevor personally prior to Trevor's coming to the Abbey."

"Then how come Roger—"

"Trevor is the son of an old friend of Roger's," Anastasia said tightly. "Roger asked Madeline to hire Trevor because the lad needed a job. Do you find something strange about that, Mrs. Dernier?"

"Nope. Not at bit. That was nice of Roger. I bet Trevor was super grateful."

This time Anastasia at least had the shame to blush and look away.

Susan Kiernan-Lewis

24

Laurent's attention to his dinner mates wavered. With Nigel snoring face down in his uneaten Floating Islands with lemon sauce and Will focused on his smartphone screen, it suited Laurent to enjoy his own thoughts while alternately observing the two men. He warned himself not to make up his mind too quickly about Nigel. It would be all too easy to assess the young man, judge him and wrap him up in a bow. For all intents and purposes, Nigel looked like a lazy, self-absorbed young man. Those kinds of people could be dangerous but usually they were the willing or unwilling dupes to smarter more devious men. Men with a plan.

It was very clear that poor Nigel had no plan.

Which didn't mean he didn't kill Roger.

The thought came into Laurent's head and it surprised him. Up until this moment he hadn't realized he was in fact looking at anyone for that particular role.

This is Maggie's doing. Laurent hid his smile in his brandy. She looked beautiful tonight—as beautiful as he'd ever seen her, glowing radiantly, her cheeks rosy, her eyes glittering with vulnerability and contrition. No, he wouldn't change a thing about his wife. *And how many men can say that?*

Her confrontational American nature amused him most of the time—except in bed where it delighted him—but he knew village politics could escalate quickly if not handled carefully. And *careful* was not a word often found in Maggie's vocabulary.

A loud sucking snore came from Nigel which startled the young man into a nearly upright position before he slid to the floor.

"Bloody hell," Will said looking up from his phone with disgust. He glanced at Laurent and then over his shoulder as if expecting one of the servants to come in and remove Nigel. "Are we going to have deal with this wanker?"

Laurent cocked his head at Will and took a long drag on his cigar. He had no memory of a single time Roger had mentioned this nephew to Laurent until six weeks ago when Roger admitted he thought there was a problem with the books.

"Roger said he was to speak to you last weekend about the business," Laurent said bluntly.

Will dropped his phone on the floor and fumbled for it before coming up and taking a quick swig of his brandy.

"We often talked business while we were at the Abbey together," Will said. But his eyes darted around the room.

Why would anyone bother with a lie detector test? Laurent thought. *All you need to do is open your eyes.*

"He mentioned to me he thought there was a problem," Laurent said.

"No biggie, mate," Will said a little loudly. "We had something to work out and we did. Bob's your uncle."

"Madeline said you and your wife did not stay at the Abbey that week."

"That's right. We only came for dinner and then went home. Listen, if you want I can ask CI Bailey to give you a copy of my deposition."

His sarcasm was a pathetic attempt to cover his anger and his fear. Both were good emotions to have elicited from someone with secrets. This was something Laurent had always known. Even before his days on the Côte d'Azur.

"Did you mention in this deposition that you returned to the Abbey that night after dropping your wife at home?"

Will's eyes enlarged and he licked his lips.

As his own darling Maggie would have said—and had said many times in the past—*bingo*! If Laurent's bluff had been called, Will's reaction would have been very different.

"Look, that's not true," Will said, continuing to lick his lips.

"You did *not* come back to the Abbey later that night to talk to Roger?"

"I...okay, I did. But it had nothing to do with...I mean, Roger was fine when I left him!"

"Did you tell the police?"

"Look, mate, I didn't kill him if that's what you're implying!"

"Then why not tell the police that you returned that night?"

"I'm sure it would be difficult for someone like you to understand but trust me, the cops can take a perfectly innocent fact and turn it into something that costs you a stretch in prison."

"That does surprise me," Laurent said, finishing off his brandy. "Only in this case it would be quite a bit more than a stretch, *n'est-ce pas?*"

⁂⁂⁂⁂⁂

Not surprisingly, Anastasia's interest in talking with Maggie cooled considerably. She stood up abruptly and walked to where Annette and Jill were playing cards, hovering over their shoulders and feigning interest.

Madeline stepped into the room with a tray holding an ice bucket, a bottle of champagne and six champagne flutes. She set the bucket down and expertly opened the bottle.

"Oh, just in time, darling Madeline," Jill said without looking up from her cards. "I was parched. The wine at dinner had gone off."

Maggie shifted to a closer seat so she might better hear the conversation of the three women.

"Don't be absurd," Anastasia said in a shocked tone. She glared at Madeline. "It tasted fine to me."

"Oh, well, then," Jill said, snickering and glancing at Annette as if to invite her to join in on the joke. "If *you* thought it was all right..."

"What was the matter with it then?" Anastasia said, blushing darkly.

Maggie didn't know whether she spoke up in support of Anastasia because she had more she needed to ask her and wanted to amend her earlier clumsiness or because it was Jill who was baiting Anastasia.

"My husband is a winemaker," Maggie said as she reached for the champagne flute from the tray after Madeline had filled the glasses. "He would have said something if the wine was off."

Anastasia relaxed visibly.

Jill shrugged. "Perhaps Laurent has lost his edge when it comes to deciding what's good or not."

Maggie smiled and counted to ten. There was no point in drawing battle lines in front of everyone. The last thing she needed was for Jill to know Maggie had felt the sting.

"Did you get a call from CI Bailey, Mrs. Mears?" Anastasia said as she sipped her champagne.

"No, Milady."

Anastasia turned to Maggie.

"I'm sure it was Violet who stole the tiara," Anastasia said. "Who else could it be? I've asked the CI to look into the woman's background...something I'm sure wasn't done when she was hired." She looked meaningfully at Madeline.

Madeline kept her back to the group as she collected the coffee cups and silver serving decanters.

"Madeline and Roger had a laudable but ultimately unfortunate habit of hiring lost waifs that has almost never worked out well for us here at the Abbey," Anastasia said.

Annette laid down what was obviously a winning hand because Jill groaned and tossed down her cards. Then Jill turned to Anastasia.

"I understand Roger's will was read this morning," she said.

Anastasia sipped her champagne. "There were no surprises."

Madeline turned to give Anastasia an incredulous stare.

"I wasn't notified that the will was to be read today," Madeline said.

"And why would you be?" Anastasia said. "It had nothing to do with you."

Madeline's face lost all its color and Maggie jumped up to put a steadying hand on her elbow.

"It was as I expected," Anastasia said indifferently. "I was left the entirety of Roger's estate, including the controlling share of the Abbey."

The effect of Anastasia's words on Madeline was profound.

She'd expected Roger to leave her the Abbey, Maggie realized. Even after everything that had happened and after all the ways he'd let her down, she hadn't expected this.

"Madeline, can I get you a drink of water?" Maggie asked.

"Pull yourself together, woman," Anastasia said. "You act as if what you had with Roger actually meant something to him. Don't tell me you're that big a fool."

"Sorry, old thing," Jill said, shaking her head at Madeline. "You know Roger. You can't really be surprised."

"Besides," Anastasia said. "I'm afraid where *you're* going a fifteen million euro estate will hardly be of use to you."

"What are you talking about?" Maggie asked.

"Didn't I say?" Anastasia said, draining her champagne glass. "I have it on good authority that the police are close to making an arrest."

Madeline looked at Anastasia, stark fear etched across her face.

Susan Kiernan-Lewis

25

Madeline bolted from the room, leaving the salon door swinging behind her and nearly running into Laurent and Will as they entered the room.

Laurent gave Maggie a questioning look over everyone's heads and all she could do was shrug helplessly.

Was Anastasia implying that the police think Madeline did it? Clearly Madeline thought so. Did they have evidence?

Jill jumped up from the card table and grabbed Laurent by the sleeve to pull him onto the couch but he didn't move. He still hadn't taken his eyes off Maggie.

"You are ready, *chérie*?" he asked, ignoring Jill

"Oh, Laurent, you can't just show up and disappear!" Jill said. "You have to play the game and this is the part where the men join the ladies in the salon after cigars and brandy." Jill poured another glass of champagne, but Laurent was already holding his hand out to Maggie.

"No more games tonight. Come, *chérie*."

Maggie hurried to Laurent and felt a rush of pleasure as he slipped his arm around her waist and drew her close.

"Goodnight, all," she called to the women behind her. "See you at breakfast."

She didn't have to look behind her to know Jill's eyes were shooting daggers between Maggie's shoulder blades as she exited the room.

Violet was standing in their bedroom with the bed turned down and the fireplace blazing against the cold night when Maggie and Laurent entered the room. She curtsied and said in a whispered voice that she would help Maggie undress. Laurent shooed the little maid away with the assurance that he was quite capable of handling that particular chore.

Maggie unzipped her frock and let it fall to the carpet, stepping out of it and into Laurent's arms.

"I am so sorry, Laurent. I do not know what came over me."

"*De rien, chérie*," he said, nuzzling her neck and lifting her onto the four poster bed.

"I guess it was just such a shock meeting someone from your past life like that."

"*Je sais*," he said. He leaned on his elbow on the bed and gazed at her.

"Well, I'm over it. Completely."

"I am glad to hear it, *chérie*."

Maggie recognized in the midst of all her apologies that it would have been nice—no, *great*—if Laurent could have admitted that neglecting to tell her about Jill was also something worth apologizing for. She tried to shake off the thought. Laurent hadn't done anything wrong. She needed to quit drifting in the direction of thinking he had.

"Why did Madeline run from the room?" Laurent asked.

"Anastasia told the whole room that not only was Madeline completely left out of Roger's will but she's the one the cops are thinking of arresting for his murder."

"I do not think the police would tell Anastasia what they are thinking," Laurent said.

"That's a good point. It really upset Madeline, though."

"Perhaps she reacted as she did because she is expecting it," Laurent said. "Food poisoning is not an alibi."

"I wonder if Anastasia has a better one," Maggie said thoughtfully.

"I assume that means you will ask her?" he said with a smile.

"What about you? You're good at getting people to tell you things they didn't intend."

"I used to be."

"Missing the old life, Laurent?"

"*Non.*" He touched one of the long curls that had come down from Maggie's updo. "You were very beautiful tonight, *chérie.*"

"You were pretty gorgeous yourself."

He leaned over and kissed her but when he pulled back, his eyes were thoughtful and far away.

"What is it, Laurent?" she asked softly.

"I did not know how Roger was living these last few years," he said. "It was not a good life."

"You're feeling bad about letting the friendship slide. That's my fault."

He shook his head.

"*Non, chérie.* I have been so busy. With the vineyard, the children. It's nobody's fault."

"If I'd have made him more welcome—"

"*Chérie*, you did not prevent Roger from visiting. I was too busy to invite him. I was too happy in my own life."

"You feel guilty for being happy?"

"*Peut-être.* But also because I was afraid."

"I can't imagine you afraid of anything."

He laughed. "I have trained you well."

"What were you afraid of?"

He drew a line down her chin and regarded her sadly.

"I was afraid for him to see me so happy when I knew he could never be."

✵✵✵✵✵

Hours later, Maggie lay in bed, too awake to sleep and listening to the rolling purr of her husband's snores. She should have known that he was processing Roger's death in light of his own past. There were so many people who had been hurt by that past—no matter how she and Laurent tried to paint it as being a good thing because of how it worked out.

Laurent wasn't one to lie to himself, that much Maggie knew. He wouldn't be able to look at the carnage that was his dearest friend's life and not see it for what it really was. A wasted life that left behind only one man who truly grieved Roger's passing.

And that man had been too busy to show it for the years when it might have mattered.

Guilt was a strange bedfellow for Laurent, Maggie knew that well. Because of his past, he'd had to come to grips with it in a way that didn't destroy his chance for a happy life with her and the children.

But it didn't mean it wasn't there or that the struggle to face it wasn't real.

As Maggie burrowed down next to Laurent she heard the unmistakable sound of a floorboard creak outside the bedroom door. She froze, glancing first at Laurent to see if it had been loud enough to wake him. He was as sensitive as a cat and slept through very little. But tonight he slept undisturbed.

Someone had walked past their door. Maggie reached for her watch on the side table. It was three in the morning. Too early for the servants to be up and too late for anyone else to be wandering the halls.

She pulled back the covers and slipped out of bed, grabbing her robe as she went to the door and stood with her ear against it listening.

Carefully, slowly, she pulled open the door. The hallway was semi-lit by vintage bronze light sconces on the wall. She stepped into the hall, sorry she hadn't taken the time to find her slippers first.

Someone was walking down the hall away from her. Every room on this floor had its own bathroom. There was no need for anyone to be up and about.

Maggie crept to the first corner in the hall and peeked around it. At first she thought it was only a shadow but as her eyes adjusted to the dimly lit passageway, she realized what she was seeing—a form stood perfectly still in front of the door that belonged to Anastasia.

The figure's head was bent toward the door as if listening. She was dressed in dark slacks and shoes and a dark hoodie.

Maggie's heart pounded as she watched the woman. If she grabbed for Anastasia's doorknob, Maggie would scream.

Finally the woman relaxed her stance and stepped away from the door. When she did, her hood fell back, revealing her blonde hair tied back in a low hanging ponytail.

Maggie only saw the side of her face but she recognized her immediately.

As Maggie watched her turn and disappear down the hall, she couldn't help but wonder....

Why was Jill wandering the halls at this time of the night?

Susan Kiernan-Lewis

26

The next morning Laurent was up again before Maggie. She wasn't sure where he went in the mornings but she thought if he wanted to tell her he would. In the meantime, she would give him the space he seemed to need.

Because he'd left so early, Maggie hadn't had the chance to tell him what she'd seen last night with Jill skulking around the hallways.

Was she listening at Anastasia's door? Or everyone's door? Maggie hadn't mistaken the sound of someone pausing outside her own door. What was Jill up to?

Maggie dressed in the day clothes that were hanging in the armoire. It was a two-piece dress, the skirt a knife pleated a-line with a matching top, both in a rich blue wool crepe. It would be warm, at least. But when she looked at the result in the mirror, she decided the look—at least on her—definitely teetered in the direction of frumpy.

Violet tapped on the door and entered carrying a large silver tray in her hands.

"Breakfast, Milady?" she said, setting the tray down on the bed. "And I will do your hair for the day."

Maggie found a piece of bacon on the tray but waved the maid away.

"I'm just wearing it down today," she said.

Violet sucked in a gasp. "Mrs. Bentley will...I mean, she..."

Maggie could see the young woman's problem.

"Fine," Maggie said. "But nothing too fancy. I'm going to walk the grounds and it'll all just come loose anyway."

"Yes, Milady."

Maggie settled into the chair in front of the dressing table while Violet brought a cup of tea to her and began brushing Maggie's hair.

"So how did you end up taking a job at the Abbey?" Maggie asked.

The young woman started at Maggie's question and again Maggie was reminded that this job must be hell for Violet who was constantly put into personal contact with strangers all day long.

It occurred to Maggie that Violet might well be a useful source of information on the night that Roger was killed.

"I guess the cops talked to you a long time about the murder?" Maggie asked.

"Yes, Milady."

"I know how upsetting that must have been for you."

"Yes, Milady." Violet scrunched up her face in concentration as she twisted Maggie's long thick hair into a chignon and began carefully securing it in place with hairpins.

"Did you know Roger very well?"

"No, Milady."

Okay, this isn't working.

"Where were you when he was killed?"

Violet knocked the teacup to the carpet and exclaimed in horror.

"Oh, Milady! I am so sorry! Let me pour you another one. I am so clumsy! Please don't tell Mrs. Mears!"

"It's fine, Violet," Maggie said as Violet dropped to her knees to blot up the liquid from the rug. "I'm sorry if I upset you."

Violet didn't answer and somehow that, in itself, felt like an answer to Maggie.

Did Violet know something? Did she have information she was afraid of revealing? Was this at all normal behavior to some pretty basic questions?

"Did you know Roger Bentley before coming to work at the Abbey?"

"No, Milady."

Maggie tamped down her frustration. Either the little maid knew nothing and was just not very good at her job. Or she knew something damning and was not very good at lying.

⚜ ⚜ ⚜ ⚜ ⚜

Trevor stood in the corner of the alcove behind the only potted plant in the hallway watching the American's bedroom door. The fury of having to do this pinged off him like radar waves. His heartbeat was racing and he felt nearly dizzy with anticipation.

The sound of the door opening made him suck in a quick breath and hold very still. He was sure he couldn't be seen from this angle. But to move would either provide an unimproved vantage point or give away his position.

The American woman came out of the bedroom first. She was wearing that ridiculous costume that Stazia made all of them wear. The Yank was shorter than Stazia—not much bigger than Violet—but she had a good figure. Nice sized bum, good rack. He watched her walk down the hall and out of sight. Just when he couldn't hear her tread on the carpet any longer, the bedroom door opened again and Violet stepped out into the hall. She held a rag in her hand as if she'd been mopping something up.

Within seconds Violet closed the door and scurried down the hall after the American.

It was true that Mrs. Mears kept all her maids and kitchen staff on a short leash, Trevor thought. And if she didn't then that frog bitch who ran the kitchen did. Which was all well and good, he thought grimly, looking both ways down the long hall before emerging from his hiding place. But it was still bloody inconvenient asking him to do this.

Not to mention dangerous.

He walked to the American's bedroom, paused, and then let himself in.

⚜ ⚜ ⚜ ⚜ ⚜

After her unsatisfying conversation with Violet, Maggie decided she needed to be more systematic in her questioning of the people who were at the Abbey the night Roger was killed. Violet was either a nonstarter as a suspect for Roger's murder or she was much more clever than she seemed at first. Maggie made a note not to rule the young woman out—at least not until she found a motive or two—but also not to spend too much time on someone who didn't, on paper anyway, look at all viable.

Gabrielle, on the other hand, reeked of motive.

But what if the police were right? What if they'd found something that directly tied Madeline to Roger's murder?

Did it matter?

The only thing that matters is finding the one who killed Roger. It's the only way to help Laurent put everything in perspective so he can move forward.

For him and for me.

It didn't take a super sleuth to figure that out.

Maggie darted past the dining room. She saw that people had begun to gather there but she didn't pause long enough to see who. She was sure Laurent wouldn't be in there, milling about, sipping tea and after last night, Maggie had had enough conversation with the others to last her a while. They were all of them just cagey enough not to answer a direct question and they knew they didn't have to answer them anyway—at least not from Maggie.

How could she determine if their alibis held up if she didn't even know what their alibis were?

The door that led to the basement kitchen was down the long main hall and around a corner. Maggie had discovered it her first day at the Abbey but hadn't gone through it. The door was propped open today, probably because—with Violet attending the ladies who breakfasted in bed—Gabrielle was on her own going up and down the stairs freshening the breakfast buffet in the dining room.

Maggie picked up the long hem of her skirt and hurried down the narrow back stairs. It was amazing to her how everything behind her was carpeted and spacious and luxurious but as soon as she went through the door that led "below," the world narrowed, turning into hard wood and plain, unvarnished walls.

The scent of breakfast cooking pulled her forward the last few steps until she came out into the middle of the kitchen. Gabrielle stood working over a large stove with her back to the door. To her right was a stack of dishes set on a wide heavy tray. A basket of soft-boiled eggs peeking out from under a gingham napkin sat beside another basket of fresh-baked scones. And next to that was a tower of buttered toast.

"Good morning," Maggie said in her most cheerful voice.

Gabrielle whirled around with a look of horror and outrage mingling on her face.

"You are not to be down here!" she said, looking Maggie up and down as if the costume Maggie wore was part of the insult.

"Before you ask, I didn't take a wrong turn," Maggie said, stepping further into the kitchen. "I wanted to meet you."

"You must go upstairs," Gabrielle said, her face flushing bright pink. "I have too much to do to talk with you."

"I'd be happy to carry something upstairs for you if that would help."

"Just go and let me do my job."

Ignoring people's arguments in order to wear them down and get to the truth was one of Maggie's main questioning tactics. She'd even used the technique a few times on Laurent with varying degrees of success. For everyone else however, it almost always worked and Maggie was confident that Gabrielle would be no exception.

"I was talking with some of the guests upstairs and was wondering how you ended up in the middle of England cooking in an old country manor," Maggie said brightly. "I'll bet it's an interesting story. Did you know Roger Bentley before you came?"

Gabrielle stared at Maggie with her mouth open. The pan she'd been attending on the stove began to bubble over.

Maggie pointed to it. "Oops," she said. "I think you're burning back there."

Gabrielle turned and snatched the handle of the hot pan from the heat then instantly screamed and dropped it onto the floor. She swore loudly in French.

"Oh, be careful!" Maggie said belatedly. "Here, let me—"

Maggie was focused on the disaster of scrambled eggs and sausage links littering the floor at Gabrielle's feet when the first dish smashed against the wall behind her.

"What the hell!" Maggie squeaked as the second dish came flying at her head.

28

Maggie made it to the door and slammed it shut just as the third dish crashed against it.

What a pyscho! she thought, her breath coming in hard, fast pants. She ran up the stairs, tripping once over her long skirt and then, grabbing the hem in both fists, climbed to the landing. Before she reached the main hall, she knew Gabrielle wasn't going to chase her through the Abbey flinging dishes at her.

Talk about an overreaction! Or a guilty reaction? Why the hell did she do that?

Maggie's heart was fluttering as she tried to steady her pulse. Of course, it was Maggie's interruption that had made Gabrielle drop the pan. Well, technically it was the hot handle that had made her drop it but clearly it was Maggie's questioning that had made Gabrielle forget she needed a potholder for the pan.

Why did she flip out? Was it me? Is she unstable? Or is she just a typical chef with a chef's temperament?

Maggie passed the dining room door and saw Laurent was inside drinking coffee.

As was Jill.

Maggie entered the room.

"Hey," she said. Both Laurent and Jill turned to look at her. They were the only two people in the dining room and they were standing on opposite sides of the room. It occurred to Maggie that the only thing more aggressive than hanging all over a guy to get his attention was to loudly and deliberately ignore him.

After last night's debacle, it looked like Jill had opted for strategy number two.

"You are just coming down for breakfast, *chérie*?" Laurent said.

Maggie went to the buffet to pour herself a cup of coffee. She was anxious to debrief with Laurent over her experience in the kitchen but wasn't wild about doing it in front of Jill.

"I am," she said, nodding briefly at Jill in greeting. "Where's Anastasia?"

"Don't you know?" Jill said smugly. "The married women of her class always have their breakfasts in bed. That's where Annette is, too. That's where *you* should be, darling. Didn't they offer it?"

"As it happens, they did," Maggie said. "I didn't want to waste one of my last remaining days lying in bed." She turned and smiled sweetly at Jill. "Not alone anyway."

Laurent gave Maggie a kiss as he walked out the door. "*Anon, chérie*," he said.

Jill shook her head after he left. "So mysterious is our Laurent," she murmured.

Maggie felt her face burn at the *our Laurent* comment but forced herself not to respond to it.

"But then I suppose everyone has secrets," Jill said. "Don't you think so, Maggie?"

"Sure. I guess."

"For example, did you know that there's a rumor that Anastasia had Nigel out of wedlock? What do you think she'd do to keep *that* little morsel from seeing the light of day?"

Maggie frowned. "I thought half the British aristocracy was born on the wrong side of the sheet."

"Don't be silly. The upper class may have their flings—not that I'm calling Anastasia upper class mind you —but very few would ever recognize the results of that fling by handing over their good name."

"How do you know this about Anastasia?"

"Well, I don't know it for *sure*, darling. But it doesn't matter. Gossip with no basis can do every bit as much damage as a DNA sample."

"Remind me never to piss you off."

"Darling, as if."

"Speaking of rumors," Maggie said, "there's one going around that has you wandering the halls of the Abbey in the middle of the night."

A glint of coldness entered Jill's eyes as she regarded Maggie. "That would be a rumor *not* based on fact," she said, appraising Maggie.

"So you were *not* wandering the halls in the middle of the night?"

"Most decidedly not."

"Good to know," Maggie said.

The fact that Jill had just lied about something that Maggie knew for a fact was the truth gave her a thrill of recognition. *Jill was hiding something. And lying about it.*

In Maggie's experience, when it came down to finding the most likely suspects for any crime—you looked at the people who were lying first.

As far as Maggie was concerned, that meant the spectre of doubt had just shifted to Jill Bentley, sister of the deceased.

Gabrielle entered the room, her arms straining under the tray of breakfast food. She thumped the tray down on the buffet table, shot Maggie a look of loathing, and then left the room.

"Goodness!" Jill said. "Whatever did you do to Madame duLuc? I do believe she might have poisoned your kippers."

Maggie selected a soft-boiled egg and a piece of toast. It didn't look nearly as good as the sausages and fried potatoes. But it was probably a lot fewer calories.

"I have no idea," Maggie said, tapping the top off her egg. "Chefs are prickly, I guess."

Jill sat down next to Maggie. They were the only ones in the dining room.

"Gabrielle hated Roger, you know," Jill said conspiratorially.

"So she knew him before coming to work at the Abbey?" Maggie asked.

"Did she ever. At risk of a repeat of yesterday's devastating faux pas, darling, I might suggest you ask your husband about Madame duLac."

Maggie put her spoon down without touching the egg.

Laurent knew Gabrielle?

"Roger insisted Madeline hire Gabrielle," Jill said.

Another employee who owes her job to Roger's generosity?

"Why would he do that?" Maggie asked.

"Seems she got into a spot of trouble in London. I don't know the details but drugs were involved and she couldn't find work after that."

"Why would she hate the man who gave her a second chance? That makes no sense."

"It does when you consider it was Roger who put Gabrielle into dire straits to begin with."

Maggie shook her head in confusion. "How?"

Jill reached over to pluck one of Maggie's toast spears from her plate. She nibbled the end of it.

"I'd say it was right about the time he bilked Gabrielle's father out of eight hundred and fifty-five thousand euros."

✻✻✻✻✻

Maggie took a deep breath and placed her hands on the table as if to steady herself.

Roger had cheated Gabrielle's family? And then thrown a bone to Gabrielle when she had trouble adjusting to it?

Oh, Roger...

"In Roger's defense," Jill said, "that con was in the days when he thought he couldn't get enough money to feel safe. It was right about the time he and Madeline bought the Abbey."

A sudden splinter of fear shot through Maggie. Was Laurent involved with that con? When did Jill say it was?

She looked at Jill who was watching her, a smirk distorting her lips.

She wants me to ask if Laurent was involved.

I'd as soon eat my rubber riding boot.

Maggie shrugged and smiled. "Oh, well," she said.

Nigel came into the breakfast room followed by Madeline and Anastasia. Maggie was surprised not to see Madeline earlier. But what with Anastasia publicly announcing last night that the cops would be coming for Madeline it was no surprise that the poor woman had taken a little time off this morning.

Nigel went to the breakfast table and piled kippers, sausages, eggs and scones on his plate before going to the head of the dining room table.

Not far enough away, Maggie thought, as she watched him methodically shovel the food into his mouth.

Anastasia nodded regally to both Jill and Maggie and simply stood at the door surveying the room. Madeline stacked empty dishes onto a nearby tray and began tidying the area.

"I'm only sorry Annette isn't here for my announcement," Anastasia said.

Jill turned to look at Anastasia. "This should be good," she said out of the corner of her mouth to Maggie.

Will entered the room without greeting anyone and went immediately to the food buffet.

Wow. Roger's relatives are just all class all the way, Maggie thought as she watched Will serve himself.

Anastasia waited until he'd taken his seat. Madeline turned and waited patiently.

"As most of you know," Anastasia said, "I am now the major shareholder of the Abbey."

Anastasia paused as if half expecting there might be applause after this statement, underscoring just how deluded the woman was, Maggie thought with amazement.

"After much deliberation and thought, I have decided that the Abbey will not take part in the ride to hounds this year."

Jill was on her feet in an instance, her teacup tipped over in its saucer.

"You can't do that!" she said.

Anastasia looked at Jill with satisfaction. "Well, yes I can. There will be no hunt crossing the Abbey grounds this year."

"Anastasia," Madeline said, "you said we would discuss it before making any—"

"I insist you not call me by my Christian name, Mrs. Mears," Anastasia said hotly. "And I'm sure I made no promises. My mind is quite made up."

"The hunt has always come across Abbey grounds!" Jill said. "For four hundred years!"

"You just made that number up," Anastasia said imperiously as she glanced over at her son who had stopped eating and was staring at her with his mouth open in astonishment. "In any case —"

"Lady Bentley," Madeline ground out, her fists clenched tightly by her sides. "You have no authority to do this. A special board meeting must be called."

"And you well know there's no time for that before the hunt," Anastasia said. "No, it's done. I called the Master of the Hounds just this morning and informed him."

"You never!" Madeline said. "You had no right!"

"I am getting very tired of you jumping up from your station, Mrs. Mears!"

"I'll jump up into your grill, you daft cow!" Madeline said. "This isn't a game. This is a business!"

"How dare you speak to me like that? I will have you sacked!"

"Don't you mean you'll have me thrown in the tower, you crazy bitch?" Madeline shrieked back.

"How dare you!" Anastasia screamed, moving toward Nigel as if for support.

Her son jumped to his feet and shouted to his mother, "You ruin everything!" before running out of the room, knocking down Violet as she was coming through the door. Maggie hurried to help the young woman to her feet.

"Are you okay?" Maggie asked.

Violet swallowed and nodded. "Begging your pardon, Milady," she said in a shaky but loud voice. She looked around the room fearfully.

"Oh, out with it, Violet!" Madeline said, her hands on her hips and still facing Anastasia. "What is it?"

"It's the police, Mrs. Mears," Violet said. "They said to say they've come for you."

29

Maggie watched in horror as the police, attended by Chief Inspector Bailey, handcuffed and led a stunned Madeline stumbling and sobbing to the police car. No one intervened. No one asked questions or rushed to Madeline's defense.

All of them—Anastasia, Nigel, Will, Violet, Jill and Maggie —stood in a small group in front of the Abbey as the police car drove slowly down the long front drive of the Abbey. It was late morning now. It was going to be a beautiful fall day with a startling blue sky and not a cloud in it.

Maggie couldn't believe how bad she felt.

Does feeling bad mean Madeline didn't do it? Should I trust my gut on these things or had I just started to like her and my gut means precisely nothing?

How Maggie wished she knew what kind of evidence the cops had that made them arrest Madeline.

As the police car drove away with Madeline, Gabrielle ran out of the front door.

"What has happened?" Gabrielle shrieked. "Where is Madame Mears?"

"Gone, Madame duLac," Anastasia said. "And now perhaps we can finally get back to normal. The *new* normal."

"The police have arrested Madame Mears?" Gabrielle said in astonishment, her eyes going to Maggie as if somehow this were her fault.

"Yes," Anastasia said. "I am making you the new Manager of the Abbey. And Violet? Where are you?"

Violet never moved from where she stood at the doorway watching everyone with a shocked expression.

"Violet, go to the stables and tell Trevor that he is to work in the house from this moment on. We will have no need of a groomsman."

"Missus?" Violet said in confusion.

"Go!" Anastasia barked. Violet fled down the front walkway in the direction of the barn.

"You have truly lost your mind, Anastasia," Jill said. "Trevor is a stable boy. You can't bring him into the house!"

"There will be many changes going forward, Jill," Anastasia said. "I won't take it badly if you decide you won't stay as a result."

"You can't get rid of your only stable hand! We have a hunt in one day's time!"

"I told you! The hunt's cancelled!"

"You can't cancel it!"

"I already have. Now if you will excuse me. Madame duLac? You will discuss the evening meals with me from now on."

"*Pardon?*" Gabrielle said, her gaze going from where the police car had disappeared and back again to Anastasia's face.

"You are *barking*," Jill said. "Gabrielle barely speaks English! How is she supposed to manage this place?"

Trevor came running from around the corner of the house. Violet was behind him, her eyes focused on the ground. He looked at the group gathered on the gravel and went straight to Anastasia.

"Milady?" he said.

"You are the new Abbey butler, Mr. Harris," Anastasia said. "Please come inside and I will outline your new duties."

"The new what, Missus?" Trevor said. He stood in front of her with horse manure on his boots and his hands dark with dirt.

"*Ce n'est pas possible!*" Gabrielle wailed, ripping off her apron and throwing it onto the gravel drive before turning and fleeing around the side of the building.

Annette stepped out onto the porch. She was dressed in jodhpurs with riding boots and a tweed hacking jacket. She held a teacup in one hand.

"I say," she said. "Has something happened?"

As he returned from his walk, Laurent watched the group. He'd taken to spending most of his time walking the perimeter of the gardens when it wasn't raining. It was quiet. In most instances, depending on which direction he faced, he could believe it was the early 1900's again. There wasn't a phone line or cell tower to disturb the fantasy.

Except living in 1910 was not something Laurent desired to do. *Why would you long to live in a time where none of the conveniences we all depend upon had yet to be invented?*

He took out his cellphone. Back home, this year's grape harvest had been their best yet but there were still many chores to do and many decisions to make for the coming year. And now for the first time since he and Maggie had begun to work the vineyard, he had the money to make those decisions based on what was the right thing to do and not merely on what they could afford. He was sorry the hunt would delay their return to St-Buvard by the extra day. But he knew Maggie was looking forward to it.

As he drew closer to the group standing at the front of the Abbey Laurent could observe everyone's reactions to Madeline's arrest. He saw that while his *femme* might prefer him by her side at the moment, she didn't need him.

And he wanted to see who was surprised by Madeline's arrest.

And who was pleased.

Anastasia of course. But that could be for any number of reasons.

Gabrielle was not happy.

Violet appeared fretful—as she was almost all of the time.

Nigel looked angry.

Will had no discernable reaction which seemed odd.

And the man Trevor? He was a cool one. Hiding something, to be sure. But a killer?

Well, everyone is capable of it, Laurent thought.

Given the right circumstance.

※※※※※

Maggie stayed outside after Anastasia and the servants went inside—followed by a still arguing Jill and a glowering, pouting Nigel.

What was his deal? If Maggie had to guess, she'd say that for some reason he hadn't wanted his mother to cancel the hunt. But how much sense did *that* make?

Will and Annette had gone to the stables. Annette was obviously planning on riding and Maggie supposed they went together so they could process the morning's events.

Poor Madeline.

Anastasia had been right. Was it possible that the police had confided in Anastasia after all? Pretty dangerous thing to do if they were at all worried about Madeline trying to escape in the night. And why *didn't* Madeline run away? Was it because she was innocent and thought justice would prevail? Or was it because she was guilty and knew how bad it would look if she tried?

Maggie decided to explore a part the part of the Abbey grounds she'd not yet seen. As she began to walk, the hem of her long day gown became drenched from the dew that had yet to burn off the lawn. Here the gardens were formal—more in the French style, with a long corridor of lawn between large sections of flowers. At the end of the lawn was an ancient wooden pergola covered with roses.

Many of the flowers were gone, the beds covered with mulch in anticipation of a glorious spring, but because the Abbey didn't close for the winter, the garden was planted with seasonal blooms. Asters, daisies and bright orange sneezeweeds filled the beds. Madeline had mentioned that they used a professional landscaping firm to tend the garden. Gone were the days when all of this would have been the life's work of one man or even a team of men who lived on the estate.

It was not a cold day but Maggie still wished she'd brought her jacket. The breeze had picked up. As she approached the pergola she saw Will sitting with his back to the house, smoking a cigarette.

"I hope I'm not disturbing you," Maggie called as she approached.

He turned and squinted at her as if not sure who she was.

"Oh, hello," he said.

"It's beautiful here," she said as she sat down opposite him. "Do you mind?"

He shrugged.

Will had to be the only person besides Nigel who Maggie hadn't talked to. He was quiet, even tending toward the grumpy side in her opinion.

"I saw you talking to CI Bailey when they took Madeline away," Maggie said, keeping her voice light and nonthreatening.

"I don't know why he talked to me," Will said. "I'm not next of kin or anything."

"Well, he probably saw you were the only man in the group."

"Maybe."

"Can I ask you what he said?"

"Not much, really."

"Did he say anything about whether or not they had evidence against Madeline?"

He shook his head. "But now that you mention it, he did say he was expecting a confession."

"Really?" Maggie sat up straighter.

"Is that significant?" He frowned and took a long drag off his cigarette. Maggie noticed the pack next to him. It was the French brand *Gauloises*.

"Well, it might be," Maggie said. "If he's hoping for a confession, it could be because his forensic evidence is weak. Possibly it's all circumstantial."

"Are you a cop?"

Maggie grinned. "No, just a hobbyist. But I've picked up a few things along the way."

"Like other people's husbands, it would seem!" Annette said as she appeared from the side of the pergola hidden by a long row of primrose hedges.

She glared at Maggie. "What are you up to? I saw you looking at Will earlier."

Maggie couldn't help the laugh that escaped her.

"Are you serious? Have you seen my husband?" That was mean but Maggie couldn't help herself. Comparing the paunchy balding Will to Laurent was flat out laughable.

"Annette, honestly," Will said. "You're making an ass of yourself."

Annette looked at Will and then back at Maggie and then clapped a hand over her mouth to stifle a groan. Her eyes watered and tears dripped down her cheeks. Her husband tossed down his cigarette and stood up to bring her into his arms.

"I'm so sorry," she whispered to him.

"It's all right, love," he said in a low voice. "We're all on edge."

Whether it was something going on between them or just the drama at the Abbey, it was pretty clear that Will and Annette were dealing with something private and difficult. Maggie felt a spasm of pity for both of them but especially Annette. Her jealous outburst had hit awfully close to home.

Is that how Maggie sounded to Laurent? She cringed to think it and began to edge out of the pergola when Annette reached out with a hand to stop her.

"Please," Annette said. "Forgive me. I do not know what came over me."

"I do," Maggie said, patting her hand. "Because it's the same thing that comes over me. Do not think another thing about it."

Annette smiled shakily at her. "Thank you. Ride with me in the hunt tomorrow?"

"I'm afraid I'm not riding in the hunt."

Up until that moment, Maggie hadn't realized how much she wanted to.

"Besides," Maggie said. "I'm sure you're loads better than I am. I'd never be able to keep up."

"Nonsense! From what Jill said, you're as good or better than I am."

Jill had praised Maggie's riding? What was that all about? Most of the equestrians Maggie knew back in Atlanta were fiercely competitive and would no more compliment someone else's riding than pull their own teeth.

Especially not someone you considered a rival.

It started to rain. Maggie said goodbye to Will and Annette and returned to the Abbey. The walk had done her good and the interaction with Annette had boosted her mood. Not just because of the much needed perspective it gave her but also because of the chance to connect to at least one person at this resort who wasn't manipulating people for her own agenda.

Seeing Annette's irrational jealousy—based only on the fact that Maggie was attractive and sitting three feet from her husband—reminded Maggie that her own reasons for worrying about Jill had nothing to do with reality.

Just because Jill had a perfect figure and not a line on her face and Laurent had never seen *her* groaning and twisted into ungainly and highly unattractive positions giving birth—*twice*—didn't mean he wanted to jump her.

Well, he's a man, Maggie reasoned, *so he probably would like very much to jump her but he won't.* Suddenly the thought of what Laurent might or might not want to do in the deepest part of his desires made Maggie flush angrily.

You call this a pep talk? She shook herself. *Stop it!*

She felt a vibration and reached into her dress pocket for her cellphone. It was a text message from Danielle with a little video she'd taken of Jemmy and Mila at breakfast. Maggie grinned and played it twice, feeling her mood ratchet up with each hit of the play button.

Remember what's important, she told herself. Helping Laurent process his friend's death—while hopefully discovering who caused it—and being grateful for all that she and Laurent had created together.

Feeling much better and more centered in her thoughts, Maggie hurried up the front steps of the Abbey and into the grand hall, humming and swinging her arms. Sudden pangs of hunger reminded her that she'd never gotten around to eating anything this morning. Wondering if there were any crumbs left from breakfast, she pushed open the door to the dining room to reveal Laurent sitting on the couch by the window.

Jill was beside him, her hand on his shoulder.

Her lips on his.

Susan Kiernan-Lewis

30

As she sat on the edge of the camel back silk divan, Anastasia thought how Roger would have laughed if he knew that the library was her favorite room in the house. No, he wouldn't laugh, she decided.

He wouldn't have believed it.

She stared out of the floor to ceiling windows and watched the rain come down. Always the rain was coming down. Worse here than in London.

A fire was blazing in the hearth of course. Every once in a while a piece of burning wood would snap and explode into a shower of tiny sparks onto the slate apron in front of the fireplace.

Anastasia tapped the ash from the tip of her cigarette into a Ming saucer.

Roger said smoking was low class. *No. Correction.* He said it was *working* class. And the way he'd said it made Anastasia believe he didn't think that was a bad thing. As if to say *what else do the poor buggers have to look forward to?*

Roger.

Anastasia looked around the library. He had loved this room. And little wonder. He designed it himself. Every book was hand picked. Every dish, every candlestick.

She set the faux ashtray on the wide marble coffee table.

She'd expected to feel more relief when the police came this morning for Madeline. Perhaps because as first steps went, now all she could think about was the second step.

Telling the Chief Inspector that she saw Madeline coming out of Roger's room that night—how perfectly Victorian for Anastasia to have insisted on separate bedrooms—had been positively prescient.

But now she needed to turn the same trick again in court. Only this time she wasn't telling a copper with a notepad. She was performing to the gallery. She'd need to properly sell it. But at least her statement had done what it needed to do. It had shone the light on Madeline and away from the grieving widow.

Dear God, how much longer must I pretend?

The eighteenth century ceramic clock on the mantel struck the hour. It was time to dress. The thought of Violet attempting to adorn Anastasia's hair brought a return of the churning in her gut over the missing tiara.

Unbelievable! That that guttersnipe felt she could steal a priceless heirloom from my bedroom—nearly from my very hands as I slept!

The door to the library jerked open—scattering Anastasia's building pique. Nigel strode in.

"There you are!" he said.

He wasn't dressed properly. And he wasn't addressing her properly either. Was that any way to greet his mother? Or to enter a room? Her expression must have shown her displeasure because his own face instantly screwed into a mask of aggression.

"Why did you cancel the hunt?" he bellowed. "Bring it back! Immediately! Why do you have to screw everything up?"

The minute she realized her mouth had fallen open, she shut it with a snap.

"I…I thought you'd be pleased," she said stuttering.

"That's because you know precisely bollocks about me or anything that matters to me," he shouted and then turned and stomped out of the room, slamming the door behind him.

Anastasia sat for a moment, her hands folded in her lap, and then opened the seventeenth century silver candy dish on the coffee table and delicately removed a single cigarette.

Two in one day broke her rule.

She lit the cigarette with a shaking hand. The rain was coming down harder now. She could hear it tapping against the leaded window panes like an insistent army of gremlins wanting to get in.

But she couldn't bring her gaze away from the closed oaken door to the library and the path Nigel had blazed in his exit.

She had thought—she had *hoped*—that with Roger gone, more than a few problems might be solved.

How is Nigel not happier now that his stepfather is out of the picture?

How does that make any sense? she thought sucking the tobacco hard into her lungs.

⁂

Maggie felt the heat creeping up her throat to her cheeks.

"Hey, I wondered where you were," she said, forcing a lightness into her voice she did not feel. Her heart was racing and she could feel a sudden coldness tingle across her skin.

Laurent turned to look at her and as usual, there was nothing to be learned from the expression on his face with the possible exception of pleasure at seeing Maggie.

Jill on the other hand jumped away from Laurent as if she'd been lit on fire.

"Oops!" Jill said with an embarrassed laugh.

Maggie forced herself to walk to them. She held out her phone to Laurent.

"You're going to want to see this," she said, hitting the play button on Danielle's video.

Laurent took her phone and as he watched the short clip a grin spread across his face. Jill wasn't close enough to see the screen but Maggie knew she heard children's laughter—and could see that it was enthralling Laurent.

Maggie glanced at Jill just long enough to send the clearest nonverbal message she could: *Score one for Team Wife and Kids, bitch.*

Maggie took the phone back from Laurent just as Trevor burst into the room.

"The hunt is back on!" he said. "But we have a broken paddock gate. Do you have time to lend a hand?"

Laurent shrugged. "I have nothing but time," he said.

"Great! That means I have some things to do too," Jill said, already on her way out the door.

Maggie stood alone in the empty salon with her phone in her hand.

What had she really seen? Laurent had been turned toward Jill as if they were talking. The image of the kiss came rushing back into Maggie's mind. It made her sick to see how possessively Jill had clutched his shoulder.

Had Jill surprised him? If she had, Laurent certainly hadn't made much of an effort to push her away. And if she hadn't surprised him? If she'd looked into his eyes and telegraphed her intention?

Maggie's ringing phone shook her out of her mounting distress. A photo of her mother appeared on the screen.

Maggie sighed. "Hey, Mom," she said into the phone. "What's up?"

"I'm sorry to bother you in London, darling," Elspeth Newberry said, her voice tight and controlled.

"We're actually in the country," Maggie said, spotting a flash of movement through the window and turning in time to see Laurent walking alongside Trevor in the direction of the barn.

"I'm just at my wits end here," her mother said. "I'm sorry to keep calling you."

"It's okay, Mom. What's Ben doing?"

"It's more what he's *not* doing. He hasn't come out of his bedroom in three days now."

"Is he eating?"

"I put a tray outside his door and he seems to take a little each day."

"Mom, I'm so sorry. I don't know what else to say."

"Even your father is worried now," Maggie's mother said, her voice catching with emotion.

Maggie heard voices out in the hallway and moved toward the sounds.

"Whatever is wrong with Ben is just going to take time," Maggie said as she poked her head out of the salon to see if she could see anyone. "We just need to be patient."

"I hope you're right, dear," Elspeth said tiredly. "I'll let you go now. When will you be back in St-Buvard?"

"We leave here day after tomorrow." No sense in telling her mother about the fox hunt. Although Elspeth had been a wicked hunter jumper in her day, Maggie didn't think even horses could distract her mother from the disaster unfolding at home.

Maggie walked down the hall until she reached the dining room. Inside she saw an orderly line of bag lunches on the dining buffet table. A carefully hand-printed placard next to the bags announced that luncheon, afternoon tea and evening cocktails had all been cancelled for the day.

Maggie imagined the changes in schedules had less reflection on what had happened to poor Madeline and more to do with the fact that Gabrielle was totally overwhelmed in her new duties as manager of the Abbey.

She took a paper bag and filled a teacup from the tea urn and went to find something to read in the library. There was no sign of Jill, Anastasia or Annette.

Where do they all go when they're not getting dressed or posing for Instagrams at cocktail hour? Maggie bit into her sandwich. It was roast beef with sharp English mustard and it was delicious. She debated the idea of running a couple of sandwiches down to the barn where Laurent and Trevor were working but decided against it.

While it was encouraging that Laurent hadn't looked at all guilty when she'd interrupted his little canoodling with Jill this morning, his innocent affect didn't exactly erase the scenario that Maggie had walked in on. She knew that as soon as she talked to him it would all make sense.

Wouldn't it?

How could a kiss on the mouth by a woman not your wife —a woman who you used to kiss on the mouth and do a whole lot more to—make sense? *And maybe it made sense to a French person because we all know how loose they are when it comes to who they should or should not kiss...but a normal person?*

An *American* person?

Deciding she wasn't hungry after all, Maggie wrapped up what was left of her sandwich and returned to the dining room.

Of all days for them not to be serving alcohol, she thought as she left the bag on the dining room table and went upstairs to see if she could reproduce the up-do that Violet had created yesterday. Something told her Violet was going to be way too busy tonight to dress her for dinner.

How long does it take to fix the stupid paddock gate? Maggie stepped into her bedroom and began pulling off her clothes. First thing she'd do before anything else was take a long hot bubble bath.

As she grabbed a thick bath towel, she stepped to the window to look down onto the front lawn of the Abbey when she realized with a start that Laurent must have come back to the room today already.

The laptop that Maggie had placed on the windowsill had been moved to the bed.

31

Dinner was agony.

And not just because there were only two people waiting on them—three if you counted Trevor whose fingernails still did not look sufficiently scrubbed.

Or because the beautiful midnight blue silk dress with the dropped waistline and lowered neck that Violet had delivered to Maggie's door was at least one size too small for her.

But mainly because Laurent had not yet returned. Maggie had waited as long as she could before boredom won out and she'd dressed and come down to dinner. As she sat down at the gigantic dining table with only Anastasia, Will and Annette she began to wonder if Laurent would even show up tonight.

It didn't help that Jill wasn't there either.

Why hadn't Trevor asked Will to help? Or even Nigel for that matter? Either of them could probably be counted on to hold a hammer. But she knew why. It was the way it always was with Laurent. He looked capable—not just because he was tall—but also because of his manner which was always confident and self assured. Whenever there was a job to do, especially one that mattered—even people who didn't know him turned to him first.

"So I understand the hunt is back on," Maggie said to Anastasia.

"Thank God," Annette said. "I was going to have to go out and do a little protest of my own!"

Maggie saw the smile from Will when Annette spoke and she was glad to see that whatever tension there had been between them seemed to have eased since their conversation in the pergola. They were both much more relaxed with Maggie, too.

Annette spoke to Maggie.

"It's true Roger didn't ride," she said, "but he loved the hunt and even Anastasia can't deny that."

Anastasia shrugged. "I readily admit it."

"Why, I wonder?" Maggie asked.

"I think it was because he saw it as an example of a kinder, more civilized time in England," Will said. Maggie was surprised to hear Will speak. It was the most he'd said at the dinner so far.

"Exactly," Annette said. "He used to say it embodied the whole idea of country living and the concept of being truly English." She looked at Anastasia. "He would have been appalled to think it had been cancelled."

"Well, now it hasn't been," Anastasia said tersely.

Annette turned to Maggie. "The time has been pushed back to the afternoon. The morning weather is supposed to be bloody anyway. Are you sure you won't ride?"

Even with visions of riding on sodden, slippery leaves with a herd of excitable horses, Maggie's pulse began to race at the thought of it. But it wouldn't be right. They weren't here on vacation.

"I'm sure," she said.

Where was Laurent?

The thought hadn't fully formed in Maggie's head before she turned to see Laurent walk through the door. His hair was still wet from the shower and his white tie was untied. He looked like he'd just rolled out of bed—but a very posh, extremely elegant bed. He shot her an apologetic look and went to hand Anastasia a small envelope before taking his seat at the table by Maggie.

He smelled of lemons and shampoo and Maggie felt her heart beat faster at his proximity.

But they still had a few things to sort out.

"Well, it appears we won't be blessed with Miss Bentley's presence," Anastasia said, tossing down the note card she'd pulled out of the envelope. She looked at Trevor standing at attention behind Will and Annette.

"Harris," she said to him. "Tell Cook send a tray up to Miss Bentley's room."

Trevor hesitated and looked around the room in confusion. "Cook…?"

"Mrs. LeDuc," Anastasia ground out between her teeth.

"Oh! Yes, Milady," he said with a grin as if he was ready to share a personal joke.

Anastasia clearly wasn't having any of it.

"*Before* our soup gets cold," she said testily.

Maggie saw a flush of annoyance cross Trevor's features. He made a jerky bow in Anastasia's direction and left the room.

"How did you get the note from Jill?" she asked Laurent in a low voice.

Laurent poured wine into his glass.

"She stopped me as I was coming downstairs," he said.

"Outside our room? Because her room is nowhere near ours."

Laurent narrowed his eyes as he regarded Maggie but he didn't answer her.

The door opened to the dining room and Gabrielle stepped in, whispered a few urgent instructions to Violet, who then left the room at a run. Gabrielle approached the buffet table and picked up one of the larger serving dishes. She went to Laurent first.

Maggie couldn't believe that this woman had begun her day by flinging crockery at Maggie's head and was now calmly serving consommé into everyone's soup bowls.

"I know this day has been difficult for all of us," Anastasia said and then stopped as Nigel came into the room and ambled over to his chair next to her before slumping into it.

"As I was saying," she said, raising her voice. "I want to thank Mr. Dernier for pitching in and helping with the repairs needed in the paddock. We are short staffed at the moment, to be sure, but that must not affect standards."

Maggie ate her soup and used every ounce of self-control she had in order to behave as normally as possible.

He knows I saw Jill kiss him! He knows and yet he has done nothing to ease my mind or explain what happened! On the contrary, he has deliberately avoided me.

That's just cowardly! There's no other word for it. He's behaved badly and he's doing everything he can to avoid the inevitable consequences of his actions.

Maggie dropped a spoonful of soup onto the white damask tablecloth. She knew she was getting herself worked up and she made another concentrated effort to calm down.

"The soup is not good, Madame?" Gabrielle asked from across the table where she was serving Annette.

"It's great," Maggie said, her cheeks burning. "I've just had enough."

More than enough. Up to here with enough!

"I have some interesting news pursuant to our unfortunate spectacle on the lawn this morning with our former manger, Mrs. Mears," Anastasia said.

Everyone turned to look at Anastasia.

"I received a phone call from a clerk at the law office of the attorney representing Mrs. Mears and it seems..." Anastasia paused dramatically and lifted her wine glass to prolong the moment. "...That in order to help with her legal expenses she has asked about the possibility of my buying her share of the Abbey."

"So you would control the Abbey outright," Annette said, frowning, as if trying to put it all together.

"Well, I control it outright *now*," Anastasia said with a smile, "but you're right, this is a little different."

"How?" Annette asked. "How is it different?"

"Well, for one thing, once the Abbey belongs entirely to me, I can dispense with the board."

Will shook his head. "You need the board of directors if you're to make intelligent business decisions about the running of the Abbey."

"That's exactly it, William," Anastasia said. "I don't intend to run the Abbey as a business."

"I don't understand," Annette said.

"I do," Nigel said, looking at his mother with what looked like growing surprise and respect. "She intends to turn it back into a private residence."

Maggie didn't think she was the only one waiting for the other shoe to drop or for the laughter to well up. When it didn't happen, Will snorted and tossed down his napkin.

"That's idiotic."

"Why do you say that?" Anastasia asked as if genuinely curious.

"You can't afford it."

"My solicitors think otherwise."

"They're only telling you what you're paying to hear," Will said, biting off every word.

"Will, darling..." Annette said in a quiet voice in an attempt to calm him.

"Do you hear what she's saying?" he said to Annette and then to the rest of the table. "Do you have any idea how much it would cost to run this place as a private residence? With servants, I suppose?"

"Wouldn't be much point without servants," Anastasia said with a smile, clearly enjoying Will's agitation.

"Well, it's bollocks," Will said, reaching for his wine. "But you'll find out soon enough."

"One more thing," Anastasia said. "The board and I have met to dissolve the Bentley Foundation. It's positively sucking cash at the moment. Without the burden of having to support the Foundation, I should be able to live at the Abbey without renting rooms out to strangers."

"*Dissolve the Foundation*?" Will said, dumbfounded.

"That's right. My forensic accountants will be in your offices after the weekend to sort everything out. On behalf of the board I have the authority to thank you, Will, for all your hard work."

Anastasia's gaze drilled coldly into Will's eyes, the smile gone from her face.

Maggie saw Will noticeably whiten but it was Annette who spoke.

"You're firing Will?" she blurted out. "Is that what you're saying? Because you know Roger didn't leave us anything."

Anastasia turned to look at Gabrielle and snapped her fingers. The French woman brought the silver serving dish and held it while Anastasia looked it over and then finally waved her away.

"Did you expect him to?" Anastasia asked Annette, her smile never reaching her eyes.

Annette burst into tears and fled the room.

Maggie couldn't help but feel a visceral reaction to Anastasia's cold words. What Anastasia was talking about was a scenario that would have taken weeks if not months of strategizing and planning.

And since Roger only died twelve days ago, the inescapably obvious question in Maggie's mind was: *Had Anastasia been planning this all along?*

32

Laurent knew he had his work cut out for him.

It wasn't going to be what she wanted to hear, he knew that. And it was likely—very likely—that waiting for his explanation was no less painful than the eventual unsatisfying reality of it.

That would be up to Maggie. But he wouldn't torture her any longer. She'd waited all afternoon to hear what he had to say. He wouldn't prolong her agony.

He'd been planning to make their excuses immediately after dinner but when Gabrielle brought in the dessert he had two reasons for delaying. The first and the least important was the fact that Gabrielle was French and had gone to a lot of trouble on a very trying day to make this dessert. The least they could do was honor the effort with their praise. And secondly, if he pulled Maggie away before dessert was served she would think it had to do with him not wanting her to eat it because he was worried about her getting fat.

Would she ever know him?

And so he waited. The *Crêpes Suzettes* were worth the wait and he thought he detected a glimmer of pride in Gabrielle from all the exclamations of appreciation around the dining table. But when Anastasia said they would not separate tonight but go straight to the salon for coffee, Laurent stood up and held his hand out to Maggie.

"We will beg your indulgence for tonight," he said in his heavily accented English. If Maggie was in the mood to notice she would detect his accent was a little thicker than usual. In Laurent's large bag of tricks was the knowledge that certain types of English and Americans were willing to forgive all manner of sins when presented with a French accent.

He had reason to know this from the many years of his past.

Never for a moment did he think Maggie would not take his hand. She was angry with him, to be sure. Without a doubt. But she was eager, too. Eager to hear the impossible explanation that would erase the episode from her mind and from the narrative of their existing love story.

Unfortunately, on that point she would be disappointed.

He gave a short bow to Anastasia.

They made it as far as the foot of the staircase. Laurent was surprised Maggie was able to wait that long.

"What the hell was going on with you and Jill?" Maggie said, whirling around to face him. The rustle of her skirt created an absurd but tantalizing sensation against his skin. It was all he could do not to drop his hand to her waist and draw her to him.

"Shall we discuss this in our room?" he said mildly.

"So you can distract me? I don't think so."

"Keep your voice down."

"*That's* why you want to go upstairs," Maggie said, her eyes snapping with fury. "So we don't create a scene."

She'd waited a long time for this, he thought with resignation. She would have her fit no matter what he said.

And she certainly would once she'd heard him out.

The library was across from the staircase. Without warning, he picked her up in his arms and carried her into it, kicking the door behind him. Maggie protested but taken by surprise as she was, her struggles were minimal.

It wasn't much to ask—that he choose the arena for this discussion—but asking always prompted the possibility that a less than satisfying answer might be forthcoming. Laurent didn't like to take the chance of getting a less than satisfying answer.

He put Maggie on her feet and watched as she straightened her dress. It was tight on her and he could see each breath strain the seams of the bodice. Her breasts heaved dangerously near to overflowing from the low cut neckline.

"I did not kiss her," he said.

Maggie was ready for that one.

"But you let yourself be kissed!"

"It is true I did not push her away or stand at arms length from her. I am not afraid of her."

"Maybe you should be! Why did you let her get so close? Were you talking about the old days?"

"I do not welcome her attentions but I will not make a scene with her. I will deal with her." He could feel the anger pulsating in his throat.

"I saw how you were *dealing* with her!"

"I will handle this without instruction from you!"

How is it Maggie could bring this fury out in him so quickly? He had lived through more than one moment where his life literally balanced on the edge of a coin toss—and all without losing his head or raising his voice. How was it that Maggie had the power to bring every emotion he'd ever hidden away out into the bright light of day?

"You say you didn't want it but somehow Jill got a lip lock on you. You're telling me it's because you're too polite to tell her no? Is that your defense?"

Laurent saw her eyes blazing with equal parts hurt and anger. She was right about that. Of course he felt nothing for Jill. But he could see that wasn't the point.

He drew Maggie to the couch and sat her down on his lap. She struggled to be on her feet but he wouldn't have it. It was difficult to be combative when sitting in someone's lap. He had learned this early on in their marriage.

"*Attends, chérie,*" he said, forcing her to look into his eyes. "You are the kindest person I know."

"Thanks a lot," Maggie grumbled. "Because that beats sexy any day," she said.

"*Oui,* it does but fortunately for me I have both. Listen to me, *chérie.* As thoughtful as you are to the lowest workman in our village, I do not understand why you are not sympathetic to Jill. You have everything she wants."

He held Maggie's chin and looked into her eyes. "*Everything.*"

She pressed her mouth in a firm line and said nothing.

"I did not throw her to the floor and denounce her overtures, yes?"

He saw the barest hint of a smile on her mouth.

"Yes," she said. "You did not."

"The kiss was not worth a show of indignation. But I would spare her my pity. Could not my kindest of wives do the same?"

He saw the realization when it hit Maggie. He saw how her view of Jill changed from the Jill who was beautiful and free with the world at her feet to the Jill who had missed the boat—all the boats, every imaginable boat—and morphed into a desperate woman willing to risk rejection and humiliation for a stolen kiss.

"You're still not off the hook," Maggie said. But he felt her relax in his arms.

✳✳✳✳✳

After they'd sufficiently made up in the library—or as sufficiently as they could with no lock on the door—Maggie suggested they take a quick walk out on the lawns before retiring.

While she didn't feel totally at peace after their talk in the library, she was at least mollified. She would have preferred Laurent to have flung Jill across the room.

But she could understand why he hadn't.

In any case it felt good to have Laurent by her side again. In many ways she felt more in sync with him since they'd arrived at the Abbey.

They walked along the main front drive with the sounds of the gravel crunching under their shoes. Laurent draped his tuxedo jacket around her shoulders.

Maggie told him about her phone call from her mother.

"She's so upset, Laurent, but I have no idea what she thinks I can do from this distance."

As she spoke Maggie was haunted by her mother's words: "If it was Jemmy, would you just sit back and be patient?"

Her mother was right about that. *No matter how old they are, they'll always be your babies.*

"You will think of something," Laurent said.

"Really? You think I should try to intervene in some way?"

182

He smiled as they walked, his arm around her. "Perhaps you can help without intervening? Just this once?"

"You are nothing but contradictions tonight."

A noise up ahead near the main entrance made them both stop. Maggie felt Laurent's arm tense around her as if ready to make a move.

"What is it?" she whispered.

A moment later, she saw a group of people in the distance moving in the shadows of the dense forest.

"Are they on Abbey property?" Maggie asked. "Who are they?"

"The hunt *saboteurs*," Laurent said with disgust. "I saw them when I drove to the village."

They turned around and began walking back to the Abbey.

"Annette was telling me tonight at dinner that Roger really loved the hunt," Maggie said.

"So English, yes?"

"In Atlanta when I was growing up, all the horse moms would take their daughters to riding lessons and competitions every weekend. It was a wonderful time and one my mother and I enjoyed together right up to my teen years."

"When boys took over as your hobby?"

Maggie laughed. "Maybe. But those afternoons after school and weekends riding with my mom were some of the happiest moments of my childhood."

"You are asking my permission to allow you to do this with Mila?"

"If you're not comfortable with me taking Mila out riding I won't try to talk you into it. But I'm asking you to think about it."

"It's dangerous even without the *saboteurs*."

"It can be," she admitted.

"Fine. We'll talk of it later," he said.

"Let's hurry back," Maggie said. "Poor Violet is probably waiting to turn down our bed and tuck us in."

"I told her not to come any more," Laurent said. "*C'est ridicule.*"

They stood in front of the massive double front doors of the Abbey and Maggie wrapped her arms around Laurent's waist.

They stood for a moment holding each other. Finally, Laurent lifted her chin and kissed her on the mouth.

"I'm sorry for our misunderstandings," he said, his voice low.

Well, that's one word for it, Maggie thought. But she brushed off her lingering annoyance.

"Me, too," she said as they turned and walked inside, "But I have one final question and then we need never talk about Jill or the kiss ever again."

"*Oui, chérie?*"

"I was just wondering if it had been *me* in the salon with an old boyfriend—"

"I would have killed him."

"Good to know," she said, laughing, and for the second time that evening, he picked her up in his arms. When they reached their bedroom, he entered but stopped short of tossing Maggie onto the bed. Instead he turned away and placed her on her feet by the window.

"Laurent, what is it?"

"It is nothing, *chérie*. Wait here a moment."

But she pushed past him to see what had stopped him.

There on the bed was the bloodied carcass of a mangled badger.

33

Jill lifted the silver domed lid off the *coq au vin* that Violet had carried to her bedroom a few hours earlier. Jill had eaten every morsel and washed it down with a lovely half bottle of Gigondas.

She was sitting on the bed with a cashmere throw around her shoulders. A massive canopy over the bed made her feel like she was one of the sultan's favored wives—or at least a typical pampered American teen. The image made her smile for a moment before the sadness of what she was doing came back to her, cascading over her like a relentless tide.

She pulled her laptop onto her knees and started it up. It had been a long day and she welcomed an evening without performance or guile or the effort of wearing any of her disguises. She looked at her computer screen and went to her browser history.

She scanned the list of website visits in the last three weeks. Ouch. Very damning indeed. No, this would definitely not help if push came to shove. She carefully deleted the sites visited in her laptop history and then turned to her emails—both sent and in the trash—and deleted those as well.

That should do it. If worse comes to worse and somebody does come looking for evidence that I was involved, there'll be no trace now.

Of course, if there was someone who knew about her crime personally, someone like, say, Laurent Dernier, that would be a different matter.

But Laurent would protect her. Jill knew he would. He might not care for her romantically—and it was painful to admit that—

but Jill knew his affection for Roger would force him to protect her.

It wasn't a rose covered cottage with a picket fence, but a rock-solid alibi was better than nothing.

She picked up her cellphone and began scrolling through her browsing history.

Can't be too careful these days, she thought as she began deleting each web address. *No matter who you think has your back.*

※※※※※※※※※

The night had taken only a minor hit.

Laurent disposed of the badger and stripped the bed while Maggie examined every square inch of the room to see if there was anything else tampered with. Finally, they wedged a chair up against the doorknob to bar any further entrance at least while they were inside.

Maggie didn't think it was necessary to mention that she'd noticed someone had been in the room because now they *knew* someone had been in the room. The dead badger was pretty much Exhibit A for that.

They slept wrapped in each other's arms until morning which broke raw and wet. The rain was coming down in grey sheets outside their bedroom window.

"Where did you put it?" Maggie asked looking around the room.

"Never mind, *chérie*," he murmured from the bed, his eyes still closed.

"I say we don't mention this to anyone," she said.

He pried one eye open to regard her.

"That way," Maggie said, getting out of bed and going to the window, "we can watch everybody to see who is watching *us* for a reaction."

Laurent snorted.

"Who do you think did it?" she asked, coming back to bed. "Practically everyone but Trevor has a reason to be upstairs and I just learned yesterday that Trevor has a reason too."

"What is Trevor's reason?" Laurent asked.

"He's having it on with Anastasia."

Now both of Laurent's eyes were open. "*Vraiment?*"

"I saw them yesterday. It looked like they'd just come out of one of the bedrooms."

"Pretty bold," Laurent said skeptically.

"Well, you can hardly expect Anastasia to be boffing him in the barn. She can't even bear to walk from the house to the limo let alone some place with horse poop piled in every corner."

Laurent didn't answer and Maggie knew he was thinking of Roger. Not two weeks cold in his grave and the one woman Roger had finally chosen to marry was carrying on with the stable boy. And probably had been for months.

"What are your plans today?" Maggie asked.

Laurent ran a hand through his hair.

"I will go to Oxford to see Madeline."

"You think they'll let you see her?"

He shrugged. "Probably not. But she will be told that someone came."

She'll be told that someone cares.

Maggie slipped back to bed and wrapped her arms around Laurent.

"I'm sorry this all sucks so bad," she said.

"We could leave today," he said.

"Before the hunt?"

"Is that so important? What more is there for us here but these people who knew but did not love Roger?"

Maggie knew this was torture for Laurent but she also knew there would be no relief from his doubts and his guilt back in St-Buvard. If they didn't sort it out here, they would just need to wrestle it out back home only then it would be with the children watching.

"Look, Laurent, we know Madeline didn't kill Roger," Maggie said. "I think the Chief Inspector is playing games to unnerve the real killer. I'd bet anything they have no hard evidence against Madeline. She's just an ex-girlfriend with a grudge."

"If not Madeline," Laurent said with a frown, "then who?"

"I don't know. *Yet.* But I do know just one more day here might help me figure it out."

He shook his head. "Let the police handle it."

"I'm astounded at your confidence in the police, Laurent. Especially since we both know they've probably arrested the wrong person."

"You said you believe they would let Madeline go."

"I said I *think* they'll let her go—but only if they like someone better. All I want to do is speed up the process."

"*Non.* I do not want you to be involved."

"Too late. This is personal for me."

Laurent groaned and put a hand on Maggie's shoulder.

"*Chérie*, Roger knew you were fond of him in your way. I promise you he did."

"Maybe. I hope so. And that matters a lot but what matters more is that I find the person who killed him. Because Roger was…he was family."

Laurent leaned over and kissed Maggie.

Her phone rang and she saw that it was Danielle.

"Hey, Danielle," she said. "Everything okay?"

"Mommy! Mommy!" a little voice chirped out. "When you are coming home?"

Both Laurent and Maggie laughed and put their heads together to say good morning to their son and hear about the day he had planned with his *Pépère* and *Mémère*.

After their conversation with the children, Laurent went to take his shower and as Maggie was putting her long hair into a single braid she heard Laurent's phone get a text. She glanced at it where it lay on the bed and saw it was regarding an email notification from the Arles post office. She scrolled down Laurent's email list and saw that he'd gotten a notice from them almost two months ago. Laurent was expert in just about every area there was to excel in—from cooking to winemaking, fatherhood and being a loving husband—but even he admitted he was disinterested in technology. Half the time he left his phone at home and it was not unusual for his emails to stack up unanswered indefinitely.

Maggie saw that the latest email notification from the post office notified Laurent that he had received a package and was encouraged to come and pick it up as soon as possible.

Using her own phone, Maggie called Danielle to ask her to have Jean-Luc pick up the package in Arles if it was still there.

"Yes, of course," Danielle said. "He will do it today."

Maggie detected the strain in Danielle's voice.

"What?" Maggie said. "What's happened?"

"It is Madame Roche again," Danielle said. "She is claiming she caught you with her husband. And he is confirming it."

Crap. This was bad. Maggie glanced in the direction of the bathroom and the sound of Laurent's shower. If Laurent heard about this there would definitely be murder in St-Buvard only there would be no question about who the murderer was.

"Please try not to worry about it, Danielle," Maggie said. "We'll be home in two days and I promise I'll sort it all out then."

"I cannot imagine how."

After Laurent left to see Madeline, Maggie dressed in slacks and a sweater and went downstairs to breakfast.

Only Will and Nigel were at the table eating. Gabrielle and Violet stood with erect backs on either side of the door like they were ready to jump and wipe up a spill or dab an errant drop of tea on the damask tablecloth. Violet's face was impassive although her eyes looked like she'd been crying. Maggie wondered if Anastasia had gotten in an early morning bullying session with her.

Gabrielle, on the other hand, was watching Maggie. Maggie thought she detected a flicker of a smirk.

Will was concentrating on his fried eggs and tomatoes and Nigel was studying his cellphone and letting his plate grow cold. If it was either of those two who left the stinking carcass of a woodland creature on her pillow, they'd clearly forgotten they'd done it.

"Sleep well, gentlemen?" Maggie asked.

Nigel ignored her but Will looked up. "Well, enough," he muttered.

"Where's Annette? Still in bed?"

"Hardly," Will said. "On hunt day? She's at the barn giving French kisses to her horse."

Maggie had never met a husband who didn't feel at least a little ignored by his horse-loving wife. It looked like poor Will was no exception.

Maggie put scrambled eggs and toast on a Worcester china plate and looked at Gabrielle who was still watching her with amusement in her eyes.

If I had to guess, I'd say you were looking to see if your late night present had any effect on me.

"Everything looks so scrummy," Maggie said with an exaggerated smile. "I don't know what to eat first."

The smirk was promptly replaced by a disappointed scowl and Maggie congratulated herself that she'd found the culprit.

But now what?

Now that she knew *who*, the big question was *why*?

※ ※ ※ ※ ※ ※

After breakfast, Maggie went outside to see what was going on at the barn. She imagined the barn would be a maelstrom of activity what with the hunt happening last minute. She had to admit that a very big part of her wanted to ride in the hunt but she would use the time to explore the Abbey without worry of running into anyone.

That whole no lock on the door thing might come in very handy, she thought as she made her way to the stables. On the other hand, the actual hunt wouldn't likely get too many people out of the way. Only Jill and Annette were riding in it. The rest of the field would ride to the Abbey right after lunch, collect anyone who wanted to join them, and go on from there.

Hearing running footsteps behind her, she saw Violet burst out of the Abbey. The little maid looked red in the face and as usual on the brink of tears. With Madeline gone, Maggie hoped Violet was finding some support from Gabrielle although the French cook didn't look much like the nurturing type.

Violet slowed when she saw Maggie. Her eyes darted from Maggie to the barn.

She's afraid of the horses, Maggie thought.

"Hey, Violet," Maggie said. "Heading to the barn?"

"Mrs. Bentley gave me a terrible bollocking," Violet said, her voice trembling, "because Trev isn't in his butler's uniform. And she's picked it out special for him."

Maggie filed away the fact that Violet referred to Trevor as "Trev." They were clearly better friends that she'd thought.

"Want me to tell him?" Maggie asked. "I'm going there."

"Oh, Missus, would you?" Violet said, already turning around to go back to the Abbey. "Tell him Mrs. Bentley is gobsmacked something awful."

"Will do," Maggie said as she hurried to the barn. She would have expected to see several horse trailers parked out front of the stables but there was only the one belonging to Annette.

She peeked in the back and saw the trailer was empty so either Annette's horse was in the barn or in the adjoining paddock which Maggie could see already held Diva and the horse that Jill had ridden two days before. A moment later she caught a glimpse of Annette in the paddock leading her horse to the water trough.

Maggie hurried across the stone courtyard, mindful of the piles of horse manure scattered all around.

Trevor must be run off his feet. He doesn't even have time to clean up the droppings. Maggie saw a wheelbarrow parked against the stable wall with a large manure shovel in it. The wagon was only half full.

The stable door was open and although the rain had stopped, the sky was gray and overcast, allowing very little light into the barn interior.

Two people were silhouetted inside, their heads close together in conference.

Coming closer, Maggie saw it was Trevor and Jill.

"Mrs. Bentley wants you in the house, Trevor," Maggie said.

Trevor jumped away from Jill. He wiped his hands on his jeans and without a word walked past Maggie and toward the Abbey.

Jill turned to face Maggie. She was wearing jeans and rubber riding boots. Her hair was tied back in one long, low ponytail giving the effect of a much younger woman.

But Jill's eyes were hard. Off to the side, one of her dogs—the mastiff—lay chewing on a piece of leather. The other dog was a bigger, Rottweiler mix. As Maggie came into the barn, he stood with hackles raised and a growl thick and threatening in his throat.

"Well, well," Jill said. "Change your mind about riding in the hunt?"

Maggie couldn't see a currycomb or a hoof pick—or any good reason for Jill to be in the barn except for possibly collaborating with Trevor.

She had a bad feeling in the pit of her stomach about what she had just seen.

"No," Maggie said, looking down the long aisle of facing stalls. "Mind telling your dog to stand down?"

The Rottweiler advanced. His growls grew louder.

"I thought you liked dogs," Jill said. "Demon is just a big puppy at heart."

Unmindful of the dirty floor or her slacks, Maggie lowered to one knee to be eye level with Demon. Instantly, he stopped growling. He wasn't in tail-wagging posture yet, but Maggie knew he wasn't far off from it.

"My, my," Jill said. "Truly a dog whisperer. Laurent must be so proud."

Maggie held out her hand and Demon sniffed it. And then wagged his tail.

"They *will* attack, you know," Jill said. "It's only because they know you intend me no harm that they're not ripping you to pieces."

Maggie glanced over at the mastiff Maximus chewing on his leather, his tail thumping happily on the ground in greeting.

"Sure, Jill," Maggie said, standing up, "if you say so. What are you doing in here?"

"Just checking on a few things to make sure everything comes off as it should."

Maggie didn't like the sound of that.

"You know, Maggie," Jill said, "Roger knew you didn't like him."

Maggie felt the insult like a punch to the stomach. She knew she must have flinched because Jill smiled.

"In fact," Jill said, "I can remember more than one or two times when I had a pint with him where he was literally tearful about the fact that Laurent's wife hated him."

"You're lying." Maggie knew Roger well enough to know—first, he wouldn't be tearful about anything and, secondly, even if he did feel that way about Maggie—he'd never have shared it with another living soul.

"Roger loved your husband as a brother," Jill said.

"I know."

"And he always thought Laurent and I would get together."

Maggie wasn't sure how to respond to that so she said nothing.

"A part of me feels like I'm honoring his memory," Jill said, "by taking Laurent from you."

Maggie couldn't help laughing. She marveled at how differently she would have reacted to this threat just eight hours ago.

Yes, Jill was trim and sexy and didn't have the weight of the world or two people under the age of five on her shoulders. But in the end it didn't matter. Maggie knew she couldn't take Laurent from her.

Her confidence must have shown on her face. But her derision faded as she saw Jill's hand curl around the pitchfork that had been propped unseen on the wall.

Susan Kiernan-Lewis

34

Forget Oxford. The traffic between the Abbey and the nearest village was wall to wall and motionless.

In the two hours that Laurent had been sitting in it, he'd not even made it as far as the M-4.

Was all this mess really because of the hunt?

The traffic comprised mostly sightseers and there was a good bit to see along the way including a crowd of pedestrians carrying placards with grisly photos of mangled fox kittens, and headlines like *Don't kill our babies!* and *Down with the Abbey Hunt!*

He hadn't been aware that the hunt was named after the Abbey. It was likely not the official name, but the Abbey was well-known enough as a luxury resort that most people probably used the name for convenience because of the Abbey's proximity

He vaguely remembered Roger talking about foxhunting once. Laurent remembered actually teasing him about the fact that Roger supported it so wholeheartedly and yet had only been on a horse twice in his life.

But then that was Roger. A series of contradictions and surprises. Laurent had never met anyone like him. All calm and reserve on the surface with the burst of humor and wit that took you by surprise.

When was it that Roger had begun trying to build this life as a country squire? When was it he'd decided to try to make amends to the people in his life he thought he'd hurt?

Madeline…Gabrielle…Trevor…even Jill.

Had Laurent seen it? Had he seen it in the last couple of years and recognized it for what it was? An attempt to have Laurent's life? Because that's what it was, wasn't it?

Laurent's cellphone rang and he saw a photo of Jean-Luc on the screen and grinned. Danielle must be forcing the old fellow to modernize. If you'd told Laurent five years ago that he'd be getting a phone call on his mobile from Jean-Luc, he would have laughed. What next? Text messages?

"Hello, Jean-Luc," Laurent said into the phone as he edged slowly forward toward the Abbey, careful not to clip any pedestrians as they dodged in and out of traffic. There were many people on horseback too.

"Hello, *mon vieux*," Jean-Luc said. "Danielle talked with Maggie this morning about a package to be picked up at the post office. Do you know about this?"

Laurent frowned. "It sounds familiar," he lied.

"I have picked it up as instructed. It has been waiting in Arles for two months. It looks important. Shall I open it?"

"Yes, of course," Laurent said. A big-bottomed woman wearing tight jodhpurs and riding a bicycle hit the front fender of Laurent's car and turned to glare at him over her shoulder. While Jean-Luc was ripping the package open, Danielle came on the line.

"Hello, Laurent," she said. "Is Maggie there?"

"No, Danielle, I am stuck in traffic. All is well with the little ones?"

"Yes, of course."

"And Madame Roche?"

Danielle sucked in a hard breath. "Oh, Laurent! I am so glad that Maggie has shared that with you. I am so worried. I do not know how we will fix this!"

It was very possible that Maggie had not *shared* the problem to the extent Danielle thought she had.

"There is something new?" he asked warily.

Danielle hesitated as if Laurent's response had just revealed how little he knew of the situation.

"Just more rumors," she said airily. "Nothing for you to worry about, Laurent."

That meant Danielle was afraid Laurent would come back to St-Buvard and kill someone. They must be very bad rumors.

"Oh! Here is Jean-Luc with the contents of your package. *Au revoir*, Laurent!"

Fifteen minutes later, Laurent was still no closer to the Abbey. His mind was swirling with everything he had learned from his conversations with both Jean-Luc and Danielle. It was all he could do not to abandon the rental car and jog the rest of the way to the Abbey.

He called Maggie instead. She picked up the phone. She sounded breathless.

"Hello? Laurent?" she answered.

"What is it?" he said. "What is the matter?"

"Nothing." But her voice was tight as if attempting to appear nonchalant. "Just having a little talk with Jill in the barn. Look. I'm taking her picture to send you."

Laurent heard the hiss "*Bitch!*"

"Oh, never mind," Maggie said. "She left. I guess she didn't want her picture taken so now it's just me. Did you get a chance to see Madeline?"

"*Non*. But I spoke with the assistant to her attorney. And Danielle called."

"Danielle called *you*?"

"*Non*, I was speaking to Jean-Luc and she picked up."

"To say what?"

"The situation with Madame Roche is getting worse."

"I'm sure Danielle is exaggerating," Maggie said. "Why is it taking you so long to get back to the Abbey?"

"There is terrible traffic. The protestors from the hunt."

"The saboteurs?"

"Not just them. It looks like half the students from Oxford are out against it."

"At breakfast this morning, I got the feeling Will wouldn't mind joining them."

"But his wife rides in the hunt."

"I think he's jealous of the time it takes from him."

"*Vraiment?*"

"It's pretty common. All my friends back in Atlanta who ride say their husbands hate the time the horses take from them."

"And yet you think this might be a good hobby for you?"

Maggie realized he'd made a good point. Anything that drove a wedge between a husband and wife was not something to pursue.

"Is her lawyer any good?" she asked, changing the subject.

"I only talked to his assistant but he sounds competent. He said Madeline told the police she thought Trevor killed Roger."

"Trevor?" An image of Trevor and Anastasia flashed into Maggie's head. Did Madeline know the two of them were carrying on?

"Are you aware of the reason Roger brought Trevor to the Abbey?" Laurent asked.

"Jill told me it was to help out an old pal."

"*Oui.* And because Trevor is Roger's son."

35

Anastasia pushed the tray of cold eggs and kippers away from her on the bed. Her stomach lurched and she ran to the bathroom to vomit up one piece of unbuttered toast and two sips of black tea, no milk.

Can this be possible? she thought as she collapsed a few minutes later in the antique Louis XV French chair by the window. *All my plans? All my careful plans?*

Her hand was trembling as she snatched up her cellphone from the nearby dressing table. By God, she wasn't going to be the only one inconvenienced by this disaster!

When he picked up, she didn't even allow him to say hello.

"It's confirmed," she said. "No, don't speak. Just listen. If word of this gets out and there's even a hint...even a whisper that it might not be Roger's...I'm not the only one who'll suffer the consequences. Do you understand me? Your fingerprints are all over this and I'll see to it that it ends up a life sentence for you. Do you hear me?"

Because she'd told him not to speak, only silence greeted her. She felt the fury well up inside her.

My God, how could I have done this with such a complete berk?

She flung the phone across the room and watched it shatter the Chinese porcelain jar on her bedside table.

Knowing how much the thing cost—nearly twenty thousand pounds—made her feel, perversely, at least a little better.

After Maggie hung up with Laurent her mind was whirling

Trevor was Roger's son? Did Trevor know? How must Madeline have processed *that*? Roger made her abort *their* child and twenty years later when their child would've been about the same age—he made her hire his illegitimate son?

This is looking worse and worse for Madeline. Maybe the police didn't arrest the wrong person after all.

As Maggie left the barn, she saw Jill had only gone as far as the outer courtyard where she would have no trouble hearing every word of Maggie's phone conversation.

Jill approached with her arms crossed. Her dogs were close at her heels.

"*Pax*, Maggie. Sorry about all that in the barn. I hope you didn't misunderstand me with the pitchfork. It just occurred to me how that must have looked to you."

"You mean because your dogs weren't interested in attacking me so you thought you might have a go at Plan B?"

"That's what I was afraid you'd think. But I'm not like that at all. I don't consider you any sort of threat to me whatsoever."

Protesteth too much, much?

"Glad to hear it," Maggie said.

The two began to walk back toward the Abbey.

"Listen, petal," Jill said, "I couldn't help but hear that Laurent told you about Trevor's paternity."

Maggie wanted to say *Couldn't you?* but she was too interested to hear what Jill had to say about the whole affair.

"So you knew about it?"

"Everyone knows."

"Does *Trevor* know?"

"Of course."

"And he's cool with shoveling horse crap when his father was a multi-millionaire?"

"I guess when you put it that way it does look rather bad for poor Trevor but in Roger's defense, while it's true he never formally acknowledged Trevor, he did pay full child support to Trevor's adoptive parents."

"I'm trying to imagine what Roger could have been thinking," Maggie said, shaking her head. "Why did he bring

Trevor to the Abbey? For what possible purpose? Did he want a relationship with him?"

"Hardly. Trevor needed a job," Jill said, shrugging. "I think it was that simple."

"In my experience so is the reason most people commit murder."

"I'm not sure the police even know about Roger and Trevor."

Well, they do now, Maggie thought. *Madeline made sure of that.*

"Besides, I know for a fact that Trevor was grateful beyond words to Roger for all his support," Jill said.

"Most people in Trevor's position would be resentful," Maggie said, "not grateful. And resentment is a *motive*. Add that to the fact that Trevor had opportunity and that he was strong enough to stuff Roger's body down a laundry chute...and, well, it doesn't look too good for Trevor."

"If you're using strength as any kind of criteria for Roger's murder," Jill said, "let me help you narrow the field." She stopped walking and put a hand on Maggie's arm. "When was the last time you saw Roger?" she asked.

"What does that have to do with anything?" Maggie asked.

"Well, if you'd seen him recently you'd know that anybody —even Violet—could have shoved him down that laundry chute," Jill said.

Susan Kiernan-Lewis

36

After Jill delivered her bombshell, she returned to the barn to lock the dogs in their kennel before going up to dress for the hunt.

Maggie stared at her retreating back, stunned at Jill's news about Roger.

It just made everything worse of course. Roger was sick. *Terminal*, if Jill could be believed. Maggie felt a thickness in her throat at the thought of him.

She looked down the long drive that led from the Abbey.

Did Laurent know Roger was sick?

It might not be the sort of thing Roger would share with Laurent.

If Roger really was dying that meant that unless it was a crime of passion whoever killed him needed him dead sooner rather than later.

That could be anyone, Maggie thought with frustration.

Anastasia was the only one to benefit from Roger's will. And she was sleeping around on him. Did those two things go together?

Nigel also benefited from Roger's will—through his mother. Perhaps he needed the money sooner than he was willing to wait?

And what about Will? Didn't Laurent say Roger was about to lower the boom on Will and his shady dealings with the business? That might make someone take action rather than wait for fate to take its natural course.

And Gabrielle? Not much sweet revenge to be had watching your tormentor die of an illness you had nothing to do with.

Maybe Gabrielle thought she was going to be cheated out of the pleasure?

There were simply too many unanswered questions.

Inside the Abbey was quiet. As Maggie entered the great foyer, she couldn't help but wonder how it must have been all those centuries past. The entranceway was so massive. Even as a posh resort, no one had made an effort to bring warmth to its décor.

Maggie went to look in the dining room but it was empty, the table set for its usual thirty. She could see the silver place settings gleaming from where she stood in the doorway.

After her last experience visiting the downstairs kitchen she decided not to check there to see where everyone had disappeared. Besides, it was unlikely anyone other than Gabrielle or Violet would be there.

Maggie went upstairs to her bedroom. At first glance it didn't look like anyone had been in there since she'd left an hour earlier. She checked the bed for more dead animals and as she passed the window she saw Trevor hurrying from the house back to the barn.

So Trevor was Roger's son. And he was screwing Roger's wife.

It wouldn't take long for the police to draw a straight line between those two facts and come up with something damning.

Could Trevor have killed Roger? He had motive, opportunity and means. In the few conversations Maggie had had with Trevor, she'd gotten precisely nothing as far as his personality went.

Maggie sat in front of her dressing table and pulled her hair out of its braid and brushed it before carefully rebraiding and wrapping it into a tight coil around her head.

What had Roger's thoughts been these last months? Maggie wondered. He'd called Laurent only two weeks ago to see if Laurent was up for a visit.

Was it to say goodbye?

Maggie fought through another spasm of guilt at the memory of how she'd initially shunned that request.

Would she ever come to terms with how she'd treated Roger? Would finding the person who killed him help?

Yes. It would help. It would help her live with herself and it would help ease Laurent's pain.

She couldn't do anything about the past but by God she could do this.

Had Roger done something in the last few weeks to change his affairs? Could *that* have triggered his killer? Anastasia said the will was read yesterday and she got everything.

What if there was another will? A more recent one? Maggie tapped her fingers on the dressing table as she mulled over the possibility. Was that the real reason Roger was coming to see Laurent?

Her thoughts were interrupted by the sound of raised voices.

One of them was Laurent's.

Maggie jumped up and jerked open the bedroom door to see Gabrielle standing in the entrance foyer confronting Laurent.

"Why should I believe you?" she screamed in French. "Why should I believe anything you say?"

Laurent had his hands up in a clear pantomime of trying to appease or calm the woman. Gabrielle looked up and spotted

Maggie watching them, then turned and fled down the hallway toward the downstairs kitchen.

✻ᕁ ✻ᕁ ✻ᕁ ✻ᕁ ✻ᕁ ✻ᕁ

Laurent saw the reason Gabrielle had bolted when he looked up and saw Maggie standing in the upstairs hallway peering over the banister. He felt weary. Moving up the stairs towards her, he could see she had questions—and something to tell him.

She followed him into the bedroom. "What was all that downstairs with Gabrielle?" she asked.

Laurent came to the dresser and tossed down his car keys.

"She thinks I know something."

"About Roger's murder?" Maggie sat down opposite him in the chair by the window. She had her hair up and off her neck. He preferred it down but had to admit she looked younger, more vulnerable with it up.

"*Non.* Something else."

"When were you going to tell me that you knew her?"

He sighed and ran a hand over his face. Between the long frustrating drive, his conversation with Danielle and Jean-Luc and then being intercepted by Gabrielle, this mini-interrogation was the last thing he was in the mood for.

"I didn't think it was important."

"You know what I'm trying to do, right, Laurent?" Maggie said as she threw her hands up in frustration. "Every person in this place could have killed Roger, including Gabrielle. Jill told me Roger cheated Gabrielle's father out of a fortune. Left him penniless. She has a serious motive for wanting Roger dead."

He could see she wanted to ask. He was relieved that she didn't.

At least for now.

"Roger thought he was helping by hiring her," Laurent said. But even as he said the words he felt his fury building.

This was just another example of how Roger tried to move people's lives around his game board as it suited him without regard for who they really were or what they needed.

"When he heard she had developed a problem with drugs, he brought her to the country," he said.

"And that was really nice of Roger," Maggie said. "But naturally she might never have *needed* his help to begin with if he hadn't impoverished her father."

"That is true."

"So she hated him."

Why doesn't she just ask me? Does she think I am like Roger?

Wasn't I?

"Why was she yelling at you just now?"

"What do you want to ask me, Maggie? If I was involved in the con?"

Her eyes widened and in his mind that's exactly what she was asking—after everything they'd done together and been together. And while he had not worked the con with Roger that destroyed Gabrielle's family, there were plenty of people in the world where he couldn't claim that innocence.

Maggie went to him and put her hands on his arms to make him face her.

"Listen to me, Laurent," she said. "If you were involved or you weren't, it's in the past. I honestly don't care."

Laurent knew he didn't deserve Maggie's love and acceptance. Not when he'd played Roger's same game for so many years and then escaped to enjoy the pleasures of a loving family and a prosperous vineyard. As if that other life had never happened.

And Roger had died brutally at the hands of someone he'd cared for.

"Laurent," Maggie said gently.

"I'm fine, *chèrie*," he said as he walked to the door. "I just need some air."

"Laurent...?"

He turned impatiently toward her. The urge to be alone was nearly overwhelming.

"Did you know Roger was sick?"

✻✻✻✻✻✻

Nigel walked to the far corner of his bedroom. He'd learned months ago the trick to getting privacy was being just far enough from the hallway where no one could overhear him—but close enough to the outdoors to get enough bars on his cellphone not to drop a call.

He glanced at the phone screen and saw the *Missed Call* icon. Just looking at it made a patina of sweat break out on his brow. He pushed the *Call Back* button and took in a long breath.

"I wondered when you'd get around to calling back," Bob snarled into the phone.

Nigel knew it had only been a few minutes but that wasn't the point with Bob. The point was he hated Nigel and nothing was ever going to be enough for him.

It reminded him of someone else he knew.

Someone dead.

"Jimmy's put together a lovely package for you then," Bob said. "We'll deliver it to the site but we'll need you there to push the button when it's time. That's all clear to you, Nigel?"

"Yes, of course," Nigel said. He knew they hated him. They all did. Bob, Jimmy, Paul and the rest of them. Even though it was Nigel taking all the chances. As usual.

"I'll feel much better when I hear you repeat back to me what's expected, Nigel."

Bob said his name mockingly, as if he wouldn't name a dog Nigel.

Nigel wiped the sweat from his face.

"I'm to meet you at the old Caretaker's place on Abbey grounds—"

"No, mate, you've cocked it up already, haven't you?"

"I..." Nigel glanced out the window and saw a single horseback rider in a scarlet coat riding down the Abbey drive in advance of the hunt. His lips began to tingle.

It was starting.

"There'll be nobody at the cottage, ye see, Nigel. We'll be leaving the package for *you.*"

"Right. Yes, I understand. I'll go to the Caretaker's cottage and set the bomb to detonate forty minutes into the hunt."

"That's the ticket."

"And nobody will get hurt, right?" Nigel said.

"That's up to you, Nigel," Bob said. "You remember how Jimmy told you to set the timer?"

"Yes."

"That's fine then. Any questions?"

The way Bob asked it, Nigel knew he shouldn't have any.

"No," he said. "No questions."

"Jolly good, mate," Bob said sarcastically and hung up.

The second Bob disconnected was the same second Nigel heard the sound of the creaking floorboard outside his room.

For one long second he simply stood there in horror and then bolted for the bedroom door, his hand on the knob.

Should he confront them? Could he say what they heard was just a joke?

The sweat was pouring off him now, making the doorknob slippery in his hand.

He pulled it open slowly, took a long steadying breath and looked into the hallway.

It was empty.

37

I take it the answer is no, Maggie thought dismally as she watched the door shut behind Laurent.

If only he'd let her console him! If only they could talk about it and piece it all out. Maggie was sure it would help

She sagged onto the bed. It was all such a mess. And being here wasn't doing anybody any good. It certainly wasn't making Laurent feel better about losing Roger, and God knows Maggie wasn't feeling any less guilty about how she'd treated Roger while he was alive.

As for who killed him, what she'd said to Laurent was true. It could be anyone! This group all had so many secrets that any one of them could be protecting themselves at the cost of shoving one sick, weakened man to his death.

She brought an image of Roger to mind. He was always so cheerful, so full of strength and life.

And lies, yes. Of course. That was Roger. A twinkle in his eye and a lie on his smiling lips. It was no surprise he had enemies. Not at all.

But it was also true that Roger was the start of most of the joy in Maggie's life. Laurent was right about that. If not for Roger, her family wouldn't have Nicole—another lie—but one they would kill to keep. If not for Roger, Maggie would never have found Elise's killer and received at least a modicum of peace over how her sister had lived and died.

If not for Roger, Maggie would never have met Laurent.

If he'd done nothing else, that alone would have been enough.

Maggie knew if she was ever going to be able to overcome her guilt and look Laurent in the eye again, she needed to find Roger's killer. She paused for a moment and glanced at the door where Laurent had stormed out. And she needed to help Laurent deal with whatever he was clearly struggling with about his own past.

A movement snagged her attention out the window and when she went to look she could see that the hunt party was beginning to arrive. The many splashes of scarlet coats jostled down the long drive to the Abbey.

From her vantage point, she could see the hounds frolicking and dancing around the horses as they surged toward the front door. Maggie felt a rush of excitement.

There was a light tap on the door and Violet entered with a stack of riding clothes. She left the clothes, curtsied and scurried out. On the very top of the clothes was a scarlet riding jacket. And a note.

Forgive me, chérie. If you want to ride today, I can think of few ways better to honor Roger's memory. L.

Maggie's eyes brimmed with tears.

Oh, Laurent.

She knew Laurent didn't want her to ride in the hunt—even when there *weren't* saboteurs ready to jump out of the bushes. That he would green light her going anyway filled her heart nearly to bursting. She looked at the clothes. She wasn't entitled to wear the pinks—not technically. But it didn't matter. She stood up and held the red jacket in front of her image in the mirror. She wasn't entitled to wear the fake tiaras she'd worn all week either.

Roger's final gift to me is the next two hours. But they're also my homage to him.

She would take two hours out of her life to race with the wind and jump everything in her path—two hours of blood pounding thrills with the wind in her face before she came back to France and once more became simply Jemmy and Mila's *Maman.*

Two hours to remember a life she'd once had and to reinforce that what she had now—for all its lack of excitement—was the one anyone might envy her for.

Two hours to say thank you to the man who had brought Laurent into her life.

As if she could ever have properly thanked Roger in his lifetime.

She dressed quickly. Trevor had said if she changed her mind about riding in the hunt that she could ride Diva. She should go down and make sure everything was ready. If she had time, she wanted to find Laurent and thank him.

She slipped out the bedroom door and then realized she might need a crop. Taking the back stairs instead of the main staircase was a more direct route to the side the Abbey where the stables were.

She moved silently in her slippers—she would have to borrow the rubber boots again—when she heard voices coming from around the last corner before the stairs to the servants' quarters. Instinctively, she slowed down.

She heard Trevor's voice—which was odd since he slept in the barn and had no reason to be in the Abbey. Not upstairs anyway. Was she walking in on another tryst with Anastasia? Maggie stopped so as not to come upon them.

"I'll just tell 'em it was you, how about that?" Trevor responded with a snarl. "Give me five hundred quid or I'll tell 'em they got the wrong end of the stick 'coz I saw who really done the deed."

Susan Kiernan-Lewis

38

Maggie sucked in an audible breath. There was a brief shuffling sound on the carpet. Should she retrace her steps? Or confront them?

Maggie stepped around the corner. But the hall was empty.

How could they have disappeared so quickly? She looked down the long hall. It would have been impossible to miss anybody escaping that way. There were no nearby bedroom doors in this section either. Somehow Trevor and whoever else he'd been talking to in the hallway had just vanished.

Maggie retraced her steps and hurried down the main staircase, her mind buzzing with what she'd heard. Who was Trevor speaking to? Was he saying he knew who killed Roger? *Was he speaking to the killer?*

If Trevor knew who killed Roger, why hadn't he told the police? Does this definitely mean it wasn't Madeline?

She went to the dining room and looked in.   Jill and Will stood together talking.   Laurent was standing at a distance by himself.

Jill wore a scarlet riding coat over beige breeches with a cream-colored stock tied close to her throat and pinned with a gold brooch. Her hair was wrapped in a tight braid around her head. She carried a black bowler in one hand.

Maggie stepped into the room. Behind her Gabrielle entered with a tray of drinks. The cook was red faced as if she'd been running and she looked immediately at Maggie.

Could it have been Gabrielle? No, surely there hadn't been enough time for her to descend, grab a tray of drinks and appear in the salon. A few seconds later Violet came into the room with a tray of canapés.

It occurred to Maggie that Trevor and Violet were the closest in age at the Abbey and they were both attractive. Plus, Violet had called Trevor by a nickname earlier—as if they had a personal relationship. If they did, was it odd they were never seen together?

Laurent came to Maggie and kissed her. "You are beautiful," he murmured.

Maggie caught her breath but her nerves began to settle at his words.

"Laurent, I am so sorry about Roger. Did you know he was sick?"

He shook his head. "*Non.* But it doesn't matter."

Maggie felt an overwhelming desire to slip into his arms and hold him close. But she knew his receptivity for public displays of affection had its limits.

As Jill began to walk toward them, Maggie said to Laurent in a low voice, "Thank you for being okay with me riding in the hunt today."

"Jill was right," he said. "Roger would have been pleased." He moved a long tendril of hair from her face.

Had Jill talked him into letting me ride?

"Please don't worry about me, Laurent. I'm good at this."

Jill paused in front of the two of them. "Just wanted to wish you a good ride today," she said.

"Thanks," Maggie said. "Same to you."

The sound of the Master of Hounds horn sounded in the outside courtyard making all of them turn in that direction.

"It's time," Jill said.

Maggie hesitated. She desperately wanted to share with Laurent what she had overheard upstairs. But it looked like it would have to wait until later.

🎇🎇🎇🎇🎇🎇🎇

There was no time for later.

Most of the hunt party had already gathered in the front court of the Abbey.

When Maggie and Laurent came out the front door of the Abbey, Maggie counted twenty riders in all. The masters and field secretary were talking to the various members from the field—all of whom were turned out impeccably, from their own attire to their horses. The hounds swirled around the horses' legs but Maggie knew they would respond immediately once directed.

Even so, the noise and the motion was dizzying. Three of the riders were young but all of them looked experienced. Today, thanks to the fact that the Abbey had closed its doors to paying guests, there would be no lawsuits waiting to happen. Except for herself, there was nobody riding in the hunt who didn't belong there.

Maggie blushed to be seen wearing the scarlet coat. She certainly hadn't been awarded her colors and everyone in the hunt knew it. She shrugged off the feeling. This wasn't about what was real, she reminded herself. It was about one day of Abbey magic.

Of being someone else, living someone else's life just for a few hours.

Trevor stood in the forecourt of the Abbey holding Diva by her bridle. Maggie smiled. Laurent must have gotten word to him that she would be riding. The horse pranced with excitement at the yapping dogs and all the other horses milling about on the front lawn. Maggie couldn't help but think it was a carnival of color with so many riders and horses of all sizes.

The weather seemed to have cleared. But although it wasn't raining, neither was it a bright fall day. Dark clouds bunched overhead in ominous threat.

Annette was already mounted and Maggie quickly lost sight of her in the crowd of riders. Assuming she had friends or acquaintances in the hunt, Maggie wouldn't hold her to her promise that they ride together.

"Are you sure, *chérie*?" Laurent asked, his hand tightening on her elbow. Before she could descend the front steps one horse reared prompting terrified but delighted squeals from some of the younger riders.

Maggie could only imagine what it looked like to Laurent— barely controlled mayhem probably—but to her and every other equestrian there it looked like the promise of an exhilarating day.

"Yes, yes, I'm sure," Maggie said. "Thank you, Laurent. I'll meet you back here when it's over." She could tell he was hesitant to let her go but she felt like Diva looked—too excited and pent up to stand still a minute longer. She kissed Laurent quickly and then hurried to where Trevor waited with Diva. He gave her a leg up onto the big mare and handed over the reins to her.

Once mounted, Maggie tried to see if there was anything in Trevor's face that might show that he suspected Maggie had overheard him upstairs in the hallway. His expression revealed nothing.

"She's strong today," he said to her. "Don't let her get away from you. Keep your leg on her."

Maggie felt Diva's muscles contract and ripple beneath her. The horse felt like a coiled spring primed and poised.

A massive two-ton coiled spring.

No sooner had Maggie mounted up than the horses and hounds began to move out of the front driveway of the Abbey. She twisted in the saddle to wave goodbye to Laurent and saw that he stood on the steps with Anastasia on one side and Will on the other. There was no sign of Nigel.

Maggie put her focus back on her riding. Trevor was right. Whether it was the excitement of the day and all the tumultuous activity or the fact that Diva hadn't been exercised recently, the mare was much stronger today. Before they even left the far side of the stable yard, Diva had jerked the reins out of Maggie's hands twice.

Could it just be all the excitement of the hunt with all the other animals? Had Diva ever ridden in a hunt before? Or was Maggie's own inexperience and anxiety being transferred to the horse?

Maggie sat up straight in the saddle to force Diva to slow down and pay attention to her.

I'm in charge, Maggie said under her breath. *We'll both have a lot better day once you remember that.*

But Diva wasn't having it. As soon as they hit the pasture, she surprised Maggie by breaking into a sudden gallop. Maggie leaned back in the saddle, then began sawing on the reins, pressing Diva's head around until her jaw nearly touched Maggie's knee.

But it didn't work.

Maggie saw the rest of the hunt move steadily away until they disappeared into the woods that fringed the pasture. She knew she had to get Diva under control before they entered the woods.

In the narrow confines of the bridle paths in the woods, there was only disaster waiting for her if she didn't.

Maggie hauled the reins hard to the left and pushed Diva's right flank with her leg to try to bend the horse between her legs.

Not only did the mare not respond to Maggie's leg, but when Maggie forced Diva's head back toward her again, she could see Diva's eyes were wide and wild with terror.

Susan Kiernan-Lewis

39

Something was wrong with her horse.

In desperation, Maggie forced herself to loosen the reins and felt them snake from between her fingers as Diva instantly claimed her newfound freedom.

Maggie worked to stay calm. Panicking would not help the situation. She knew if she could drive Diva in ever widening circles she could avoid the woods and maybe even tire the animal out in the process.

Assuming we don't hit a pothole first and both go cartwheeling across the pasture.

Maggie watched the ground rush by beneath her. She was looking at a broken arm or worse if she couldn't hang on.

Could she hang on?

She tugged the reins to the left and felt a throb of relief when Diva began to turn.

What was the matter with the animal? What had terrified her? This wasn't the normal skittish behavior of a horse who'd been spooked by a scuttling piece of paper across the hard ground.

If anything, Diva's terror was getting worse and her movements more erratic.

Maggie glimpsed a flash of red as the last rider in the hunt disappeared into the woods. It took all the strength Maggie had to keep Diva from following.

The circles Maggie was attempting to force Diva to ride were larger and wider than Maggie intended—bringing them both closer to the edge of the woods.

Maggie's shoulders cramped with tension as she continued to push Diva relentlessly into another arc. Normally when riding a horse in circles in order to regain control, as soon as the horse was facing the barn it would slow down and then speed up again when he was pointed away.

But Diva wasn't slowing down for any part of the circle. Her mad gallop was unmeasured and urgent with no sense or purpose of where she was or what she was doing.

If there had been a cliff in the pasture Maggie had no doubt Diva would ride straight off it.

What was the matter with her?

They were again getting too close to the woods. Maggie could see no opening into the woods—just dense bush and shrub. If she couldn't get control of Diva before the next circle headed them back to the direction of the woods, Maggie would have to jump.

The ground rushed by beneath her in a visual threat. At this speed a fall or a jump would be a disaster. Broken bones were a given.

Her face was clammy and she knew she was clutching Diva's mane in a death grip. She couldn't help it. All of her muscles were tensed and rigid. She was having trouble breathing.

Instead of tiring as she raced in the ever widening circles, Diva seemed to be channeling energy from somewhere. As they rode the final circle together Diva cut the corner hard, unbalancing both of them for one horrifying moment.

Up until then Maggie had been sitting tight in the saddle in an attempt to slow Diva down. Now with fear ratcheting up with every stride, Maggie lifted out of the saddle and balanced in two-point position—with only her feet in the stirrups and her knees touching the horse. She knew the move would destroy the last bit of resistance to Diva's speed.

But it was either that or risk both of them crashing down on the next turn.

As the woods loomed closer, Maggie kicked free of her stirrups and let go of the reins, gripping only Diva's mane.

Suddenly two figures leaped out of the woods. They waved their arms and screamed, smashing trashcan lids with sticks.

Diva reared, pawing the air with her hooves. Her piercing scream vibrated down Maggie's spine.

Maggie wrapped her arms around Diva's neck as the animal rose up on her back legs.

The two men dove into the bushes—inches from Diva's hooves—only seconds before she thudded back to earth.

The panicked horse swiveled on her back hooves and charged into the woods.

Susan Kiernan-Lewis

40

The rain was coming down harder. It was impossible to believe the hunt would carry on in this downpour. Laurent and Will were standing in front of the Abbey, staring down the long front drive. Will was smoking.

"They will end it now, surely?" Laurent said as the sound of thunder rippled through the air.

"Oh, no, mate. Not at all," Will said. "You underestimate the obsession of the average horseman—or in our case, horsewomen. Nothing will stop them. Certainly not a bit of a sprinkle."

Laurent could not see how the grey sheets of cascading, pounding rain could be considered *a sprinkle* in anyone's estimation even as classic understatement for the typical Englishman.

"How long will it last?" he asked, watching the dark skies.

"There's no fox to worry about whatever that crackpot Nigel says," Will said. "And the rain will wash away the chemical scent that was dragged. The dogs will lose the scent if they haven't already."

"And then they will return to the barn?"

Will laughed and tossed his cigarette out.

"Don't you know? It's not really about chasing anything," he said. "It's about being out there in that mess, getting drenched to the bone and jumping over everything and anything in sight." He shrugged. "Nothing stops them. Not weather, not a sick child. Trust me," he added bitterly, *"Nothing."*

Will's phone rang and he pried it out of his jeans pocket, read the text on the screen and then laughed.

"I stand corrected," he said putting his phone away with a grin and moving off the porch into the rain. "A horse that loses a shoe will stop them. I'm off. Annette's waiting for me along the main road. She'll be easy to spot. She'll be the drowned rat walking beside a limping horse."

Laurent watched Will disappear around the building. A few minutes later he reappeared pulling the horse trailer which he maneuvered down the long front drive before disappearing from view.

Laurent looked up at the sky.

Surely no one sane would willingly be out in this?

⁂

The time to jump had come and gone.

Maggie clutched Diva's mane as the horse thundered into the thick underbrush. There was no path. No trail. The branches from the trees attacked them from every height as the horse plunged wildly through the thicket. The branches carved thick wheals into Diva's chest and front quarters.

Maggie was gasping for air as the animal drove deeper into the woods. The horse was out of her mind. Any second Maggie knew she would be impaled on a branch or flung into a tree.

She couldn't wait any longer. Praying her feet wouldn't tangle in the flapping stirrups, Maggie covered her face with an arm and leapt from the saddle.

The world came up suddenly to crash into her face in her sickening plummet to the ground. The earth stopped moving abruptly when she hit but the sky and the canopy of trees continued to swirl above Maggie's head.

She landed on her side, her left arm trapped under her. She lay still a moment, her body humming in pain and shock.

She said a prayer of thanks that came out half a sob.

As Maggie lay on the wet ground she felt the vibrations of Diva's hooves pounding away from her. The tremors in the ground grew fainter by the second.

Maggie tried to sit up and a sharp pain in her side answered her movement. It was her rib. She forced herself to move slowly and saw she was sitting in a bush. Now that Diva was gone so was

224

the booming sound of Maggie's panicked heartbeat reverberating in her head.

She realized then that it was totally quiet in the woods.

Where had the men with the trashcan lids gone?

Those bastards! If only she could have seen a face—or been in any condition to even try to look at their faces. *They were Nigel's friends, that's for sure.*

Maggie got to her knees, her ribs screaming as she moved. The ground around her was slick and muddy. She was surprised to realize it was raining. She used a nearby sapling to pull herself all the way up to her feet. Her side shrieked in agony when she did.

The horse had been drugged. There was no way Diva would have behaved like that without some kind of chemical inducement. That wasn't normal horse fear.

That was equine terror on steroids.

Maggie felt wetness on her face and wiped her chin. She was shocked to pull back a hand covered in blood.

She quickly assessed her physical situation. Her ribs were sore but she was breathing fine. Her left wrist was tender but didn't seem to be broken. She had a cut on her temple. It didn't hurt much but it was bleeding a lot.

The rain was coming down in sheets. Maggie looked around but had no idea which direction the Abbey was. She began to walk, hoping to find a road or a pasture or something that might reveal her location.

After five minutes she was still surrounded by nothing but woods. She was amazed that she and Diva had gotten so far into the forest. Maggie thought it had just been a few seconds but she'd obviously stayed on her longer than she realized.

She kept her hard hat on for protection from the rain but her clothes were soaked through.

The rain splashed up from the sodden leaves as she leaned against a tree and shook with the cold. At least the scarlet jacket she wore—although useless against the cold and the rain—would make it easy for her to be seen in the thick woods.

She lifted her head when she heard the sounds of a horse moving through the trees behind her. With hope it might be Diva, Maggie's stomach fluttered. She whirled around, wincing at the effort.

"Hello?" she called. "Is anyone there?"

Jill appeared on horseback fifty feet away. Her Rottweiler walked beside her on the narrow path.

"Is that you, Maggie?" Jill called. "Where's your horse?"

Maggie pushed out of the thicket. She was trembling violently now from the cold. She wiped the rain from her face.

"As if you don't know," Maggie said. Why wasn't Jill surprised to see her? Was it possibly because she had arranged this disaster?

Why else would she be here now when the rest of the field was long gone?

"What are you talking about?" Jill said.

"You drugged my horse!" Maggie said breathlessly, holding her sore ribs. Every word felt like a knife in her side.

"Give me a break," Jill snorted. "You're just another arrogant Yank who misjudged the amount of horse she could handle. Nobody will be surprised to hear you got dumped."

"I can prove it," Maggie replied hotly. Wherever poor Diva was—dead or alive—tests could be run to show she'd been drugged.

"You're mental," Jill said with a sneer.

"Oh, really? Any particular reason why you're here in the middle of the woods and so far from the hunt?"

"I didn't see you with the other riders," Jill said. "I wanted to make sure you were okay."

"All I need is my horse to prove what you did. Or the feed bucket you used to do it."

Jill looked up at the thick latticework of branches as the rain came down harder.

"The storm's getting worse," she said. "I'll ride back to the Abbey to tell them where you are."

And get rid of the evidence, Maggie thought.

"There's a place up ahead where you can stay dry and maybe not get hit by lightning," Jill said.

Maggie hesitated.

"Or you can stay here and drown," Jill said. "It doesn't matter to me."

"Where are you taking me?" Maggie asked as she followed Jill. Her shivering had turned into full blown shaking.

"It's the Abbey's old caretaker's cottage," Jill said.

Susan Kiernan-Lewis

41

Laurent wasn't sure of the route of the hunt. He knew most of it was over private property—pasture and woodlands and nowhere near roads. But still, he should be able to see the riders returning.

Why had he listened to Jill? He should never have allowed Maggie to ride in the hunt. It hadn't taken Jill long to convince him that encouraging Maggie to participate would be a great way to honor Roger.

It was a stupid, sentimental miscalculation. Jill had caught him at a vulnerable moment, right after his fight with Maggie and his discovery that Roger had been ill.

Even thinking about Roger's illness—and how he'd kept that fact from Laurent—made Laurent want to put his fist through a wall.

He'd not been there for his friend. Laurent had been too busy reveling in his own joy—his own blessed and happy life—to spare a thought to his oldest friend.

Laurent slammed the car into third gear and had the satisfaction of hearing the spray of gravel as he gunned it down the front drive.

Regardless of what Will said, it was not possible to believe that sane people would continue any activity in this kind of weather.

Once Laurent left the driveway and Abbey grounds, he drove slowly in order to peer down both sides of the country road into the thick woods. It was fortunate that so many of the riders wore the bright red coats.

It was unfortunate that none of them were visible at the moment.

He wasn't sure why Maggie wasn't answering her phone. It was possible she hadn't even brought it with her.

Will was right about one thing, Laurent thought. To ride in this miserable weather was nothing less than an obsession. An illness of the mind, even. Laurent couldn't imagine Maggie was seriously contemplating riding as a hobby.

Suddenly, he saw a rider up ahead. Since anyone riding in the hunt would not be on the main road his first thought was that the rider was one of many day riders in the area who were either protesting the hunt—or the Abbey itself—or just out for a ride in truly terrible weather.

The English, Laurent thought. How could this day not be made infinitely better by a seat near a blazing fire with a hot cup of buttered rum?

As he drove up behind the rider, she turned and he was surprised to see it was Jill. He stopped the car and since she clearly appeared to have no intention of dismounting and joining him in the dry car, he flipped his collar up and stepped out into the deluge.

"What are you doing here?" she said to him as the rainwater cascaded off the bill of her derby hat.

"I could ask the same of you," he said.

"You did a good thing today, Laurent," Jill said, "letting Maggie ride in the hunt. I'm sure it's an experience she'll always treasure."

Laurent snorted and wiped the rain from his face.

If she doesn't catch pneumonia first.

Even in just the few minutes that Laurent stood beside Jill's horse, he was already drenched to the skin. He noticed her Rottweiler was with her.

"Since it was *your* idea," he said, "I'm not sure how much credit I deserve. Or in this case," he said pointing to the dark skies, "blame."

"Well, whoever's idea it was I'm sure she's having a great time."

"You have seen her?"

"Sorry, no," Jill said.

"Why are you out here alone?"

"I had to fix my cinch," Jill said. "That's why I'm on the road. I'm trying to catch up. Look, Laurent. About what happened earlier, I'm asking you as a special favor to leave it alone."

"I am no special friend of the police."

"Good. Besides, I'll be gone soon and none of this will matter."

Jill turned her horse as if to leave.

"If you see Maggie—" Laurent called after her.

"This isn't like you to be so over-protective," she called to him over the sound of the rain. "For pity's sake, let the woman have a moment to call her own. Demon, come!" Without another glance at him, Jill kicked her horse into a fast trot down the road.

Laurent watched her for a moment. Then got back in his car to return to the Abbey.

❀❀❀❀❀

It was more of a shack than a cottage, Maggie thought as she approached the structure, but it was still some place to ride out the downpour. Maggie couldn't help think how odd it was that Jill hadn't taken cover in the cottage herself.

Not that Maggie would have enjoyed her company but it did seem a whole lot safer than riding back out into the storm.

A caretaker's cottage to be positioned here, Maggie thought, must mean the Abbey wasn't far away. Although she hated the fact that it would be Jill telling Laurent of Maggie's mishap—and no doubt embellishing it to enhance herself—Maggie had to admit she was grateful for the respite from the deluge.

Her wrist throbbed, her side ached and her head hurt. She was fairly sure she hadn't hit her head coming off Diva but everything had happened so fast.

The door to the cottage was ajar. It was probably too cold for snakes—something a southern girl was always mindful of when tramping about abandoned shacks back in Georgia—but that didn't mean something else just as nasty hadn't taken up residence.

Maggie picked up a stick on the way to the door and hobbled inside. Her eyes strained to adjust to the darkness. There was only one room with one small window and a pot-bellied stove. An old painted table and two chairs—wooden and rough-hewn—lay turned over beside the stove.

Maggie wondered how old the place was. It was pretty clear it had not been lived in for a good while. Still, all she needed was shelter until Laurent arrived. She regretted the fact that she'd left her cellphone back at the Abbey.

She reached out to grab one of the chairs to right it when she saw a dark shape on the floor behind the table. The pit of her stomach began to throb.

She stepped around the table and caught her breath in horror.

42

It was Nigel.

Maggie knelt and reached for his wrist to take his pulse, trying to stop the sound of the blood pounding in her ears long enough to tell if he was alive.

What was he doing here?

She thought she detected a pulse. But now that she was close to him, she could see there was blood under him. Not that much. But not a little either.

"Nigel?" she asked softly, knowing he wouldn't answer.

She looked around for his phone. Her jaw clenched when she saw it clutched in his hand.

"Hang on, Nigel," she said as she reached for the phone. "I'm calling for help. You're going to be okay."

Had Jill made it back to the Abbey yet? Was Laurent on his way even now?

Where was all the blood coming from? Was it a stab wound? Had he hit his head somehow?

She pulled the phone from his hand and was relieved to see there wasn't an access code on it. But she frowned as she looked at the screen. It was already in use. Oddly, the phone's stopwatch was on the screen.

And it was counting down.

A cold worm of dread crawled down her back as she looked around the area where Nigel lay. She held her breath until she saw it and when she saw it, she stared at it unbelieving.

Next to his body was a large copper pipe rough cut around the edges as if it had been sliced into with a wide-tooth saw. The pipe had black wires snaking out the top. Inside, she could see the edge of a white block of what appeared to be modeling clay.

Or a plastic explosive.

It was a bomb. A homemade bomb.

Maggie stared at the phone in her hand.

It's a detonator. He's planted a bomb to disrupt the hunt.

Sweat coated Maggie's cheeks in spite of the breeze cutting straight through the cottage.

The timer read 00:60.

Then 00:59.

Then 00:58

Dear God. The bomb is going to go off in less than a minute.

Could she turn it off? Or would the attempt detonate it?

Carefully, she set the phone back down. Her heart was pounding and the urge to run was nearly overpowering. But Nigel wasn't dead and he wasn't going to be able to save himself.

She grabbed his arms and tried to drag him across the wooden floor. He was heavy and for a minute she thought he must be tied to something.

She looked frantically on the floor where he'd lain but there was only a wide smear of blood. She could hear the phone's silently ticking timer in her head.

Maggie pushed past the burning in her side as she grabbed Nigel under his arms and dragged him as far as the door of the cottage.

Dear God, how many more seconds?

The sounds of the hunt with the hounds in full cry came to her faint and muted in the distance.

Were they coming this way? She sucked in a long painful breath and put her whole strength into making her legs move across the entry steps with Nigel—his legs dragging behind him.

Move! Move! Move! she cried silently in her head as images of Jemmy and Mila and Laurent came to her.

Stay alive for them! Be strong for them!

The hounds were louder now but Maggie forced herself to shut them out.

She forced herself to shut out the sounds in her head of the seconds ticking off and of Mila's laughter and Jemmy's throaty chuckle. She shut out the sounds of Nigel's body heavy and lifeless scraping across the flagstone entry until it hit the dirt and grass forecourt.

She prayed her legs would hold her. If they gave out, if she went down even to one knee, she would never make it back to her feet again.

And they wouldn't make it.

She closed her eyes and put every ounce of energy and force she had into what she needed to do to get back to her babies and her husband.

She gritted her teeth and pushed past the pain in her side and the fear ricocheting around her brain and didn't stop until she hit the verge of the woods outside the cottage clearing.

She didn't stop until she felt the ground rumble beneath her and the heavens roar in agony.

Until the sky filled with debris—boards and bricks, stone and gravel—flying through the air.

And still she didn't stop.

Susan Kiernan-Lewis

43

Laurent was standing in the front of the Abbey again watching the rain come down when he heard the blast. It was muffled by the tree line behind the stables. His heart began to race.

Had it come from anywhere near the riders?

Anastasia came out the front door behind him with a cup of tea in one hand.

"What on earth was that?" she said, peering down the Abbey drive.

"It's not normal?" Laurent asked. "Perhaps construction in the area?"

"Oh, it's probably just a blown transformer," Anastasia said.

"Out here in the country?"

"Do we not have transformers in the country?" She frowned and then shrugged, turning to go back inside the Abbey

Laurent set off at a jog, digging his car keys out of his pocket as he went.

❈ ❈ ❈ ❈ ❈

The blast knocked Maggie off her feet. She saw the tree in front of her but didn't have time to put an arm up to protect her face. When she hit, she felt the breath leave her body in one awful discharge. She slid to the ground. The earth seemed to vibrate beneath her. Her feet and legs ached with the thrumming as it shot up and down her spine.

She turned and threw up in the bushes. She felt the solidity of the tree, rough and real, where she gripped the jagged surface, bruising her fingertips.

She was alive.

She looked around. The clearing looked as if a tornado had touched down. The roof of the cottage was gone—scattered into pieces across the clearing and into the woods. Small fires were visible inside the damaged cottage walls.

Maggie crawled to Nigel's body. She sat there, too weak, too shocked to do anything but stare at the destruction before her.

A sudden thought niggled its way into her head.

Jill knew there was a bomb about to go off here. She had tried to kill her.

Maggie's shivering threatened to overwhelm her. She rubbed her hands up and down her arms to warm them.

"Hello! Anybody there?"

Maggie turned to see two teenage girls on horseback. She struggled to her feet, using the tree behind her for support and staggered into the clearing.

"Help!" she said.

Both girls backed away fearfully. One of the horses snorted and pawed the ground. *Horses don't like fire and they don't like feeling people's fear.*

This place was full of both.

"Please," Maggie said. "Lend me your phone. I need to call for help."

The two girls looked at each other but the older of the two suddenly pried her phone out of her coat pocket.

"Catch!" she said to Maggie and tossed it to her.

Maggie's fingers were too numb with the cold and fear to catch it and it fell into the tall grass at the edge of the woods.

"Ten eight one one," the girl called, and Maggie quickly keyed in the access code and then Laurent's number.

"*Allo?*" he answered suspiciously, not recognizing the number.

"Laurent, it's me," Maggie said, her voice trembling with relief to hear his voice after everything that had happened. She forced herself not to cry. Plenty of time for that later.

"*Chérie*, where are you? I heard an explosion."

"I'm at the old caretaker's cottage," Maggie said breathlessly. She glanced at the two girls who had now dismounted.

"Off Trinity Road, first turn before the Abbey," one of the girls said.

"Did you get that?" Maggie said. "Call for an ambulance first and then meet me on Trinity Road."

She could hear Laurent moving as he spoke. "You are hurt, *chérie*?" he asked, his voice tight with tension.

"No, the ambulance is for Nigel. Please hurry…and Laurent?" Maggie turned her back on the girls so they couldn't hear, "*do not* call the cops."

She handed the girl her phone.

"Thank you so much," Maggie said. "Do either of you know first aid?"

"I'm a doctor," a voice called out. Maggie looked up to see Jill riding up with an elderly man in a red hunt coat. He swung down from his horse and hurried over to Maggie beside Nigel.

There was no way Jill could have gone for help at the Abbey and then be here this soon after the explosion.

"Come back to pick up the pieces?" Maggie said leaving the doctor to his work and walking to where Jill sat on her horse. Her Rottweiler was sniffing at a smoking piece of rubble.

"I heard the explosion," Jill said, looking around at the demolition. "Wanted to make sure you were okay. For the second time today I might add. I met Ian on his way back to the Abbey. Goodness, what a mess. There's nothing but match sticks left."

"What did you expect would happen?"

Jill turned her attention back to Maggie. "You're not suggesting I knew about this?"

"Pretty convenient otherwise, wouldn't you say?"

Jill laughed. "For what possible reason would I lead you here knowing there was a bomb about to go off? So I could get Laurent from you? Trust me, darling, I don't need to kill you to do that."

"Maybe you thought I was getting too close to the truth about how Roger died? Maybe you had a conversation with Trevor in the upstairs hallway today? And you knew I'd overheard it."

"I know you're crazy," Jill said, but her eyes looked wary.

"It occurred to me that you are the only one at the Abbey who never talks of Roger," Maggie said as she began to move across the clearing. "Did you know that? You don't say you hated him or loved him or missed him. Just nothing. I think that's strange for a sister."

"You don't know anything."

"I know I saw you wandering the halls of the Abbey one night. I know you lied about it."

Jill's eyes narrowed.

"I know you were whispering with Trevor virtually moments before Diva was poisoned."

"Trevor had nothing to do with anything," Jill said. "He was asking me for some investment advice."

"Oh? About to come into a chunk of change, was he?" Maggie asked. She turned to one of the girls who were watching the doctor tend to Nigel. "Which way is Trinity Road?" she called.

The older girl pointed to the trail behind Jill.

"You have no proof your horse was poisoned," Jill said as Maggie moved past her toward the trail.

"I will have as soon as I find the bucket you fed her from. Forensics can do amazing things these days."

"You won't find anything to implicate me."

Maggie turned and faced Jill. "You mean because there won't be any fingerprints on the bucket? Cops don't need that nowadays. As soon as I tell them my suspicions you'll be vacuumed from head to toe and forensics will find traces of the poison that made Diva go crazy. Don't you ever watch CSI? Maybe you should come in from the barn now and then. Well, you'll have plenty of time for Law and Order reruns where you're going."

Maggie turned to walk away. She wanted to be long gone before the ambulance arrived—or the cops.

"You know, accidents happen out here in the field all the time," Jill said to Maggie's back.

"I think you'll be hard pressed to show that a cottage blowing up was an accident," Maggie said over her shoulder, "*or* a normally mild-mannered horse going berserk."

"I was talking more about the adverse affects the scent of the chemical drag and the baying hounds can have on a normally obedient dog."

Maggie turned and saw the Rottweiler was watching her. His eyes were alert, his ears perked. The sound of her own heartbeat crashing in her ears drowned out all other noise.

She looked around at her tactical environment. She was too far from the caretaker's cottage and nowhere near a tree with low enough branches to climb.

Surely, Jill wasn't seriously considering...?

Jill wheeled her horse around and as she galloped past Maggie, she screamed out,

"Demon! Attack!"

Susan Kiernan-Lewis

44

Maggie had only enough time to put both hands out. The dog hit her hard in the chest and knocked her onto her back. Her head hit the ground with a thud, her throat exposed. She held a forearm up and felt the grinding, sudden pressure as the dog bit though her jacket sleeve.

His snarls were loud in her ear. His breath hot against her cheek. Maggie felt the second bite go into her shoulder like a sledgehammer. She grabbed the dog's fur with both hands and felt his head jerk spasmodically from side to side, his teeth snapping.

"Demon, no!" Maggie screamed. "Demon, NO!"

He stopped. The dog stood panting with his front paws on Maggie's chest.

Maggie opened her eyes and looked into his. She saw the confusion there. She forced a thick timber in her voice. She willed it to come from a place deep within her—threatening and strong.

"Bad dog!" she snarled. The pain of the attack vibrated through her body. "Get back!"

The dog stepped off her and looked in the direction that Jill had gone. Maggie sat up and grabbed his collar and jerked it hard.

"Hey!" she said loudly.

He lowered his eyes. His tail was clamped between his legs.

She stood up, shakily, and kept one hand wrapped around Demon's collar for support.

She couldn't believe Jill had sicced her dog on her! And then had fled the scene so she could claim she knew nothing of it. Demon looked up at her with worried eyes.

She heard the sound of an engine over her shoulder and quickly moved into the woods. The ambulance drove up the grassy drive toward the ruined caretaker's cottage. The cops wouldn't be far behind. She had to hurry.

Jill had ridden in the opposite direction of the Abbey. Did that mean she *hadn't* poisoned the horse?

Because that was pretty chill behavior for someone who had a tainted bucket or used syringe to dispose of.

Could it be someone *else* who'd poisoned the horse? Was it possible Jill *didn't* know about the plot to blow up the caretaker's cottage?

But then why did she lead Maggie there?

In the end Maggie knew it didn't matter. The first thing she had to do was find the bucket or other evidence of the poisoning. The second thing was to find Trevor and see who he'd been talking to this morning in the hallway.

Maggie ran to the main road with the Rottweiler at her heels and saw Laurent's rental car only a hundred yards away. He was standing beside it, his hands on his hips, scanning the woods.

"Laurent!" she called. "Over here!"

He turned in her direction. Based on the expression on his face, she must have looked a sight. He ran toward her and when he reached her instead of pulling her into his arms as she expected —and was braced for—he gently lifted away her hair and touched the side of her face.

"I know I look a little rough—" she said.

Demon growled menacingly.

"Demon, no!" Maggie said harshly.

"What happened?" Laurent said, ignoring the snarling dog. From the look on Laurent's face, he appeared perfectly capable of snapping one annoying Rottweiler in two without much fuss. In fact, he might welcome the opportunity.

"I fell off Diva and then went to the…listen, can we talk about this in the car? We need to get back to the Abbey," she said breathlessly.

"*Quoi*? You fell off your horse?"

"It's a long story. Please, Laurent. We have to get to the Abbey."

"You are holding your side."

"It's nothing really," she said, as they hurried to the car.

"Why are you with Jill's dog?" Laurent asked.

The sounds of police sirens grew louder.

"Hurry," Maggie said, holding her side as she hobbled painfully to the car, "before Jill can destroy the evidence."

"Evidence? What are you talking about?"

"I think Jill drugged my horse but I need its feed bucket to prove it."

"I met Jill on the road forty minutes ago," Laurent said. "She said she hadn't seen you."

"That would have been right around the time I was wrestling with Nigel's unconscious body—*after* she led me to the cottage that was wired to explode."

Laurent swore under his breath.

"Laurent, hurry! The cops will be here soon and we need to avoid getting caught in their dragnet."

She pulled open the car's rear door and the dog jumped in. As they got in the car she saw the look of confusion and concern on Laurent's face.

"Laurent," she said as patiently as she could muster, "we are about thirty minutes from finding out who killed Roger but first we've got to get back to the Abbey to talk to Trevor."

"Why?" Laurent said, his fury at Jill's lies emanating off him in waves.

"Just before I left for the hunt I overhead him blackmailing someone," Maggie said. "It sounded like he was accusing them of killing Roger."

"Did he say so?"

"Well, no. Ergo my need to question him. Can you drive a little faster?"

Laurent gunned it over the bumpy stone roadway and every bounce in the road was like a jackhammer to Maggie's side. While Demon hadn't broken the skin on her shoulder, she knew it would soon blacken and bruise.

She bit her lip and tried not to react to the jolting ride. Laurent was already watching her more closely than the road.

They saw at least a dozen riders on the side of the road. A few were dressed for the hunt but most were in regular riding clothes

—jeans and paddock boots as if out for a day ride. Some carried *Down with the Hunt* signs. Others carried picnic baskets.

"Rubberneckers," Maggie said, trying not to gasp with pain as she spoke. "Could you hear the explosion from the Abbey?"

"Yes. Anastasia said it was a transformer. But it was one of the Abbey's outbuildings?"

"A caretaker's cottage. Nigel was obviously trying to create havoc by planting a homemade bomb. He must have had a fight with someone because when I found him he'd been stabbed and left to die."

"*Incroyable.*"

"Well, you hang out with murdering scum, you can't be too surprised when they turn on you," Maggie said.

They drove up to the front of the Abbey. The rain had slowed but lightning still punctuated the grey skies in the distance. The front parking lot was empty. Annette's horse trailer wasn't in front of the stable and neither was Jill's horse.

Has Jill come and gone? Could I have been wrong about her poisoning Diva?

Maggie jumped out of the car and ran to the barn with Demon again at her heels. Maximus stood up and barked as they passed his cage.

Maggie plunged into the dark interior of the barn and felt the coolness of the stables as she did.

"Trevor?" Maggie shouted.

She went first to the tack room. Over the feed bins was a line of hard rubber feed buckets, each with a horse's name written on it in black marker. Each bucket was hanging on its hook.

All except one.

Maggie stopped and stared at the gap in the line of buckets. Diva's bucket was missing. She felt a tingle start in her hands and she rubbed the feeling away against her riding pants. In all the excitement, she'd briefly forgotten the pain in her side and her shoulder.

Both began to throb now.

Whoever poisoned Diva had already disposed of the evidence.

Maggie turned in time to see Laurent enter the barn. Even though the barn doors were a good two feet taller than his height, he still stooped from habit as he entered.

"Maggie?" he called, not seeing her in the dark.

"Over here," she said as she left the tack room and walked toward him down the main aisle of stalls.

One of the stall doors was ajar which wasn't unusual since most of the horses were either in the paddock, the pasture or out in the hunt.

Maggie would later wonder what made her stop, what there had been about that half open stall gate that had made her hesitate and look inside...

...where she saw Trevor lying face down in the straw bedding.

Susan Kiernan-Lewis

45

"Oh, my God," Maggie whispered.

The back of Trevor's head was covered in gore. Next to him lay the manure shovel. The blade was crimson with blood.

Laurent reached the stall door and grabbed Maggie just as she stepped into the stall.

"Maggie, *non!*" he said, pulling her back.

"But I've been in the barn a lot," Maggie protested. "My DNA will be all over here."

"Not in the puddle of blood beneath the body," Laurent said, pulling her toward him into the aisle.

The Rottweiler sat watching them.

"How did this happen? Could it possibly be an accident?" she said, bewildered.

"We must go. *Maintenant,*" Laurent said.

"Aren't we calling the cops?" Maggie's head was spinning. *How could this have happened?*

"Not unless you want to spend the rest of the day at the police station answering questions."

Laurent took her by the arm and led her down the long aisle. "Later, *ma chérie.* We were never here. Hurry now."

Maggie knelt in the aisle to look at something.

"Maggie, I will carry you out," Laurent growled.

At Laurent's tone Demon's snarl erupted low and threatening in his throat. He positioned himself between Maggie and Laurent.

Maggie pointed to the item that had stopped her.

"It's an unsmoked cigarette," she said. "There's no smoking allowed in the barn."

"*Don't* touch it," he said firmly.

Maggie stood up and began moving in the direction of the exit. "It's Will's brand," she said.

Laurent again clamped a hand on her arm and they hurried out of the stable.

"Demon, come!" Maggie called over her shoulder.

"Lock up the dog," Laurent said as they stopped at Maximus's crate.

Maggie bent down to take hold of Demon's collar.

"On second thought, no," he said. "They'll know we were here if they see him caged."

It was all too horrible to imagine. Poor Trevor lying in his own blood. Maggie got a sudden thought like a splash of ice water down her back. *Trevor was killed by Roger's killer.*

It was so obvious. Trevor was blackmailing whoever killed Roger.

Everybody knows this is what happens to blackmailers!

Laurent led Maggie to the garden behind the stable and away from the Abbey. Demon loped happily beside them.

"I can't believe it," Maggie repeated. "He was so alive just a few hours ago. When are we calling the police?"

"We aren't. Whoever reports the death becomes an instant suspect."

There were definite benefits to having a former criminal as your fellow sleuth, Maggie thought grimly. But in that case how were the cops going to be notified?

They sat down on a stone bench beside a heavily mulched herbaceous border. Through the branches of an ancient beech tree they could see the front of the Abbey as well as the long drive leading up to it. But they themselves were hidden.

"It has to be whoever killed Roger," Maggie said. The Rottweiler came to her and she put her hand on his head.

"Why do you say that?" Laurent said.

"Isn't it obvious? Trevor was about to reveal the identity of Roger's murderer!"

They both happened to be looking toward the Abbey when Anastasia appeared at the front door with a cocktail her hand. The hem of her long chiffon frock dusted the wet pavers of the threshold. Gabrielle stepped out of the house with a silver tray. Anastasia thumped her empty cocktail glass on the tray and went back inside with Gabrielle close behind.

Maggie shivered. "Think of it, Laurent. Who had the opportunity for both deaths? Who could have killed both Roger and Trevor?"

"It couldn't be Madeline—she's in police custody."

"And it couldn't be Annette, Nigel or even Jill—unfortunately —because they were all out in the hunt. That leaves Will, Anastasia, and the servants."

"You think Roger's murder was committed by one of those?"

"Yes, because I'm sure Roger's murderer killed Trevor. The timing of his murder is too convenient otherwise."

Laurent nodded begrudgingly.

"So ask yourself do you really think Anastasia would have killed her own lover?"

"You had no problem believing she might have killed her own husband."

"But like this? It's so brutal."

"Anyone can swing a shovel at a man who is looking the other way," Laurent said.

"But they'd have to be in the barn to do it. Even if Anastasia could bring herself to go in the barn—and that's a big if—I can't see her picking up a *manure* shovel."

Laurent nodded. "She is not pretending about her aversion to horses."

"So I'm ruling her out at least for now," Maggie said. "But what about the servants? Especially Gabrielle?"

"Gabrielle did not kill Roger."

Maggie looked at Laurent with surprise. "Mind telling me why you think so?"

"She does not have the stomach for killing."

The memory of Gabrielle chucking a full shelf of crockery at her made Maggie beg to differ.

"She seems plenty violent to me, Laurent. All it would take was one crime-of-passion kind of moment...and you know how passionate you French tend to be."

He gave Maggie a side glance and one corner of his lip turned up in a near smile.

"Gabrielle does not have that kind of passion," he said. "Besides, she has an alibi."

"She told you this?"

"*Oui.*"

"She could be lying."

"Madeline will confirm it."

Maggie hesitated. "So Madeline *didn't* have food poisoning the night Roger was killed?"

"It appears not."

"Jeez. Madeline would rather go to jail for murder than reveal she and Gabrielle have a thing?"

Laurent shrugged as if he had come to the end of any information he might know.

"Well, what about the other servants?" Maggie asked. "The Abbey had a full roster of employees the night Roger was killed."

"Except for Violet, Gabrielle and Trevor, they all live off premises. Madeline told me they were all accounted for during the time of the murder."

"You know, Laurent, some of this information would have been helpful earlier on. You don't really grasp the concept of *teamwork*, do you?"

"You already knew the murderer was not Madeline. So there was no reason to expose more of her secrets."

Maggie shook off her annoyance. "Well, fine. So if we take the servants out of the equation and we say it's unlikely that Anastasia could've bashed Trevor over the head with a manure shovel, then we're looking at Will. He had motive. *And* his cigarette was at the crime scene. So he had opportunity."

"*C'est vrai.*"

"It's just hard to believe he would kill his own uncle though," Maggie said as she tapped her finger against her lip in concentration.

"They were not really related."

"What?"

"Annette is the orphaned daughter of Roger's younger brother, Geoffrey."

"See, this is the kind of thing I mean when I talk about *sharing information*, Laurent," Maggie said testily. "Where is Geoffrey now?"

"He died years ago in prison. The mother was already dead."

"Tell me he wasn't in prison for something he did with Roger."

"It is possible."

"Wow. Motives are now literally coming out the ying yang."

"What is this ying—?"

"Never mind. So the bottom line is Will is *not* related to Roger?"

"*Non.*"

"Well that seals it then. It has to be Will. Was he out of your sight at any time while you were waiting for us to return from the hunt? Even for a few minutes?"

Laurent frowned. "When he went to get his horse trailer, he was gone for at least fifteen minutes before driving away."

"That would be plenty of time for him to slip into the barn and kill Trevor." Maggie found herself growing excited. "Will had motive, opportunity and means for both murders plus direct evidence that places him at the crime scene. It's got to be Will."

Laurent stood up as Will and Annette's horse trailer came into view on the drive leading to the Abbey.

"Speak of the devil," Maggie said.

Susan Kiernan-Lewis

46

Laurent picked up Will and slammed him against the side of the horse trailer. Annette shrieked and a horse inside the trailer whinnied loudly. Annette began pounding on Laurent's back.

"Stop it! What are you doing? Help! Help!" she yelled, looking wildly around.

Maggie stood watching, her heart pounding.

"Making friends again, I see," said a voice behind her.

Maggie turned to see Jill had ridden up behind her and was dismounting. The rain had eased to a light patter.

Demon ran to Jill.

"Should I even ask?" Jill said as she tousled Demon's ears and then turned away to lead her horse to the barn.

Maggie held her tongue. After possibly poisoning Diva before putting Maggie where a bomb was set to go off and then siccing her dog on her...yep, she would definitely let Jill do the honors of discovering Trevor's body—*if it was a surprise to her at all.*

Maggie watched as Jill walked to the barn. Annette ran over to Maggie.

"Stop him! He's killing Will!"

"Someone poisoned my horse," Maggie said as she removed Annette's clinging fingers from her jacket.

"And you think it was Will? He's afraid of Shetland ponies, for heaven's sakes!"

"He wouldn't need to get very close to lace a bucket with a chemical," Maggie said.

"You're crazy! Why would Will want to poison one of the horses?" Annette was looking from Maggie to Laurent who was holding Will against the trailer.

"*My* horse," Maggie said testily. "The horse *I* was riding."

"What…what possible reason would Will have for poisoning your horse?" Annette sputtered.

"My first guess is he was afraid I heard something incriminating about his involvement in Roger's death."

"Are you mental? You're trying to pin Roger's murder on Will?"

Annette turned and ran back to where Laurent stood holding Will by the throat.

"Did you poison the horse?" Laurent asked.

"No! God no. I swear!" Will choked out.

Annette slapped Laurent's arm. "Unhand him this instant!"

Laurent surprised her by releasing Will, who immediately sagged to his knees. Annette knelt by him and threw her arms around him.

"Tell me the truth, Will," she said in a hoarse whisper. "Let's get this out in the open. Did you…do anything?"

"Nothing! I swear!" Will said and instantly flinched as if sure his denial would trigger Laurent to go for him again. "Maybe Jill did something! You know how she hates Laurent's wife."

Annette shook her head. "But why would Jill—"

"Oh, my God!"

The scream came from the barn and trailed out in a long howl as Jill ran from the barn's entrance, her dog at her side. She reached the group and went straight to Laurent and grabbed him by the arms. Her face was white with shock.

"Find something interesting in the barn?" Maggie said as she focused on Will's face. Unless he was the world's best actor, Maggie was sure his reaction would reveal he'd killed Trevor.

"You *knew*! You knew he was in there!" Jill said twisting away from Laurent. He grabbed her around the waist just as she tried to launch herself at Maggie.

"I don't know what you're talking about," Maggie said.

"Who?" Annette said. "Who's in there?"

"Trevor!" Jill screamed at Annette. "He's dead!"

The very words seemed to weaken her. She covered her face and turned to sag against Laurent's chest. "In the barn," she said. "He's dead."

Laurent caught Maggie's eye over Jill's head and frowned.

Will leaned against the side of the trailer with his hand to his mouth.

"Oh, my God," he moaned. "What is happening?"

Maggie frowned. He looked authentically shocked.

"Someone should call the police." Laurent said. He looked at Jill huddled against his chest. "I hope you didn't touch anything?"

"I...I..." She looked at him and bit her lip.

"Because that would not look good for you," Maggie said sweetly.

"What are you saying? I didn't kill Trevor! Why in the world would I? Are you mad?"

But Maggie could see that Jill knew the police wouldn't think it was a mad idea at all. No, they would be very interested in talking to the person who had her foot and handprints all over the spot where Trevor died.

"Well, the silver lining," Maggie said to Jill, "is that the cops will now seal the barn off and go over every inch of it with a nit comb. They'll be able to find out who killed Trevor *and* who poisoned my horse and do you know what I think? I think that will lead them straight to whoever killed Roger."

"I didn't kill Roger," Jill said as she spun around, her eyes on Laurent. "Laurent, look at me. You know I didn't kill him."

But as usual, Laurent's expression revealed nothing.

Susan Kiernan-Lewis

47

Detective Chief Inspector Bailey stood in the doorway of the salon. Laurent thought he looked tired—but also expectant—as if he knew his case was coming together. The detective nodded at Laurent as he stood and waited for everyone to quiet down. Not for the first time, Laurent wondered if Bailey knew who he was.

Knew his past.

The police had arrived barely a quarter hour after Laurent had made the phone call. They had a unit investigating the bomb site at the caretaker's cottage. A pair of detectives was already on their way to question everyone at the Abbey when the call about Trevor's murder came in.

Laurent sat in one of the padded Edwardian salon chairs with Maggie on his right. He couldn't help wondering if Maggie was right that the forensics from the barn would finally tell them who'd killed Roger. And why.

Looking at Detective Chief Inspector Bailey as the man stood, rocking back on his heels in the picture of confidence, somehow Laurent wasn't at all sure.

As soon as the police had arrived, everyone was herded into the main salon of the Abbey. Yellow crime scene tape already festooned the driveway, the stable courtyard and the barn.

From the salon window, Laurent could see at least twenty police in booties and gloves photographing the gravel, raking the grass, and exiting the barn in a steady stream holding baggie after baggie of collected evidence.

Jill sat in one of the police cars where she'd been ever since Bailey showed up.

As soon as she'd gotten the news about Nigel, Anastasia was driven to the hospital in Oxford by one of the constables. While at least alive, it didn't look like he was going to be waking up anytime soon and naming his assailant.

All the horses had been moved out of the stable to the outdoor paddock—all except Maggie's horse, of course, which was still missing. Laurent knew Maggie was counting on them finding the horse soon—or at least the feed bucket.

No one needed to tell her that the more time that elapsed, the less likely it was that they would find either in time to prove that the horse had been drugged.

Violet, Gabrielle, Will and Annette had all had their statements taken—what few bits and pieces they had to tell. They'd all pled ignorance to the knowledge of the body in the barn —all except poor Jill.

Will sat on a divan sporting a dark bruise over his cheekbone. Annette had not let go of her husband's hand since the moment they'd been ushered into the salon three hours earlier.

Gabrielle and Violet sat beside each other in silence.

Bailey cleared his throat and addressed the group. "What is it about this place, do you think? Two murders in two weeks?"

Laurent squeezed Maggie's knee. It would be just like her to respond to the man and Laurent did not want to do anything that kept them here even ten minutes longer than they needed to be.

"Well, you've all had a very busy day," Bailey said when nobody responded. "Are you all staying on the premises?"

Everyone nodded.

"Very good. We are finishing up here for the night. As soon as the body is removed..." he said, looking at his watch, "which should be any moment now, we'll be gone."

"So you've finished with the crime scene?" Maggie asked.

Bailey zeroed in on her. "Mrs. Dernier? Is that right?" he asked, but he was looking at Laurent.

Maggie nodded.

"No, Mrs. Dernier. We are finished for the night. We will resume our onsite investigation tomorrow."

"Will you be leaving a guard?" Maggie asked. It was all Laurent could do not to roll his eyes. If both of them weren't sitting on a couch, he would have stepped on her foot to shut her up.

"Should I?"

"Well, I don't want to tell you your business," Maggie said, "but as I've mentioned to you earlier, there's a missing feed bucket and I didn't see any of your men carry one out of the barn."

"How do you know there's a missing feed bucket?"

"Oh," Maggie said, frowning, "of course I don't know for sure. I didn't see with my own eyes, if that's what you're asking me. But I'm pretty sure the culprit wouldn't poison my horse and then leave the incriminating bucket for all to see."

"The culprit?"

"Do they not have that word over here?" Maggie asked innocently.

Laurent was a second away from kicking her and it didn't matter who saw.

"I will do my best to keep you apprised of all buckets missing or otherwise," Bailey said.

"*Merci*," Laurent said firmly as he frowned at Maggie.

She shrugged.

"Jill Bentley will be coming with us for more questioning," Bailey said. "Everyone here is advised to stay in the house. Under no circumstances will you go near the crime scene. If we discover your DNA there we will have to assume the worst."

"What does that mean?" Will asked. "*Assume the worst?*"

Bailey turned to look at Will as if seeing him for the first time.

"It means, Mr. Fitzhugh, that we will have to assume your DNA was in the barn before or around the time of the murder."

"That's not true, is it?" Annette said. "It's a contaminated crime scene in that case. Isn't that true?" She looked at Bailey who smiled at her.

"Why don't we not try and find out?" he said as he left the room.

When the police left, everyone in the salon seemed eager to leave too.

In direct defiance of the Chief Inspector's directives, Annette went out to the paddock to throw a flake of hay to the horses. Maggie wouldn't put it past her to go to the barn to get her tack tools. Most of what Annette had complained about while they waited for the police to finish their initial investigation was that she wasn't able to groom her horse after riding him all day.

As they watched everyone else leave the salon, Laurent stood up, holding his hand out to Maggie.

"*Tu a faim, ma chérie?*"

"Starving, now that you mention it," Maggie said. "Do you think they'll be serving in the dining room tonight?"

She followed him out of the room.

"*Non*," he said. "We will eat in the kitchen."

Will was standing in the front doorway watching Annette fuss over her horse but he turned around when Maggie and Laurent crossed the foyer.

"Laurent is making us something to eat," Maggie said to him.

Will hesitated and then called to Annette before following Maggie and Laurent down the hall through the door to the lower staircase. A breathless Annette appeared behind them before they were all the way downstairs.

Gabrielle looked up in surprise from the carrots she was chopping as the four of them entered the kitchen. Violet sat at the long wooden table flipping through a celebrity magazine. Her mouth fell open when she saw them.

Laurent went to the wall of copper pots and examined two of the larger ones. Gabrielle watched him but didn't interfere. Even so, the expression on her face looked as if a highly undesirable rodent had just crawled into the flour bin.

Maggie went to the table and sat down opposite Violet. Will and Annette sat beside her.

"We're not working tonight," Violet said with the first hint of sullenness that Maggie had heard from her. *Was this the real Violet?*

"No worries," Maggie said with a smile. "I brought my own personal chef with me."

Laurent went to the refrigerator and began pulling out tubs of leftovers. He found a package of ham, sniffed it, shrugged, and put it on the counter with a few other items he deemed acceptable.

As he worked, Annette and Will settled down at the long table.

"I want you to know," Annette said to Maggie, "that I can see why you thought it was Will. But I think you owe him an apology."

Maggie snorted. "The fat lady hasn't even gotten out of her chair to make her way to the microphone yet," she said.

Will and Annette looked at each other in confusion.

Maggie looked at Violet. "Who feeds Jill's dogs?"

"How should I know?"

Yep. Definitely got a whole different attitude.

Gabrielle wrenched open the refrigerator behind Laurent and pulled out a bag of meat scraps and dumped the bag on the table in front of Maggie. "Mademoiselle Bentley feeds them from the stable," she said. "We cannot go there tonight, *ainsi...*" She gestured to the meat scraps.

"Lucky dogs," Maggie said.

"Let's go together," Annette said. "That way we don't have to worry about a situation turning into your word against ours."

Will grabbed the meat sack. "Let's just feed the buggers and keep each other in sight," he said.

Later Laurent made *croque monsieurs* for everyone. The dish was a favorite of Maggie's and easy to make in a short amount of time.

"Oh, my God, this is the best thing I've ever eaten," Annette said with a chunk of the golden crusted cheese sandwich speared on her fork.

"You're just hungry," Will said around a mouthful of his second sandwich.

Gabrielle worked side by side with Laurent to create the meal, buttering the bread and grating the cheese while Laurent worked the griddle.

Maggie wouldn't put it past Laurent to have deliberately created a meal that Gabrielle was bound to know well in order to spur the solidarity and companionship that cooking together can foster.

And while not exactly friendly, Gabrielle appeared to have temporarily lost her signature sneer.

Annette groaned as she finished off her sandwich and washed it down with a glass from the Côte du Rhone Gabrielle had brought in from the pantry. There hadn't been much conversation—there was too much distrust and shock in the room for that—but at least they weren't hungry any more.

And the rain had stopped.

While they ate Maggie watched Will closely.

"I heard one of the cops say a *Gauloises* cigarette was found by Trevor's body," she said.

Will blanched.

"Maggieee…" Laurent said in a low voice.

"You're lying," Annette said, looking at Will as if for confirmation. "The cops would never reveal something like that. Besides you were with us in the salon the whole time."

"I…I loaned Trev a fag," Will said.

"Will!" Annette said, her voice laced with dismay.

"So now giving a fag to a bloke means I killed him?"

"It might when it's his pool of blood the fag is found in," Maggie said.

Annette snapped her head at Maggie.

"How did you know where the cigarette was found?"

"I'm just guessing," Maggie said, blushing. She glanced at Laurent. He was not happy with her.

In the end, she knew it didn't matter. Will hadn't killed Trevor. His surprised reaction to Trevor's death had been too authentic.

As Maggie stood up to gather the dirty sandwich plates and carry them to the sink, it occurred to her there was someone sitting right here at this table who hadn't looked at all surprised to hear of Trevor's murder. Someone nobody ever gave a thought to. Someone who blended into the woodwork but who was always there—upstairs in the bedroom hallways, on the grounds, in the kitchen—always there but unnoticed.

Violet.

Violet had access to all the bedrooms. And she had no alibi for the time of Roger's murder.

Violet had means and opportunity, Maggie thought with excitement. Plus she was mysteriously missing for precious minutes the afternoon right after Maggie had heard the whispered blackmailer in the hallway. It would be tight but she would definitely have had enough time to get from upstairs to the salon.

The only thing Maggie didn't know was a possible motive for Violet.

"Maggie?" Laurent said.

She broke out of her thoughts and looked at him. He crooked a finger at her.

"A word?"

She followed him outside into the brisk night air.

"What are you doing?" he asked.

"Until the police release Madeline and arrest the right person," Maggie said earnestly, "we can't assume they're going to get it right."

"I thought you said once they gathered all the forensic evidence in the barn..."

"Yes, but we can't assume they'll put all the pieces together correctly. How many times have the cops back home put two and two together and gotten five?"

Laurent grunted. He knew she was right.

"I don't think Will killed Roger," she said. "He appeared genuinely surprised to learn about Trevor's murder. That doesn't fit if Will's the killer."

"So then who?"

"Well, it occurred to me that one person who is not even on anybody's radar had access, opportunity and means for both murders. And she knew Trevor and could easily have been the one in the hallway he was talking to when I overheard them. Plus since she knows the house so well, she would know where all the secret panels were too."

"Violet?" Laurent frowned. "She seems so shy and... *incapable*."

"I know, right? But tonight I saw a glimpse of a different side of her. A much less shy side."

"So it is Violet? *Mais pourquoi?*"

"That's just it. I can't think of a motive. The one thing everybody else in this house has in spades."

"I do not know, *chérie*. She seems too timid to me."

"You're not looking at her properly, Laurent. You are looking at her act—the one she's carefully performed for all of us ever since we arrived.

"So what are you looking to find? A connection between Violet and Roger?"

"That's just it," Maggie said excitedly. "I think we need to find a connection between Violet and Trevor."

"*Comment?*"

"Don't you see? If Trevor's murder is connected to Roger's as I'm sure it is, then finding the reason why Violet killed Trevor will lead us to why she killed Roger."

An hour later after each of the six people in the Abbey went to their separate rooms for the night, Maggie looked out the bedroom window and saw the bright lights of a car coming down the front drive.

"Laurent," she said, pulling on her robe. "Someone is coming!"

Laurent was still dressed and out the door. He turned to hold a finger up to Maggie.

"Stay here," he commanded.

"But Laurent, I…"

He pointed to where the bedroom hall became a balcony over the foyer—the same place Maggie had stood when she saw Laurent and Gabrielle arguing the day before.

"*Bon,*" he said. "Watch from there."

Without waiting to see if she'd obey him, he turned and went downstairs. Gabrielle must have heard too because she came up the back stairs.

The pounding on the front door seemed to reverberate through the whole mansion. Laurent pulled the door open to reveal four detectives and four police officers on the threshold.

They pushed past Laurent who immediately went to bar them entrance to the stairs but they were not interested in going upstairs.

Will and Annette ran down the hallway and joined Maggie on the balcony.

"What is happening?" Gabrielle shrieked as the cops walked past her to the door that led to the kitchen.

"We are here, Mademoiselle," Detective Chief Inspector Bailey said to Gabrielle, "with a warrant for the arrest of Violet Cunningham on the suspicion of murder in the first degree."

Susan Kiernan-Lewis

48

Pushing past Annette and Will who stood with their mouths open, Maggie rushed back into her bedroom and quickly pulled on jeans and a sweatshirt. She ran downstairs just as the police were bringing Violet—her hands handcuffed behind her—through the grand foyer.

Laurent stood beside Gabrielle who was wringing her hands and speaking rapidly in French to anyone who would listen.

Maggie joined them as the front door swung open and both Jill and Madeline entered the foyer ahead of a uniformed policeman.

What was going on?

Gabrielle pushed past Maggie and went to Madeline and embraced her. Laurent put an arm around Maggie.

Violet looked so small. She stood between the two policemen who held her elbows as if even handcuffed she might somehow manage to escape. Her eyes were wide and stunned. Exactly how anyone would feel who was sleeping one minute, Maggie thought, and then thrust into her worst nightmare the next.

CI Bailey turned to speak to Jill.

"I am sure you were told not to leave the country," he said briskly.

"But I still don't understand why," Jill said. Her face was flushed and every hint of makeup was gone. She looked tired and years older than when Maggie had last seen her. "Or is this all for show?" She pointed to the quaking figure of Violet standing between the two policemen.

Anastasia came through the front door next and hesitated as if surprised to see everyone up and about. Maggie had never seen her look so disheveled. Her makeup was smeared across her face. Her hair—normally twisted up into elaborate curls—was held back in a simple ponytail. She marched over to Bailey.

Maggie wanted to ask her how Nigel was. She wondered if Anastasia looked this bad because her son had died. But would she really be driving around the countryside if he had?

"Are you arresting my kitchen maid for the murder of my husband?" Anastasia said in a strident voice.

Jeez, would she never stop? The same thought must have formed in Bailey's head too because he gave Anastasia a disdainful look.

"Miss Cunningham is coming with us," he said, "for questioning."

"So she is not under arrest?" Madeline asked.

"She was sleeping with Trevor," Anastasia blurted out. Her lips trembled as she spoke. "Have you discovered *that* yet?"

Maggie exchanged a look with Laurent. The words were silent but unmistakable between them: *Motive.*

"And she stole my tiara," Anastasia said.

"You don't know that for sure," Jill said in exasperation. "Besides, wasn't it recovered?"

"How did you know that?" Anastasia said.

"So it was recovered?" Maggie said. "Why didn't you tell anyone?"

"Because that wasn't the point," Anastasia hissed. "She did the crime. She can't undo it by giving it back."

Bailey turned to one of his men.

"Go upstairs with Mrs. Bentley and get the tiara," he said tiredly.

"What? Why?" Anastasia moved in front of the policeman as if she would block him.

Bailey shrugged. "Unless you are not going to report the theft? But if you are, we'll need it as evidence as we go forward with the investigation."

"I...well, there's no point now, is there?" Anastasia said, wringing her hands.

"As you wish." Bailey was about to turn away when Violet shouted: "Lady Bentley was sleeping with Trev! Ask her about *that*!"

Violet, no, Maggie thought. *Everyone will only see it as another reason why you'd want to kill Trevor.*

"Horrible creature!" Anastasia said as she turned back to Bailey. "Did I mention I sent her to the barn before the hunt? To the barn where Trevor was. Alone?"

Bailey narrowed his eyes. "No, this is the first I'm hearing of this."

Maggie's mouth fell open.

"Except she never made it to the barn," Maggie said. Laurent squeezed her shoulder in a warning gesture but she shrugged him off. "I told Violet to go back to the Abbey and I would speak to Trevor."

"It was later," Anastasia said to Maggie, her eyes glinting with threat. "*After* everyone had left for the hunt. I personally watched her enter the barn."

"Violet doesn't have enough on her plate, Anastasia?" Jill said, shaking her head in disgust.

"People who do bad things should be punished," Anastasia said imperiously.

I entirely agree, Maggie thought.

Bailey gestured to his men and they walked out of the Abbey half dragging Violet between them.

"We will leave you all for a second time this evening," he said to everyone gathered in the foyer. "Again, let me remind you to stay indoors and *under no circumstances* are you to go to the stables or anywhere you see the yellow crime scene tape." He turned to Anastasia.

"Mrs. Bentley, if you would be so good as to come with me."

"What? Why in the world for?"

"I believe because of your son's injuries we failed to get a complete statement from you. I'm afraid I must insist." He held out his hand and Anastasia brushed past him in frustration and stormed out the front door.

Bailey looked at Maggie as if trying to make up his mind. He glanced at Laurent's face before shrugging and turning to leave the mansion.

※ ※ ※ ※ ※

"Is there a reason why you cannot allow a single silent space to go unfilled?"

Laurent stood in their bedroom staring out into the night. The rain had begun again.

Maggie was already in bed. She knew he wasn't happy about the questions she'd brought up tonight and she had to admit it had looked for a moment like Bailey was thinking of dragging her to Oxford too along with Anastasia.

"I just hated to hear Anastasia lying like that and making it worse for Violet," Maggie said.

"The police will discover all of Anastasia's lies," Laurent said, turning to look at Maggie. "*Without* your help."

He stripped off his clothes and slipped into bed with her.

"Any word from Danielle?" he asked.

"I talked to her briefly when I said goodnight to the kids. She said there was nothing new on the *destroy-Maggie's-life* front."

"You will need to deal with that when we get back."

"Haven't I said that all along over and over again? Gosh, Laurent, you're worse than Danielle. And *she's* an old woman."

He pulled her in close.

"We leave first thing in the morning," he said.

"I can't wait."

"And you are done with horses."

"Look, Laurent. About that. I know it was a terrible day…"

"No," Laurent said firmly. "No horses. Not for you, not for Mila. *Non.*"

"You're just upset right now."

"I'm putting my feet down, Maggie."

There was no way she could argue this. Not tonight. Not with a horse running amok somewhere in the countryside and her with at least one bruised rib to show for her day. She couldn't even blame it on the dog attack.

They were silent for a moment, enjoying the sounds of the rain light against the windowpane. Laurent turned off the bedside light.

"You were right about Violet," he said. "You said all she lacked was a motive."

"Yeah, well nothing says motive better than finding out your boyfriend is screwing your boss." She gave Laurent a slow kiss on the mouth.

"So now it is done," he said.

"It is," Maggie said. "Except for one small detail."

"And what is that, *ma petite?*"

Maggie rested her head on his chest and sighed loudly.

"Violet didn't kill Roger."

Susan Kiernan-Lewis

49

Laurent sat up in bed and snapped the light back on.

"*Quoi*? But I thought you said—"

"I know what I said, but when I gave it more thought I realized that what I overheard in the hallway was Trevor threatening to reveal what he knew unless he got money."

"Yes," Laurent said impatiently, "I understand the concept of blackmail."

"Well, Violet had no money! He said *five hundred quid*. So he couldn't have been talking to her."

"Then *qui*? Who else was *not* in the salon when you came downstairs immediately afterward?"

"That is the million dollar question, isn't it?"

Laurent frowned. "Jill and Will were both there. And Gabrielle and Violet."

"But not Anastasia, Nigel or Annette."

"So our murderer must be one of those three."

"I'm pretty sure Annette was in the barn at the time."

"That leaves Anastasia and Nigel."

"It also occurred to me that we are letting Anastasia off the hook just because she made us think she was too dainty to go into a barn."

"If you are intent on killing someone, a barn might be overcome."

"Exactly."

"And Anastasia doesn't have an alibi for Roger's murder."

"*And* she was sleeping with Trevor."

"So it could be Anastasia. What about Nigel?"

"I have no idea where he was when Trevor was blackmailing the killer but everybody knows he was in the Abbey the night of the murder. *And* he hated Roger."

Laurent shook his head. "So the police have arrested the wrong person. Again."

"Did you get a chance to talk to Madeline tonight?" Maggie asked.

"*Non.* I do not know what I would say."

"Well, at least she's off the hook."

He nodded but didn't turn the light off.

"I was a bad friend to him," Laurent said.

"Oh, Laurent, no," Maggie said. "That's not true."

"I was so happy and I had no time for him."

Maggie touched Laurent's face.

"He knew how you felt about him, Laurent. You lived different lives and he understood that."

"He wanted what I have."

"I know."

"He gave you to me."

"And I'll love him forever for that. If he didn't share the same first name of a certain French detective back in Aix-en-Provence, I'd happily name our next child after him. As long as it's a boy, of course."

Laurent smiled. "Our next child?"

"*No*, I'm not saying I'm pregnant. I'm pretty sure I'm not. I'm just saying Roger will always be a part of us and our family. He wouldn't want you to feel guilty about how things ended between you two, Laurent. He'd hate that."

"*Je sais.*"

Grimacing past the pain in her side, she leaned in and kissed him. They weren't there yet. But as far as being able to look back at their friendship with Roger and accepting how it ended Maggie was pretty sure they were both well on their way.

Maggie waited until she heard the telltale sound of Laurent's snores. She'd covertly set the alarm on her cellphone just in case but she needn't have. She was too wired to sleep.

As she got out of bed, careful not to wake Laurent, Maggie felt the anticipation of her night's work humming in her chest. What she'd said to Laurent was true. Every bit of it.

Violet wasn't the killer.

But after she'd seen his exhaustion and his eagerness to be done with everything here—even, if she had to guess, at the expense of the truth—she knew she couldn't suggest the rest of it to him. Not yet. Not without proof.

She pulled on her jeans and sweatshirt again and laced up her sneakers. She wished they were waterproof. There was no doubt they'd be coated with mud—or worse—by the time the night was over. But it would be worth it if she could catch the killer tonight.

She put her cellphone on vibrate and slipped it into the pocket of her rain jacket, then opened the bedroom door and looked out in the hall. Since she knew Jill could be outside at this hour, it wouldn't do to be too eager. The whole point was surprise.

It occurred to her that when she sleuthed with Grace she never really worried about protecting Grace. They both just focused on finding the killer.

She had no idea how other husband and wife detective teams worked together but between Laurent wanting to punch anyone who looked askance at Maggie, and both of them holding back information that could reveal the killer—perhaps it was just as well that this was their last case together.

Because what she *hadn't* mentioned to Laurent tonight was the one thing that seemed to be of interest only to her. And that was the fact that the bucket still hadn't been found.

When the police were examining the scene Maggie had stood glued to the salon's south-facing window and watched every baggie and every wheelbarrow that the police had carried from the barn. But nothing looked remotely like the missing bucket. The police had even impounded Will and Annette's horse trailer after thoroughly examining it. No bucket.

Not that Maggie expected them to find it. She was sure the killer would've hidden it a bit further away from the crime scene even if there had been no time to dispose of it properly.

Until tonight.

It had to be tonight. Only Maggie and the killer knew that simple fact. Once the bucket was found—unless Maggie was dead or incapacitated—she would press to have it forensically examined and the killer would be revealed.

Once the bucket was found.

Maggie crept silently into the dark hall and held her breath as if that might silence the soft noises made by her footfall. It was faster to go to the barn by way of the bedroom hall and then down the back stairs—but it was riskier too.

Maggie needed to catch the killer in the act of trying to destroy the bucket. What she did not need to do was meet the killer in the hall. They could always claim they were merely having trouble sleeping.

She walked down the main staircase, mindful of any creaking floorboards she'd discovered in the three days since she'd been in the Abbey. She was tempted to snap on her cellphone light, but resisted.

The foyer was nearly as large as a gymnasium and almost as empty. The light could be seen too easily from a distance. She felt her way across the foyer to the narrow hallway that led to the basement staircase and finally the anterior exit.

The bucket was still here somewhere at the Abbey.

The cops worked the barn today. They would do the grounds tomorrow.

That leaves only tonight to get rid of it.

As Maggie moved, she was ever mindful of sounds—behind her, in front of her, above her where the upper bedrooms hallway opened up in various spots to overlook the grand foyer. She thought of what she hadn't told Laurent

The fact was, there was approximately thirty minutes from the time Maggie saw Trevor alive as he was helping her mount her horse for the hunt to the time when she was at the caretaker's cottage holding Nigel's bleeding body.

It would have been impossible for Nigel to have been at the barn smashing Trevor over the head with a shovel before racing back to the caretaker's cottage in time to fight off his own knife-wielding assailant.

Nigel hadn't killed Trevor.

Maggie pushed open the exterior door just a crack and peered out. The rain was light but insistent and it was cold.

The painful truth was there wasn't just one person who fit all the criteria for motive, opportunity and means for both murders. That was what had confused Maggie for so long. She'd wanted the pieces to fit neatly.

The person who killed Trevor must also be the person who killed Roger.

Because why kill Trevor unless you were in danger of being revealed as Roger's murderer?

Why indeed?

How about if someone *you loved* was in danger of being revealed as Roger's murderer?

Maggie stepped outside and ran silently through the stable courtyard to the paddock. One of the horses nickered loudly. There were no security lights on this side of the stable. And because of the horses, no motion sensors either.

Maggie touched her cellphone for comfort and slipped under the wooden slat rails into the horse enclosure.

There were only four horses in the paddock. Maggie fought down a pang of anguish at the thought of Diva still wandering the countryside or dead in a ditch somewhere.

She heard sounds of muffled movement—guarded and careful—coming from the far side of the paddock—where the manure pile was. Maggie smiled grimly.

That's exactly where *she* would've stored the bucket for safekeeping too.

A low whine came to her from the east side of the paddock closest to the stable door. Glancing in that direction, Maggie could see the faint flutter of crime scene tape.

Another whine, louder than the first, came from the shared crate of the two guard dogs. They'd either seen or smelled her.

The sounds from the manure pile stopped.

Maggie crept through the horses to the other side of the paddock. She knew she had to move quickly now.

The killer knew she was here.

Maggie climbed the paddock fence and snapped on her cellphone light, illuminating the pile of horse manure twenty feet away.

"I see you found the missing bucket," Maggie said.

50

Laurent wasn't sure what had awakened him up but when he reached out for Maggie's side of the bed and felt only her pillow, he knew it was her absence.

He sat up and listened. She wasn't in the room or the bathroom.

There was a part of him that wasn't surprised. Cursing, he got out of bed and reached for his jeans.

He'd known there was something unfinished in her manner when they'd said goodnight. He'd just been so tired, so ready for it to all be over, he hadn't pushed it. As he pulled on his sweater he went to the window.

A half moon murkily illuminated the grounds. From their bedroom window at the front of the Abbey, he could make out nothing in the dark shapes below.

Will she have gone to the basement?

Surely not outside?

Of course she's outside. She is looking for the damn bucket.

Laurent opened the bedroom door and slipped into the dark hall. Again he paused to listen.

Down the hall, he saw a shaft of light from an open bedroom door. He walked slowly towards it.

Whose room?

Laurent reached the door just as Will emerged.

"Oh!" Will said, taking two steps back into the bedroom.

Laurent followed him into the room and looked around. The bed had not been slept in. Will was fully dressed.

"Going somewhere?" Laurent said.

"No," Will said. "Not at all. What are you doing up?"

Will was nervous. His eyes jumped around the room and past Laurent. He wanted to leave the room. Badly.

Where was Annette?

"I am looking for my wife," Laurent said. "I thought you might know where she was."

"Bloody hell," Will said as he rubbed his hands nervously against his slacks. "Why the devil would I know where she is?"

Maggie had said there were three suspects. And Will wasn't one of them. He wasn't one of them because he had been in the salon precisely when Trevor was delivering his blackmail threat to the killer. So why is Will acting so guilty?

Will glanced around the room at the drawers and closets as if there were something hidden in them he wanted—something he might—if given the opportunity—make a grab for.

Laurent put his hands on his hips and blocked the doorway.

"She's obviously not here," Will said, licking his lips, his eyes darting around the room, "I'll ask you to get the devil out of my room."

"*Non.*"

Laurent wasn't sure why he said it. He only knew that if Will wanted out so badly, he was pretty sure he shouldn't let him go.

"Fine. Have it your way," Will said, reaching into his jacket and turning away as if suddenly disinterested.

Will stopped, turned abruptly and launched himself at Laurent.

In his right hand, he held a dagger.

Laurent blocked the arm with the knife and heard it thud to the carpeted floor. He backhanded Will across the face, knocking him to the floor.

Laurent picked up the knife. Will crouched on the floor, a stream of blood pouring from his broken lip. The look he gave Laurent was one of guilt and fear.

And all at once Laurent knew he was looking at Roger's murderer. Although he had no real evidence to support it, the knowledge came to him as swiftly and surely as a signed deposition.

"You killed Roger," Laurent said.

"It was an accident!" Will said as he stood up. "I didn't mean to. We argued and he pushed me! I pushed back, rather harder than I expected to. I was just so angry...and Roger fell backward against the wall. I had no idea he was that bloody fragile!"

Laurent listened and saw it in his head like an old time newsreel. Roger's last moments. Roger's sad, desperate last moments.

"His eyes went all funny," Will said, talking faster now, "and he started to fall. You have to believe me! I didn't mean to hurt him. I didn't!" Will wiped the blood from his chin and shook his head.

"But he wasn't dead," Laurent said. "He was only knocked unconscious."

"Well, I didn't know that, did I?" Will said, his eyes wild with fright. "I panicked. I saw the open chute and I put him into it. I just needed some time to think."

"How did you get out of the Abbey without being seen?"

"There are a couple of secret passageways. I took the one nearest to me and was in my car and gone within minutes."

"And no one saw you. Except Trevor," Laurent said.

It all fit. All except for the blackmail piece. Will had been in the salon with Laurent at the time Trevor was blackmailing Roger's killer. So it couldn't have been Will upstairs.

But it could have been his wife.

A heavy weight seemed to descend on Laurent's shoulders as he watched Will. A *pathetique*, mealy-mouthed small-time crook who took advantage of Roger's guilt and weakened state, then panicked and let Madeline and then Violet take the fall for what he'd done.

It was all Laurent could do not to heave the little *merde* out the Abbey window right here and now.

Suddenly Will looked past Laurent's head. His face contorted into a mask of shock.

"Annette, no!" he screamed.

Laurent turned his head. He saw no one behind him. But the crushing pain that erupted in the back of his head turned the room to a spinning eddy of agony.

And then everything fell into black nothingness.

51

Annette stood in the beam of Maggie's light, stood at the crest of the dung heap, the bucket clutched in her arms. Behind Annette in the distance, Maggie could see the rays of the half moon shimmering on the rippling surface of the Abbey's fishpond.

"Where are you going with the bucket, Annette? Because if you're thinking of throwing it in the pond you should know that won't erase your DNA." She hoped Annette wouldn't know enough science to know that was probably not true.

"I don't know what you're talking about."

"I mean it's pretty hard to claim ignorance with Diva's bucket in your hands," Maggie said. "But I would dearly love to know why you did it."

Annette walked toward Maggie. She was wearing the rubber boots that Maggie had worn all day. A warning sensation stirred in Maggie's stomach when she saw them.

"Don't take it personally," Annette said. "I would have done Jill's horse but I thought a less experienced rider on a runaway horse would create more havoc in the field. Plus, Trevor said he thought it was you who overheard us in the hallway. Neat and tidy, I say. No loose ends."

"You were trying to disrupt the hunt? But why?" Maggie said in a disbelieving voice.

"Surely you didn't think the best the saboteurs could do was *Nigel*?" Annette laughed and set the bucket down. She pulled out a rag and began cleaning her hands.

"Once I talked Jill into putting a word in your husband's shell-like to let you ride in the hunt, it was all set. At the very least,

I knew we'd get major headlines if an American got hurt in the hunt," Annette said. "You didn't have to die. You paralyzed from the neck down would have worked just as well."

"Sorry to disappoint. I sprained my wrist."

"A pity. I was looking forward to visiting you in hospital."

"And Nigel? You came upon him on horseback at the caretaker's cottage, didn't you?"

"Saw the horse prints, did you? Yes, well, I knew the wanker was going to lie down on us. He only ever did it to get attention from Roger. Can you believe how pathetic that is? If I hadn't come up on him when I did the bomb wouldn't have been set."

"You stabbed him."

"Took him by total surprise. You see, it was never about the foxes with Nigel. With Roger gone, he just didn't care any more."

"That was you talking to Trevor in the hallway the day of the hunt, wasn't it?"

"Clever girl."

"But since Trevor was talking blackmail to the *killer* and since *you* weren't at the Abbey the night Roger was killed, he must have been talking about Will."

"Trevor was sneaking out of a spare bedroom where he'd been having it off with Anastasia when he saw Will pushing Roger's body through the chute."

All the pieces were falling neatly, painfully into place.

"Why did Will kill him?" Just the words felt like lead weights in Maggie's stomach.

"He claims it was an accident—although he certainly had enough reason."

"Wasn't Roger your uncle?"

"Yes, he was the uncle who was also the reason my father died in prison and left me an orphan. And he was the uncle who put me in foster homes because he couldn't be bothered. He was that uncle."

"Sounds like you were doing pretty well with your own motives," Maggie said.

"In any case, they argued about the business. Will got angry and gave him a bit of a shove. Roger wasn't too steady on his feet. He hit his head and went down." Annette shrugged. "Will stuffed him down the laundry chute and raced back home. Bob's your uncle. And because Anastasia had her own secrets to protect she didn't know Roger was missing until the afternoon of the next day. By then we all had our alibis firmly in place. Except for me, of course. I wasn't even at the Abbey the night Roger was killed."

"But you were when Trevor was killed. I saw you mounted in the front lawn of the Abbey just as the hunt started."

"When the rest of the field left, I held back. You might not have noticed. I saw you had your hands full with Diva. I dismounted and went straight to the barn."

"Where you killed Trevor."

Annette picked the bucket back up and stepped down from the manure pile toward Maggie.

"Well, you heard him!" Annette said. "The bugger was blackmailing us! Anyway, after I sorted him out—"

"And by *sorted him out*, you mean…"

"Yes, petal, I mean I killed him. You Americans are so literal about everything. Anyway, *after I killed Trevor*, I remounted and went straight to the caretaker's cottage where—just as I suspected —Nigel was sitting there staring at the bomb."

"And if Nigel survives long enough to name you as his attacker?"

"First, he was stabbed with his own knife. Suicide much? And of course I was wearing riding gloves. In any case, it'll be his word against mine."

"Your word won't hold much credibility when I have Diva tested to prove you tried to cause an accident."

Annette shook the bucket.

"You are obsessed with this bucket! Trust me, nobody is going to have Diva tested…even if she's ever found. The horse belongs to the Abbey. By the time you get a judge to issue a warrant for the test—if you even can—the poison will be gone from her system."

"Which just leaves the feed bucket," Maggie said. "And unless you can destroy it between now and when I walk over there and knock you on your ass and take it from you, the DNA traces will still be there to prove you drugged the horse I was riding."

"I love the way Americans talk. So tough. You want the bucket? By all means, come and get it."

"On second thought," Maggie said, holding up her phone. "I'll just call the police and let them deal with you."

"By all means call them. I'll tell them how I awoke because I heard the sound of something going on in the paddock and when I came out to investigate, I saw *you* out here trying to get rid of the bucket."

"Why would I drug my own horse?"

"I don't pretend to understand how Americans behave or why. I'm sure any British jury would agree with me."

"Good point. But since most Brits watch American TV, I bet they'll have no trouble understanding this."

Maggie pushed a button on her cellphone and held it up so Annette could hear.

Annette's voice came out of the small speaker: *"...after I killed Trevor, I remounted and went straight to the caretaker's cottage where—just as I suspected—Nigel was sitting there staring at the bomb."*

The color drained from Annette's face and she took a step toward Maggie.

"That won't hold up in a court of law!"

"Oh, I think it will but all I really need is to give the cops reason to dig in your direction. Once they start matching all the forensic evidence, my work will be done."

The crack of a stick snapping on the ground behind Maggie made her whirl around with her flashlight to see a figure approaching. Maggie scrambled down from the fence, careful not to turn her back on Annette until she saw that it didn't matter.

It was Will and he had a handgun pointed at her.

52

"Sorry to ruin your best laid," Will said. He was bleeding from his lip. "Come on, Annette. It's time to go."

"The cops took the trailer," Annette said as she stepped toward him.

"The American and her husband have kindly offered us the loan of their rental," he said. "The keys are in my pocket."

Maggie couldn't take her eyes off the gun pointed at her. Its barrel gleamed in the moonlight.

"What are we going to do about her? She knows you killed Roger. And there's still the bucket!"

"We need to leave right now, love," Will said. "Bring the bucket and get her phone. Come on, Annette. We need to *go*."

"Will, we can't run. What about the boys?"

"We don't have a choice!"

"Yes, we do! Shoot her and I'll say I found her out here trying to throw the bucket in the pond to destroy evidence. We fought and you came upon us. At worst it'll be manslaughter. You won't serve any time!"

Will licked his lips and looked at Annette. "Will they believe that?"

Listening to them plan to murder her made Maggie's fingers go icy cold. Why was Will's mouth bleeding?

"Does anyone know you're out here?" Maggie asked.

"What?" He looked at Maggie and then Annette. Annette seemed to see his face for the first time.

"You're bleeding," Annette said. "Did something happen in the house?"

"Does it matter?" Will said angrily.

"Yes, it matters! Do you intend to shoot everyone in the Abbey?" Annette said. "Who knows you're out here?"

"Will you shut up and get the bloody phone from her? Will you just do this one bloody thing?"

Still holding the bucket in her arms, Annette turned to grab Maggie's phone. Maggie held out the phone to Annette and then let go of it a split second before Annette touched it.

"Oh!" Annette said as she watched the phone drop into the mud.

Maggie grabbed the hard plastic rubber bucket from Annette's hands and smashed her hard in the face with it. With a groan, Annette buckled to her knees.

"Annette!" Will stood between Maggie and the Abbey. He looked at his wife on her knees in the mud. Blood was streaming from between her fingers that she held to her face.

For Maggie, there was nowhere to run, nothing to hide behind. She turned but hadn't taken a single step when she heard the gunshot. The impact knocked her forward. The bucket flew from her arms.

The ground rushed up and slammed into her face in a nauseating assault of manure and mud.

She felt the pain vibrating through her, pushing her deep into the earth, into her own grave. Her breath came in shallow gasps as she waited for the final blow that would send her over the edge into the abyss.

Then, like an escalating buzzing in her head, she heard the roar of the ocean as it rose up to pummel her. The sound grew louder and louder.

But the wave didn't crash on top of her.

The roar wasn't the ocean. It was too real and too near. It was the sound of a pack of wolves tearing apart their prey. Snapping and snarling.

"Maggie!"

She used every ounce of energy she had to twist her body in the direction of Laurent's voice. A glimmer of light over the trees told her morning was coming. Then she saw the dogs.

And under it all the sound of a human scream.

The dogs had Will on the ground.

Maggie got to her knees and watched Laurent vault over the top of the paddock fence. He skirted the skirmish on the ground with the dogs and ran to Maggie.

"Call them off! Call them off!" Will screamed.

Laurent knelt by Maggie's side. "Are you all right, *chèrie*?"

"For the love of God!" Will screamed.

Maggie tried to answer him. Her throat was dry.

"Maximus! Demon!" Jill shouted.

Maggie saw Jill standing at the fence in her bathrobe.

"Laurent, he has a gun," Maggie said breathlessly.

Laurent picked up the gun from the ground beside Will. Then he returned to help Maggie to her feet. Her ribs definitely felt broken this time, every breath an agony. But there was no blood.

Will squirmed on the ground in pain, his clothes ripped and torn. He was bleeding from bites on his hands, arms and legs. Annette sat beside him moaning and rocking.

Jill called her dogs to her and then knelt to carefully examine each of them as if they were the injured party. Maggie picked up her phone from the ground.

"We need to call the cops," Maggie said.

"Jill already did," Laurent said.

"What made you think to open the dogs' crate?"

"It was Jill's idea. She knew they'd get here before we did."

"You're hurt!" Maggie said, touching the side of Laurent's face where the blood ran down to his chin.

"*Ce n'est rien*," he said, holding her tightly against him. "Nothing at all."

Susan Kiernan-Lewis

53

The sun was up by the time the police arrived. Gabrielle and Madeline had just come outside in their bathrobes to see what was happening.

Maggie, Laurent and Jill had given their statements and were standing by the front door.   Will and Annette were both being loaded onto stretchers onto an ambulance.

Detective Chief Inspector Bailey waved his hands at Madeline and Gabrielle.

"Go back inside," he said. "If we need to talk to you we will."

The two women hurried back into the Abbey.

"There are already enough people tramping around my crime scene," Bailey grumbled as he walked over to where Maggie and Laurent stood.

"Will another ambulance be coming?" Laurent asked with his arm around Maggie.

"Laurent, I'm fine," she said.

"Well, *are* you fine?" Bailey asked, peering into her face. "Or not?"

"I am."

Jill snorted. "*She* didn't get shot," she said. "The *bucket* she was holding got shot."

Maggie made a face at Jill. "It still wasn't very pleasant."

"But you hardly need a doctor," Jill said, rolling her eyes.

"Isn't that what I just said?"

"Are you finished with us, Chief *Inspecteur*?" Laurent asked impatiently.

"For now."

"We have a flight back to Marseilles today," Laurent said.

"Yes, yes. We have all your information. You may return to France."

Bailey looked up at the looming façade of the massive estate. "I'll be glad to see the back of this place, I can tell you." He turned and went to his car. Within moments the car pulled away.

Maggie looked at Laurent. "Did he say when they'd release Violet?"

"He said she is free to go."

"They probably would have let her go even if we hadn't caught Will and Annette tonight," Jill said. "I'm sure their evidence was circumstantial at best."

Maggie decided to let the whole *we caught Will and Annette comment* pass. At least for now.

"How do you figure?" Maggie asked.

"I assume Violet went to the stable during the hunt to confront Trevor and found his body."

"And was probably less careful about not leaving behind evidence of her visit," Maggie said.

"By *less careful* you mean than you and Laurent were when you discovered the body before me?" Jill said giving Laurent a hard look.

"Gosh, don't be a such a sore loser, Jill," Maggie said. "I still have the bite marks on my shoulder from your attack dog."

"As I've told you a hundred times already, I had no idea he'd actually bite you."

"What did you think he'd do? Give me a shampoo?"

"Both of you, *arrêtez*," Laurent growled. "My head hurts and you are making it worse."

They turned to watch the police processing the newly enlarged crime scene. For a few moments, no one spoke.

"So exactly *why* did Will kill Roger?" Jill asked.

"Roger learned that Will was skimming off the top in the foundation," Maggie said. "That's why they fought. Will said it was an accident. And maybe it was. Anyway, that's his defense."

"And Trevor?"

"Trevor saw Will kill Roger. He was blackmailing him. Annette did the honors for Trevor."

"I always thought Annette was such a wimp."

"Yeah, because you're such a good judge of character."

"What about you? Accusing me of trying to kill you!"

"I still think it's awfully coincidental that you led me to the very place that was wired to blow up."

"You just can't let that go, can you?"

Maggie ignored her. She thought about the long day ahead of them and the flight back to France. If she knew her husband, he'd be making breakfast for everyone soon. She tugged on his sleeve.

"How's your head?" she asked. "We probably could have used the medic to make sure you don't fall asleep tonight and never wake up again."

"I am fine."

"That's what Natasha Richardson said," Maggie said ominously.

"I wouldn't worry too much about the kind of damage that *Will* could do," Jill said sarcastically.

"Well, Laurent did lose consciousness," Maggie reminded her.

Minutes after Will had hit Laurent and fled, Jill had come upon a groggy Laurent in the doorway of Will and Annette's bedroom.

"Our Laurent has a very hard head," Jill said, smiling at Laurent.

Maggie bit her lip. If she offered any kind of retort at all Jill would just know she'd struck a nerve. Maggie wouldn't give her the satisfaction.

"I have another question," Jill said. "Why did Anastasia say she saw Violet go in the stable? Was she lying? Why was she trying to implicate Violet?"

"I wondered about that myself," Maggie said, "and then it occurred to me that Anastasia probably had told Trevor secrets and so when it looked like the cops had Violet for the murder Anastasia jumped on to help make it stick."

"Do you know any secrets she was afraid Trevor might have told Violet?"

"Not a clue."

❈❈❈❈❈

Maggie had been right about the breakfast.

Between Gabrielle—who displayed a much improved countenance beyond what Maggie had ever witnessed in the woman before—and Laurent, the spread for breakfast in the servants' kitchen was impressive.

There were scrambled eggs with chives and sausage, Moroccan baked eggs, blueberry pancakes with maple syrup and a tray of caramel apple cinnamon rolls the fragrance of which drifted through the whole Abbey.

Laurent even invited the policemen who were working the crime scene to join them. And while none took him up on his offer, they all went about their work with mugs of French pressed coffee and egg and bacon sandwiches—Laurent's version of the portable Croque Madame.

Jill and Maggie sat with Madeline at the long servants' table while Laurent and Gabrielle worked shoulder to shoulder in the kitchen.

As Maggie took the last pancake she noticed that Jill had put two cinnamon rolls on her plate. That was at least some consolation.

"So I guess you're ready for all of us to leave," Maggie said to Madeline.

"In truth, I am," Madeline said. "Nothing personal, of course. Gabrielle will collect Violet this morning and I think the three of us will enjoy a quiet week here with nothing to do but recover from what we've been through."

Maggie turned to Jill. "Don't you have a job or something to go to?" she asked.

"I don't, no," Jill said, biting into a cinnamon roll. A thick curl of caramel fell onto the table. Jill wiped it up with her finger which she then licked clean.

"You're welcome to stay, Jill," Madeline said stiffly.

"I appreciate the offer, Madeline. But no thanks. When are they bringing Diva back?" she said as if eager to change the subject.

Diva had been located in a nearby farmer's pasture. She was filthy but otherwise unharmed. As soon as Madeline got the call, she made arrangements for the mare to be trailered back to the Abbey and scheduled the local vet to ensure there were no ill effects from her experience.

"What about Anastasia?" Maggie asked. She hated to be the one to mention the fly in the soup but Anastasia was bound to make her way back to the Abbey before long.

"She's been delayed in Oxford, as it happens," Madeline said with a small smile.

"Delayed?" Jill asked, her eyebrows shooting up. "How so?" Laurent and Gabrielle both came to the table and sat down with mugs of coffee.

"It seems her attorney contacted Anastasia with some rather bad news, I'm afraid," Madeline said.

"Not about Nigel?" Maggie said.

"No, while he will be charged with felony mischief and destruction of property, I was informed this morning that it is expected he will make a full recovery."

That's good, Maggie thought. *Besides it means he can testify against Annette.*

"Well, what's the bad news then?" Jill said impatiently.

Madeline's eyes filled with tears. "Bad news only for Anastasia," she said. "It appears a more recent will has been discovered."

Maggie watched as Madeline looked at Laurent. He smiled.

No way.

"A new will?" Maggie said to Laurent. "You knew about this?"

"Roger mailed it to me nine weeks ago," he said.

"The package that's been waiting at the Arles post office?"

"*Oui.* I had Jean-Luc open it and send a copy to Anastasia's attorney and the executor for Roger's estate."

"Well, you have us on tenterhooks. Is it very different from the one before?" Jill asked.

"*Oui*," Laurent said with a smile. "Very different."

"Roger bequeathed almost his entire fortune to the Home for Abandoned Children in Covington."

"No wonder Anastasia's still in Oxford. She must be freaking out. What about his half of the Abbey?"

"He left that to me," Madeline said.

"Oh, Madeline," Maggie said. "That's great. I'm so glad for you."

"There's more," Laurent said.

"He bequeathed a cash gift to one other person," Madeline said, nodding at Gabrielle. "In the amount of eight hundred and fifty five thousand euros."

The exact amount he'd bilked out of her father, Maggie thought.

"Well done, Roger," she said softly.

An hour later Gabrielle had gone to Oxford to pick up Violet. Laurent was loading their suitcases in the rental car while Madeline and Jill stood chatting with Maggie on the front drive. Jill's dogs cavorted nearby.

Maggie shook Madeline's hand. "I'm glad it all worked out," Maggie said.

"Yes," Madeline said, nodding in Laurent's direction. "For all of us. You are of course welcome to visit at any time."

"Thanks," Maggie said. "I'm pretty sure the kids will love it once they're a little older."

"We're changing it to a straight up B&B, you know," Madeline said. "None of this toffee-nosed upper crust stuff. Just riding with a proper spa thrown in and of course world class cuisine. I already told Laurent he has a job here if he ever gets tired of running a vineyard."

Laurent walked over and embraced Madeline. To Jill he nodded and said, *"Au revoir et bonne chance."*

As she and Laurent got in the car, Maggie couldn't help but wonder why he was wishing Jill luck.

"You know, Jill," Maggie said, "it did occur to me that we probably could have solved this a lot faster if we'd worked together."

"Actually, darling, that thought occurred to me too," Jill said.

"Yeah, I agree," Maggie said with a grin. "It would never have worked."

⁂ ⁂ ⁂ ⁂ ⁂

At the departure gate at Heathrow, Maggie and Laurent put in one last phone call to St-Buvard to talk to the children and hear

Jean-Luc's news that a famous American chef had moved into the village.

They sat for a moment in the relative peace of their gate before boarding began. Maggie could tell Laurent was in good spirits and more than ready to be home again.

"What will you do about Madame Roche?" Laurent said as he flipped through a magazine about the twenty best grapes in the world. "How will you make amends?"

"I don't know that I even will," Maggie said. She checked to make sure she had enough snacks and magazines for the two-hour flight to Marseilles. "I'm not sure I have to be pals with everyone. I've decided that people are allowed not to like me."

"That is blackmail, yes?"

She looked at him in surprise. "How do you figure that?"

"Madame Roche and her husband want the benefits of what your travel blog can do for them, yes?"

Maggie wondered where he was going with this.

"Their only crime is that they do not personally like you."

"And vice versa," Maggie said quickly.

Laurent gave her an admonishing look.

"Must everyone please Maggie to receive her favors?"

"Isn't that generally how the world works?"

"Not in a village the size of ours, no, *ma chérie*."

"Are you suggesting I just let anyone and everyone join the guild?"

Laurent smiled at her. "I think. Perhaps. Yes."

Now she felt completely discombobulated. She hadn't really had much time to figure out exactly how she was going to deal with the Madame Roche problem back home but she'd pretty much assumed strategy, planning and carefully thought out tactics would be involved.

Laurent was suggesting an altogether different approach. And one that was nowhere as easy.

"I know why you and Grace do this now," he said, oblivious of Maggie's consternation.

"Why?"

"Because capturing the person who killed Roger…it helps."

Maggie settled next to him and laid her head on his shoulder. He put his arm around her and they sat quietly for a moment.

"It does, doesn't it?" she said.

54

As homecomings went, Maggie and Laurent's was stellar.

By the time they'd driven down the long winding driveway to Domaine St-Buvard, it was nearly dinnertime. Although not as cold as the English countryside, autumn in Provence was still brisk and Maggie was happy to see smoke coming from the chimney as they arrived.

The children spilled out of the house to greet them along with their adult caretakers, Petit-Four and even Laurent's hunting dog, Arlo.

As Maggie hugged Jemmy and Mila both at the same time she knew she could never leave them again for so long. Both seemed to have grown in just the six days since she'd seen them last.

Danielle had made dinner, a simple farmer's supper of *cassoulet* with duck confit, a crusty baguette and a hearty Côte du Rhone. It was heavy, filling, and perfect.

Maggie was delighted to hear about all the children's' antics from Danielle and Mimi and to be able to forget her looming chore of dealing with Madame Roche. Even Danielle seemed to realize that tonight was not the night for strategizing. Except for one or two pointed glances, no reference was made to the trial Maggie had ahead of her.

That first night was a delightful return to family and friends and Maggie would let nothing spoil it.

The next morning, she awoke early. Petit-Four was sleeping contentedly beside her. Laurent was already downstairs making breakfast for the children.

Looking out the window, Maggie could see Mimi coming up the drive on her bicycle.

Maggie came downstairs and Laurent swept her into his arms for a dramatic kiss to the squeals and laughter of both Jemmy and Mila. He handed her a steaming cup of coffee.

"What is your day like?" he asked. He was already looking out the window at his vineyard and Maggie knew he could hardly wait to get out there. Although with the harvest now months behind them, it was a mystery to Maggie what he would have to do.

"I thought I'd make chocolate chip cookies," Maggie said after Mimi had taken the children to the back patio to play.

Laurent frowned. "Cookies?"

"Chocolate chip cookies," Maggie said. "I make the best. Everyone says so."

"Everyone *American*," he said."

"Yes," Maggie said patiently, "but only because the French palate hasn't evolved enough to appreciate chocolate chip cookies."

Laurent nodded and gave a last cleaning swipe to his immaculate kitchen counter tops.

"You are preparing an apology for Madame Roche."

"If you want to put it like that."

That afternoon Maggie held back a single dozen cookies for the children and wrapped up the rest—big as saucers and oozing with chocolate and toasted pecans—in wax paper and tucked them into a large basket lined with a simple red plaid napkin.

As she dressed it occurred to her that the idea of bringing a goodwill offering like this was also helpful in that it gave her something to hold onto as she confronted Madame Roche.

She frowned as she gave her appearance in the mirror one last look. Perhaps *confronted* wasn't the word she wanted to focus on.

In any case, as difficult as Maggie knew this visit was going to be—Madame Roche did not strike her as the forgiving type—she also knew it was her only option besides doing nothing.

And she was pretty sure Laurent and Danielle wouldn't allow *that* even if Maggie could talk herself into it.

Laurent had spent the day in the vineyard until just after lunch when Maggie lost sight of him. He was likely in the village at the little café bistro Le Canard where he liked to hang out with his other vignernon friends—particularly Jean-Luc.

That was just as well. Having him here would only make her more nervous. She had to do this. And that was all there was to it.

She went to the patio French doors and waved to Mimi to signal that she was leaving. Mimi waved back.

There was nothing left to do. Maggie went to the kitchen, picked up the basket of cookies and straightened her shoulders. She went to the front door just as the doorbell rang.

Surprised, Maggie opened the door to find Madame and Monsieur Roche standing on her doorstep.

Madame Roche was holding a large casserole pot covered with foil. Maggie could smell the garlic and ginger. Monsieur Roche stood solemn and silent behind his wife. He wore a large white bandage across his nose.

Madame Roche glowered at Maggie as if she'd been dragged to Domaine St-Buvard by force. Her eyes held malice and resentment.

Maggie shook off her surprise and held the door wide for them to enter.

"I am so glad you came," she said. "I was just coming to see you. I want to apologize for any misunderstanding. And I would very much like to begin again."

An hour later, Maggie was on the phone with Danielle. She sat on the couch with Petit-Four as Mimi fed the children their afternoon snack.

"No! You are not telling me she came to you?" Danielle said.

"She did. And eventually just as sweet and friendly as if she'd never told the whole village I was sleeping with her husband and poor Monsieur Picou too."

"I am astonished, *chérie*. What did Laurent say?"

"I haven't told him yet."

"I am so glad it is over!" Danielle said. "I cannot believe you are friends with her now."

"Well, I wouldn't go that far. We're just close enough to keep village harmony and that's what counts."

"And Monsieur's berries?"

"I figure if Americans are dumb enough to order fresh strawberries from France in October who am I to stop them?"

That evening after a fragrant roast chicken that Laurent served with a luscious gratin Dauphinois, Maggie bathed and settled the kids down for the night. Laurent came up after the dishes were done to read to them.

He'd returned from the village late and had gone straight to the kitchen so there hadn't been much time to talk. But Maggie often thought those were the best times—when they were both brimming with their observations of the day.

After her visit with Madame Roche, Maggie had spent the afternoon working on the promotion she was doing for the village *fête* and Laurent's upcoming wine tour. She'd been careful not to read emails while in the UK and now she was inundated with requests to add special promotions to her upcoming blog post.

Once the kids had goodnight kisses and were on their way to sleep, Laurent and Maggie went outside to the patio. Laurent kindled a blaze in the outdoor fireplace which they sat beside and sipped glasses of warmed Calvados.

While normally taciturn, Maggie could tell Laurent was still processing what had happened in England. And what had happened to Roger. No matter how well things had turned out, there was always a sadness and a feeling of loss that all the right answers in the world couldn't assuage.

She knew Laurent well enough to let him bring up the subject of Roger if he was going to. She chattered easily about the cute things Jemmy had said during the day and the various new products she would be touting in the newsletter.

"Oh! You'll be happy to hear I buried the hatchet with Madame Roche today," she said.

"I am very glad to hear it. May I know the details?"

"Basically, she took one bite of my chocolate chip cookies and said '*we must be best friends forever!*'"

Laurent smiled. "I see."

"It was beautiful. Very touching."

"And so you will advertise Monsieur's *framboises* in your blog?"

"With a smile on my face."

"I am proud of you, *ma chérie*."

"Oh! Did you know that Monsieur Roche got his nose broken?" she asked.

"Did he? I am sorry to hear that."

Maggie knew Laurent wouldn't tell her if he'd done the honors himself or if it had been one of his friends in the village on his behalf. Spreading gossip about infidelity was a serious matter, especially in a small village.

In the end it probably didn't matter who broke whose nose. It hadn't just been the nose-breaking that had done the trick, although there was no doubt it helped.

If Maggie hadn't been willing to step forward and offer the proverbial olive branch in spite of everything Madame Roche had done, the problem would still be there ready to crop up another time.

"Jill called this morning," Laurent said. He looked at her to see how she would react.

"Oh? What did she have to say?"

"It appears that Anastasia tried to pawn her tiara only to discover it was a worthless copy."

"What? But I thought it was returned? Oh! A *fake* was returned? Oh, my God! It was a con?"

"Don't look at me like that," he said arching an admonishing eyebrow at her. "It wasn't me."

"*Jill?*"

"She worked a few jobs with Roger in the old days. They'd originally stolen that tiara several years ago. But he'd given it to his new bride. I think perhaps Jill is a little sentimental."

"You're saying she stole it from Anastasia to remember Roger by?"

"*Exactement.*"

"When did you know Jill was running a con?"

"I had my suspicions at the wake. Then she confided in me that day in the salon."

"When she kissed you."

He cleared his throat. "Yes. She wanted to be assured I would not give her away."

"And that's the reason she was wandering the halls in the middle of the night when Will attacked you?"

"*Oui.* She was leaving Anastasia's room."

"Because she was stealing jewels out from under Anastasia?"

"I do not know the details. Which is as well."

"That's for sure."

"You know, *ma chérie*, I am convinced Jill did not intend to hurt you."

Maggie nearly spilled her drink. "You're joking, right? She tried to blow me up just prior to having her dog attack me!"

"She insists she did not know about the bomb. The cottage was a well known resting spot used during every hunt. And Annette confessed that *she* was the one who drugged the horse."

"That just leaves the little matter of Jill siccing her attack dog on me."

"It is true that Jill lost her temper. But she told me she was confident because of your prior interaction with the dog that no harm would be done. Her intention was only to scare you."

"And her lying to you when you went out looking for me?"

Laurent shrugged. "She is no angel. I don't mean to suggest that. *Pas du tout.* I only suggest perspective."

Was he really defending Jill after everything she'd done? Maggie fought down her annoyance. She took a long breath.

"Look, Laurent, just so you know, here's where I stand on the subject of Jill. I don't care *what* happened between the two of you in the past, okay? That's over and done with. But if I ever see her near Domaine St-Buvard, I'm getting out your dove hunting rifle."

Laurent laughed as he took her hand. "We did not live together, *chérie*. She only told you that to make you jealous."

"Really? Well, I know it shouldn't matter, but I'm glad."

Laurent looked like he was about to say something else but hesitated.

"There's more?" Maggie asked.

"About the kiss."

Oh, no. Here's where he comes clean that it was really him who initiated it. Maggie's body stiffened.

"Yes?" she said tensely.

"It is true she took me by surprise."

Because you are totally clueless when it comes to how hot you are and how devious some women can be, Maggie thought, fighting to keep her face impassive.

"But I was wrong. I should have reacted more...*definitement* in rejecting her. And for that I am sorry."

Maggie smiled and then leaned across and kissed him. "Thanks, darling. I appreciate that."

He cleared his throat to signal that he was ready to drop the subject.

"So," he said, "you have heard back from Grace, yes?"

"I did. She's asking if she can come back for awhile and stay with us."

Laurent didn't respond.

"I told her no."

"Vraiment?" He looked surprised.

"Grace needs to focus on her family right now."

"Not that it is any of your business."

She slapped him lightly on the arm. "I am not trying to run people's lives, Laurent."

"Of course not. You have your hands full with mine."

"I would however like to ask Ben to come stay with us. If that's okay."

Laurent was silent for a moment as he considered it.

"That is a good idea," he said finally.

"I was hoping you'd think so. Ben needs a change of scenery and my folks and Nicole need a break."

As Maggie got up to go inside, Laurent stopped her with a hand on her arm. Looking into her eyes, he said, "I don't want to give Roger too much credit."

"What do you mean?"

"It's true Roger introduced us. But *you* were the key to making sure my life didn't turn out like his."

Maggie felt a flush of pleasure at his words.

"Roger wanted what I had—what I was lucky enough to have," he said, squeezing her arm lightly.

Maggie vibrated with the pleasure of the moment: the brisk wind against her skin, the touch of her husband's hand on her, and the warmth of the whiskey in her veins.

"It's a good life, Laurent. Better than I could ever have hoped for."

"*Pour moi aussi, chérie,*" he said. "Definitely, for me as well."

About the Author

Susan Kiernan-Lewis lives in Ponte Vedra, Florida and writes mysteries and thrillers. Like many authors, Susan depends on the reviews and word of mouth referrals of her readers. If you enjoyed *Murder in the Abbey*, please consider leaving a review saying so on Amazon.com, Barnesandnoble.com or Goodreads.com.

Check out Susan's website at susankiernanlewis.com and feel free to contact her at sanmarcopress@me.com.

Maggie Newberry Mystery #9
Murder in the Bistro
will release May 2016.

Murder in the Bistro brings our intrepid sleuth back to Provence for a thrill ride nobody saw coming—least of all Laurent. I hope you come along for the ride!

Susan Kiernan-Lewis

Made in the USA
Middletown, DE
17 December 2016